GUARDED PASSIONS

GUARDED PASSIONS

Rosie Harris

severn
House

This first world hardcover edition published 2013
in Great Britain and in the USA by
SEVERN HOUSE PUBLISHERS LTD of
19 Cedar Road, Sutton, Surrey, England, SM2 5DA.
First published 1986 in mass market format under the
title Soldiers' Wives and pseudonym Marion Harris.

British Library Cataloguing in Publication Data

Harris, Rosie, 1925- author.
  Guarded passions.
  1. Widows--Fiction. 2. Mothers and daughters--Fiction.
  3. Great Britain--History--George VI, 1936-1952--
  Fiction.
  I. Title II. Harris, Marion, 1925- Soldier's wives.
  823.9'14-dc23

ISBN-13: 978-0-7278-8419-0   (cased)

All Severn House titles are printed on acid-free paper.

Severn House Publishers support The Forest Stewardship Council ™ [FSC™],
the leading international forest certification organisation. All our titles that
are printed on FSC certified paper carry the FSC logo.

Printed and bound in Great Britain by
TJ International, Padstow, Cornwall.

For Pam and Tony

Chapter 1

Two uniformed men stood looking at her, their faces solemn. Their lips moved but no sound was coming from them. Yet she heard the words drumming inside her head, over and over again:

'We've bad news ... bad news ... bad news ... There's been an accident ... an accident ... an accident ...'

It was just as if she was actually there and it was all happening in slow motion. She felt her gorge rising at the sight of the mutilated face that had taken the full force of the explosion. Red rivulets of blood flowed from the multiple gashes, dripping in slow, fat blobs onto the khaki uniform. They glowed richly, like enormous jewels, before turning into an obscene smear as his life-blood drained away.

His glazed eyes were a dark pit of pain and terror; his mouth gaped wide in a soundless scream.

Alone and frightened, Helen Woodley tried desperately to control her trembling limbs as tremor after tremor racked her body. Sobs tore at her throat as she groped for the bedside-light switch. Drenched in sweat, she pulled the quilt up to her chin and sat huddled beneath it, breathing hard, waiting for the spasms to end and the stark terror in her mind to subside.

Gradually, the drumming inside her head eased, the runnels of sweat between her breasts became a cold clamminess. She shuddered violently. Why, oh why, did she have to endure this awful recurring nightmare? It had all happened such a long time ago.

1

She buried her aching head in her hands, rocking backwards and forwards, shuddering violently. On each previous occasion the nightmare had heralded some dire disaster. What had fate in store for her this time?

A tall, slim girl, her dark brown hair tied back in a pony tail, her huge grey eyes shining like molten silver in her sun-tanned oval face, stood poised on the top step of the coach, looking for a familiar face in the waiting crowd.

'Ruth! Over here!' Helen Woodley called.

'You're as brown as a berry,' she exclaimed as they hugged enthusiastically. 'Brecon must have suited you.'

'It was great! I had a wonderful time.' She looked around eagerly. 'Where's Lucy? Hasn't she come with you?'

'No, she wanted to stay and help Mark with the milking. She's missed you, though. It's been a long ten days. Come on, let's collect your case and get home.'

'Just a minute.' Ruth laid a detaining hand on her mother's arm. 'There's someone I want you to meet.'

They stood together, grey eyes on a level, so similar in looks and build that, but for the obvious age difference, they might have been sisters, not mother and daughter.

'Mum, this is Hugh . . . Hugh Edwards.'

Helen found herself looking up into a pair of dark eyes under straight black brows, set in a strikingly arrogant face. His firm, chiselled lips widened into a smile as he greeted her.

Helen felt strangely disturbed by the animal magnetism of the young man and the immense power of his strong handshake. She was equally unnerved by the velvet brown eyes studying her so intently, and she was suddenly conscious of how frumpy she must look. She wished she had remembered to put on some lipstick, or even found time to change, before coming to meet Ruth.

'I've invited Hugh to come and stay, Mum.'

For a moment Helen could only stare disbelievingly at the tall, handsome man and shake her head negatively.

2

She had no idea who he was or why his hand was resting so possessively on Ruth's shoulder. His self-assurance annoyed her.

Aware that curious glances were being directed at them, Helen pulled herself together and made an effort to hide her hostility. 'I see. Well, in that case, you'd better both fetch your luggage then. I'll wait for you in the car.'

Her mind numb, Helen watched Ruth and Hugh walking across to join her. Hugh was carrying both Ruth's heavy case and his own hold-all in one hand, as if they were featherweight, while his other hand held hers. And Ruth was looking up into his eyes, hanging on to his every word, as if they were the only two people in the world.

Once they reached the farm, Helen left them to unload the car while she went to lock up the chickens. She wanted to be alone. She needed time to think, and to plan how to handle the situation.

'Damn Hugh Edwards, damn him, damn him,' she muttered fiercely, as she marched angrily across the meadow to see to the hens. Ruth obviously believed herself to be in love with him. It was written all over her face and in every look she gave him. He was certainly attractive, Helen thought, grudgingly. He must be at least six foot tall and, with those massive shoulders and slim hips, he had a magnificent physique. She could well understand Ruth falling under the spell of such a man.

It was at times like this that she missed Adam most and felt more desperately alone. Those days when he had been there to help shoulder her problems, and love and cherish her, seemed light years away – another life altogether. At night, when she was too weary to sleep, she tried to imagine he wasn't gone from her forever, but was only away on a tour of duty, or on an exercise somewhere, and that he would be home again soon. At any moment he would walk in, sling down his khaki hold-all and sweep her into his arms, kissing her tenderly, a long, lingering union that was full of promise for the passionate loving that was to follow.

Such sweet retrospection had an hypnotic effect. She

3

would drift into a sleep that was filled with erotic memories. She would feel Adam's arms around her, his firm lips hot on her flesh, caressing and exploring, rousing her need of him to fever pitch. Then she would wake, sweat-soaked and trembling, to the cold loneliness of her bed, knowing there would be no fulfilment, no easing of the ache within her.

So often at such times she would find Lucy standing at the side of her bed, as if intuitively drawn there. And, instead of sending her back to her own bed, Helen would gather the four-year-old to her, gaining some measure of comfort from the feel of the child's small, soft body curved trustingly against her own. Poor little Lucy; she'd never even known her father.

Ruth and Mark missed Adam, too, but Mark most of all. At sixteen he seemed to find it hard to accept her guidance and authority; he needed a man to relate to . . . Helen had seen the resentment in his eyes when she'd had to reprimand him. He never answered her back, but his top lip would curl superciliously and his voice would be harsh and mocking.

Ruth was laying the table for their evening meal when Helen got back to the house. As she heard Mark and Hugh laughing, her anger flared up afresh. That was all she needed, that Hugh should win Mark over to his side.

As she took out of the oven the casserole she'd prepared earlier in the day, Helen paused, a half-smile hovering on her lips. It was a long time since she had bothered to change for their evening meal, but this, she felt, was an occasion that demanded it.

She chose a blue silk dress with a flattering low-cut draped neckline, and high-heeled black sandals. She brushed out her light brown hair from its tight pleat, turning the ends under and letting it frame her face. As she outlined her mouth with a light pink lipstick, and dabbed some perfume on to her wrists, she felt much more confident about facing Hugh Edwards.

As she took a final look in the mirror, her face flamed.

What on earth was she doing! Ruth and Mark would think she had gone crazy. Ruth would know she was trying to impress Hugh.

With a feeling of resentment, she tore off the silk dress, kicked off the high-heeled sandals and tossed them into the back of the wardrobe. Then she put on the green and white cotton dress she had intended to wear when she went to meet Ruth, and put her hair back into its usual style.

Listening to the excited chatter and banter that went on around her all through the meal, Helen realized she would have to take a strong line. Hugh Edwards was fast becoming 'one of the family'. Mark was soaking up every word he said and she had never known Lucy to have so much to say for herself; usually, she was very shy with strangers.

After she had washed up, and Ruth had put Lucy to bed, Helen told Mark to take Hugh upstairs and show him his record collection. Then she called Ruth into the sitting-room and closed the door.

'I think we'd better have a talk, Ruth, don't you?'

'If you want to. Only look, Mum, don't preach or try and reason with me. I know what I'm doing.'

As their eyes met, Helen struggled to keep her temper in check. She had an overwhelming urge to slap some sense into Ruth, but realised it would serve no useful purpose and would only antagonise her.

If only Adam were here, Helen grieved inwardly, Ruth would have listened to him. And Adam would have known how to put Hugh Edwards in his place.

'Perhaps you'd better tell me how you came to meet this boy,' she said as calmly as she could.

'Hugh's a man, not a boy, Mum,' Ruth said, exasperated. 'He's six years older than me, so even if you think I don't know my own mind you can't say the same about him.'

'Where did you meet him?'

'In Brecon, of course. I haven't been anywhere else now, have I?' Ruth snapped impatiently.

Helen bit back the sharp retort that rose to her lips. She was shocked that Ruth had become so involved in such a very short time and furious with Hugh Edwards for playing on the emotions of a girl so naïve.

'And where was this, at a café or something?'

'Oh, Mum!'

The irritation in Ruth's voice rankled Helen and she felt her temper rising. 'Look, young lady. I wasn't at Brecon so I don't know what went on. If I had been there,' she added pointedly, 'I would have made quite sure you didn't go around getting picked up by the local men.'

'Picked up! What's that supposed to mean?' Ruth flared. 'I didn't get "picked up" as you put it. The vicar had arranged for Hugh to come and give us a talk . . .'

'And, at the end of his talk, he asked you for a date . . . just like that!'

'Mum! You're being quite impossible. If you can't discuss the matter sensibly then let's leave it.'

'I'd like nothing better than to drop the subject and never hear it mentioned again,' Helen told her coldly.

Ruth shook her head despairingly. 'How can I make you understand?' she implored. She walked over to where her mother was sitting, and knelt on the floor beside her. Taking Helen's hands in hers she looked up into her mother's face, her own eyes pleading. 'Mum, Hugh and I love each other. Don't say anything more until you know him better.'

Helen's heart ached as she looked down at her daughter. With her hair in a pony-tail, her sun-tanned face devoid of make-up, she looked so very young and vulnerable.

'Ruth, you've only known this man for a week,' she protested. 'We know nothing about him, or his background.'

'Mum, Hugh is a soldier,' Ruth said impatiently. She stood up, moving away from her mother's side. 'And he's in the Guards, the same as Dad was!'

Helen felt bemused. Suddenly it all fell into place. Now she knew what it was about Hugh Edwards that had seemed vaguely familiar. The man's arrogant bearing, the square shoulders and straight back, the clean-cut look of his short hair and his highly-polished shoes should have given her the answer. They were all trademarks of a trained soldier, especially of a Guardsman. She should have realised that the moment she met him!

'How did you come to meet a Guardsman on Brecon Beacons?' she asked in bewilderment.

'I told you, Mum, only you weren't listening. You were too busy being sarcastic. Hugh came to give us a lecture on self-survival and afterwards he stayed on to have coffee. Well . . . that's when I met him!' She gave a deep sigh of satisfaction. 'It was love at first sight.'

'Love! You may be infatuated, but I can promise you it's not love,' Helen said scornfully. 'Oh, I admit he's good-looking, very charming and . . .'

'You must be talking about me!'

Helen looked up, startled. She hadn't heard the door open. Hugh was standing only a few feet away from her. She felt herself colouring as she met his intense stare.

'Yes,' she said stiffly. 'As a matter of fact we were. I was asking Ruth how she came to meet you . . . and when.'

'And has she told you all you want to know?' he asked with exaggerated politeness.

'I'm not at all reassured by what she's told me.'

'Really!'

Helen was aware of the laughter in his dark eyes. She wanted to hate him, but his sheer animal magnetism made him a formidable adversary. As she forced herself to return his gaze, refusing to bow to his male superiority, she could readily understand how Ruth had become so infatuated.

Instantly they recognised each other's strength. His dark eyes narrowed fractionally, as if conceding that she was a worthy opponent.

'Is there anything more you want to know?' he asked coldly. With studied deliberation he reached into his hip pocket for his Army pay-book and held it out to her. 'This may help. Name, number, rank, date of birth, length of service. Oh, and married status, of course. At present that reads "Single" . . .'

'But we plan to change that.' Ruth smiled, linking her arm through Hugh's.

'Do stop talking so silly, Ruth. You're going to university. And that's that!'

Ruth's face fell, but she was not to be deterred. 'I know that's what we agreed, providing my exam results were good enough, but things have changed now,' she argued.

'Of course your results will be satisfactory,' Helen snapped defensively. 'If they're not, then I'll certainly want to know why.'

'No, Mum. It really isn't important. I'm in love and I want to get married as soon as possible.' Confidently, Ruth looked up into Hugh's eyes. His arm went round her shoulders possessively, as his lips brushed her brow.

'Three years is nothing, it will fly past,' Helen persisted. 'Think about it, you'll still only be twenty-one when you graduate and you'll have achieved something that will stand you in good stead for the rest of your life.'

With tears misting her grey eyes, Ruth made one last plea. 'Try and understand, Mum,' she begged. 'Hugh and I may have only just met, but we are deeply in love.'

'Rubbish!'

'No, Mum. We truly are. We both know we will never feel this way about anyone else.'

'Then prove it!' Helen exclaimed triumphantly. 'Go to university and, at the end of that time, if you both feel the same way about each other, then you can marry . . . with my blessing.'

'It's no good, Mrs Woodley. Our minds are made up,' Hugh said firmly. 'We intend to marry right away. I want Ruth to come with me when I'm posted to Northern Ireland.'

'When you are what!'

Ashen-faced, Helen rose from her chair and stared at

Hugh. 'No!' Her voice cut like a lash. 'I don't want to hear any more. You're the first man she's been out with! It's sheer infatuation on her part. In three months' time she'll have forgotten what you even look like,' she added relentlessly.

She felt full of remorse as she saw Ruth's eyes brim with tears and her mouth begin to quiver. She longed to hold her close, to comfort and warn her – she had long experience of Army life and she didn't want Ruth to go through the agonies of loneliness and uncertainty that she had endured.

'There's no need to raise your voice or make a scene,' Ruth told her coldly. 'You can't stop me from getting married. I *am* eighteen, you know!'

'And you're going to university.'

'No, Mum! I only agreed to go because I wanted to get out of this dead-and-alive hole. Don't you understand? I feel trapped. I need to meet people of my own age, see some life, and have fun.' Her voice rose hysterically. 'It was the only way I could find out if others think like I do and want to sit up all night drinking coffee and talking non-stop about the things they believe in and care about. I want to be able to do crazy things, like drive to the beach for a midnight swim without people raising their eyebrows, or trying to stop me.'

'Ruth! Listen to me . . .'

'No, Mum . . . *you* listen. Life was great when we lived in the barracks. There was always something happening, like discos and parties. There's not even a youth club in this dump.' She flung her arms wide. 'I want to live again!'

'Ruth, stop it!'

'You don't understand Mum, do you? It's all right for you, you don't need excitement. You don't even like music. Look at the fuss you make when Mark has his stereo on.'

'Leave me out of your row, I can fight my own battles.'

Ruth and Helen both swung round at the sound of

9

Mark's voice. He was standing in the doorway, frowning angrily.

'But she doesn't understand, does she?' Ruth yelled. 'She always makes you turn it down. Neither of us ever has the guts to stand up to her. Look how she creates if you want to go into Winton to a football match. And so you stay at home. You've got no real friends. You spend all your time working on the farm.'

'Just shut up, Ruth,' Mark growled. 'If *I* don't mind, then why should *you* care?'

'That's just the point, Mark, you ought to care. You have an even worse life than I do. You haven't made any friends at all since we came to live in this dump. Don't forget we only moved here because Mum wanted to. She was all right . . . she had Donald . . .'

'Shut it, Ruth! You've said enough.'

'In fact, more than enough,' Helen snapped, her cheeks flushed with anger. 'I think it might be a good idea if you went to your room and stayed there until you're ready to apologise.'

'There you go again, treating me as if I'm a child. I'm a woman, Mum. I'm going to get married . . . that's final.'

'If you do marry this man it won't be with my blessing,' Helen shouted. 'I won't encourage you to throw your life away. And as for you,' she exclaimed bitterly, turning on Hugh, 'go! Get out of my house! I never want to see you again.'

'How can you talk like that, Mrs Woodley?' Hugh said quietly. 'I understand from Ruth that you were married at eighteen. You didn't throw your life away, did you?'

For a moment Hugh's dark eyes held hers in an hypnotic stare, as if he could read the secrets in her very soul. Then the muscles round his mouth tightened and, with a slight shrug of his shoulders, he moved towards the door.

'No!' With a startled cry, Ruth grabbed his arm. 'If Hugh goes, I shall go with him,' she sobbed.

Helen knew from the expression on her daughter's face that she meant it. She glanced quickly at Hugh, expecting

10

to see triumph in his eyes. But he wasn't even looking at her. His arm was encircling Ruth, holding her close. And the tender devotion on his face tugged at Helen's heart.

As Hugh's dark head bent slowly, almost reverently, until his lips gently touched Ruth's, Helen turned away, tears in her eyes. She was defeated and she knew it.

Helen remained downstairs late into the night knowing it would be impossible to sleep. It was as if someone had turned the clock back . . . back to 1943 when she had been eighteen and just as adamant as Ruth about marrying the handsome soldier who had captured her heart.

Memories of her life with Adam came flooding back, some joyous, some sad. There were the long hours of loneliness, when they'd been separated, for weeks or even months. There were also the treasured moments of passion, when need and desire had made their love a burning fever, almost too wonderful to endure.

Chapter 2

As the morning sun sliced the blue-and-white floral curtains and cast dancing shadows on the peach-coloured velvet headboard, Helen Price opened her eyes, looked around her pretty bedroom and sighed blissfully.

The day that had been ringed in red on her calendar for so many months had dawned at last and she was home. Her school-days were finally over. She had finished with crowded, noisy dormitories, living by the bell, lessons and compulsory games.

She stretched lazily, before checking the time on her bedside clock. Not that it mattered, she reminded herself; she could lie in bed until mid-morning if she wanted to.

Exams were over, school was over, and the future stretched ahead like an endless reel of blank paper. She smiled to herself, wondering if Miss Butts, her former English teacher, would have approved of such a simile. It seemed strange to think she would probably never see her again, or any of the girls she'd lived and studied with for seven years. Most of them were going straight into the Forces. In fact, she seemed to be the only one not exchanging her gymslip for a uniform, she thought, wistfully.

The last time she had been at home she'd tried to persuade her parents to let her join up, but neither of them would even consider the idea.

'Don't you think this family's done enough to help the war effort?' her father had snapped. 'My chauffeur's in the RAF, the gardener's in the Navy, our cook's working in a munitions factory, and even the housemaid has joined the WRNS. Your mother's done more than her share of war work as well. When she was Billeting Officer she sorted out all the evacuees sent down here from London and now she's so involved with Red Cross work that I'm left with no help at all in the surgery. And *you're* talking about volunteering! Well, you can forget it. University for you, my girl.'

Helen stretched again. University was months away; there was still time to try and make them change their minds.

She heard her father unlock the door to the surgery, which had been built onto the side of their rambling, old stone house. Even the war hadn't managed to interfere with his strict routine, she thought, as she threw back the bedclothes and padded over to the window. Leaning out, she noticed how overgrown the garden looked. Before their gardener had gone into the Navy, the lawn had always been as smooth as a bowling-green and the flower beds a riot of colour. Now, the borders were full of weeds and even the grass needed cutting.

Jimmy will have a fit when he comes on leave, she

thought, as she pulled on a pink linen skirt and hunted for a blouse to wear with it.

The house had the same neglected air. It was clean and tidy, but there were no welcoming bowls of flowers anywhere and no savoury smells coming from the kitchen.

As she rinsed her breakfast dishes, Helen saw her father hurrying towards the garage.

'You've finished surgery early, Dad,' she called through the open kitchen window. 'Do you want a coffee before you start your rounds?'

Dr Price stopped. A tall, spare man, he was neatly dressed in a dark grey suit, offset by a crisp, white shirt and striped blue and grey tie. As he passed a long, thin hand over his greying hair, he stared at her in surprise from over the top of his gold-rimmed glasses.

'I'd quite forgotten you were at home, Helen. Your mother has just telephoned from Bulpitts for this medicine,' he said, holding out a wrapped bottle. 'Could you take it along to her?'

'Yes, of course I can, but who's ill?' she asked in alarm. Bulpitts was owned by the Bradys who were family friends. Donald and Isabel, though a few years older than Helen, were almost like her brother and sister.

'Didn't you know, they've turned the place into a military hospital?' Dr Price said in surprise. 'Your mother has taken on the job of Matron. I hope it's only going to be temporary,' he added in a worried voice, 'she has enough to do here with all the servants gone.'

Sturbury has certainly changed since the war, Helen mused as she walked past the Post Office and General Shop. Instead of their usual colourful displays, the windows were full of official-looking notices about ration books, clothing coupons and blackout regulations.

Since Sturbury was surrounded by farms, it was hard to believe that the people living there had to put up with shortages of dairy foods and meat, just the same as those who lived in towns.

13

Even the gardens of the grey stone cottages she passed, which should have been a riot of colourful sweet-smelling flowers at this time of the year, were either neglected or turned over to vegetables.

Up until now the war hadn't really affected her life very much. She was occasionally shocked by what she read in the newspapers about bombing raids and the injured, but she hadn't actually come face to face with any suffering. The nearest bombs had been in Bristol, thirty miles away.

In fact, until now, the only disturbances they'd known in Sturbury had been the arrival of the evacuees, and being asked to donate their iron gates and railings to help in the war effort. Now, it seemed to be catching up with them.

At St Margaret's she'd grumbled along with all the other girls if butter was in short supply and when, twice a week, on meatless days, they were served Woolton Pie, a concoction of vegetables topped by a fatless pastry crust that tasted like cardboard. That, and being expected to economise on hot water and remember about blackout regulations, had been all the discomforts she'd experienced.

As she reached Bulpitts, it seemed incongruous to see ambulances and army vehicles, all camouflaged with mottled green markings, parked on the wide, gravel drive. At the front door of the gracious old Georgian building, an armed soldier challenged her to stop.

'It's all right,' she told him, 'I've come to deliver some medicine.'

'May I see your identity card?'

'I'm not carrying it,' she said in surprise.

'Wait here. You'll need an escort.'

'You needn't bother. I know my way around this house blindfold,' she announced airily.

'Sorry. We have our orders,' he told her in clipped tones. 'Please follow me.'

He escorted her to the Guard Room, where the sergeant in charge seemed equally suspicious even though she showed him the medicine. He insisted on accompanying her to one of the large front bedrooms to find her mother.

Helen couldn't believe her eyes when she went into the room that had been Isabel's. The lace drapes had all been replaced by heavy blackout curtains. All the carved oak bedroom furniture, even the canopied four-poster bed, had gone and in their place were eight narrow, iron bedsteads. Mrs Price, in a blue print dress covered by a starched white apron, a red cross emblazoned on the front, was leaning over one of the beds, dressing a young soldier's leg wound.

'I'll be back in a second,' she said, taking the medicine from Helen. 'Find someone to talk to – they all need cheering up.'

Shyly, Helen stood in the middle of the room, conscious that eight pairs of eyes were watching her. Colour rushed to her cheeks as several low whistles reached her ears, and someone called out theatrically, 'Water! Water!'

'Why don't you start with me?' a voice said from the bed nearest to her, and a pair of vivid blue eyes, under a thatch of thick dark hair, met hers challengingly.

For a moment she was tongue-tied as she studied the long, broad-shouldered figure lying on top of the bedcovers. Then, with a cautious grin, she shook her head. 'You don't look ill to me,' she told him.

'What *do* you mean by that?' he exclaimed in mock dismay. With an exaggerated groan he made a pretence of lifting his left arm, which was encased in a plaster cast, then letting it fall back heavily onto the bed. Before Helen could reply, her mother had returned.

'Come along, dear, and have a look around. Poor Donald won't know the place when he comes home.'

Helen felt a mounting mixture of sadness and exhilaration as she followed her mother through the various rooms and saw all the changes that had been made. The sight of so many young soldiers lying there, some heavily bandaged, brought home to her the reality of the war.

15

'Isabel was horrified when she saw it all,' Mrs Price said, as if reading her thoughts. 'She looked very smart in her WAAF uniform. That greyish-blue colour suited her. She came to collect some of her personal belongings before everything went into store. She says that from now on she'll spend any leave she gets in London.'

'In London?'

'With her parents. Colonel Brady is something at the War Office,' her mother told her briskly. 'He and Margaret have a flat in London. She decided that if he was going to be at the heart of things then she wanted to be there as well.'

'And Donald?'

'I'm not too sure what he's going to do. We've stored his things up in one of the attics.'

As they reached the hallway, Mrs Price looked at her watch. 'I must get back to the wards. Now, what are you going to do for the rest of the day? You'll have to see to your own lunch, I'm afraid. I don't finish work here until mid-afternoon.'

'I haven't really made any plans. I might go and see Aunt Julia.'

'Well, I'm not sure if you'll find her at home. She's very involved with civil defence these days and always seems to be out organising ARP wardens and so on.'

'Whatever for? There haven't been any bombs near here,' Helen said in surprise.

'Not yet, but you never can tell. Jerry seems to be coming further and further inland these days. If he does strike then we want to be ready for him. The Civil Defence help with ambulances, too, so it's very useful work your Aunt Julia is doing.'

'Yes, I'm sure it is,' Helen said hastily. 'I think I'd better go,' she said, grinning, 'before you find work for my idle hands.' In her starched Red Cross uniform her mother seemed so different, so full of her own importance. It was almost as if she was actually enjoying the war and the role she was playing.

16

'We could certainly do with some extra help,' her mother agreed. 'Still,' she added, giving Helen a gentle push, 'you run along and enjoy yourself. When we know which university you'll be going to we can decide how you fill in your time until the new term begins.'

Out of curiosity, and because she needed time to think, Helen wandered around the gardens at Bulpitts. She was dismayed to find that the once sweeping green lawns had been rutted by army lorries and the flower-beds had all been ploughed up and planted with potatoes and cabbages.

Even the box hedges that lined the path leading to the water-gardens were ragged and overgrown. And, when she reached the ponds, she found they had been cleared of lilies and turned over to watercress. The pagoda summer-house, where in the past they had taken afternoon tea, was now being used as a storehouse for the flat, wide baskets used to harvest the watercress.

Despondently, she made her way to the Silent Pool. The smallest of the ponds, it was shaded by a willow tree and hidden away in the far corner of the gardens. When she and Donald had been quite small, Isabel had told them a terrifying story about a child that had drowned there and how its ghost still haunted the spot.

After Isabel had gone away to boarding school, the Silent Pool no longer held any terrors for them, and the stories they built around it were much more romantic. Donald claimed there was an old legend that said if you stood at the side of the Silent Pool, closed your eyes and concentrated hard, when you opened your eyes again you would see the face of the one you were to marry, reflected beside your own in the water. It was a game they often played, and always it was each other's face they saw when they gazed down into the mysterious dark depths.

Now, as she walked towards the pool, through the tangle of weeds and overgrown grass, Helen felt the old compelling urge to 'test the magic'. The willow fronds swept down over the water, almost completely cutting

17

out the sunlight, obscuring the brilliant July day and making it shadowy and mysterious. She shut her eyes as she counted to a hundred. Then she opened them and stared down into the mirrored surface of the dark pool.

She saw the smooth oval of her own face, framed by long hair that was brushed back from her brow and spread like a fan over her shoulders. As she smiled at her reflection she was startled to see a man's face reflected beside her own. It wasn't Donald's round, full face, but one that was strong and lean and topped by a shock of close-cropped hair.

She turned quickly, then jumped as she saw the khaki-clad figure standing next to her.

'Sorry! I didn't mean to scare you.'

'Are you following me?' she asked sharply, recognising the young soldier who had spoken to her in the ward.

'Of course!'

His answer took her by surprise. She studied his tall, lithe figure, the broad shoulders and slim, tapering waist. Standing there in the shadows, with the sun behind him, he looked like the statue of a Greek god. His disarming smile, revealing strong, even teeth, made it difficult for her to remain aloof.

'You're trespassing, you know.'

He shook his head, his blue eyes twinkling. 'No, we are allowed to walk in the grounds. I've never been to this spot before though,' he admitted. 'Quite spooky here, isn't it?'

'You're not afraid, are you?' she teased.

'No, but there *is* something eerie about the place,' he said. Frowning, he looked around at the riot of weeds and shivered slightly.

Helen looked at him with interest, surprised that he should be so sensitive about atmosphere. Shyly, she found herself blurting out the legend.

He listened intently, nodding from time to time.

'I've never told anyone before,' she said, a little awkwardly. 'It's ... it's a secret shared only with Donald.'

18

'Donald?'

'Donald Brady. His people own Bulpitts. He and his sister Isabel have always been friends of mine.'

'A wonderful playground. You must feel sad to see it taken over by the Army.'

She looked at him sharply, wondering for a moment if he was laughing at her, but his blue eyes, as they met hers, were full of understanding.

'I must be getting back,' he said, looking at his watch. 'Are you going to stay here a little longer?'

'No, I'll walk part of the way with you and you can tell me how you were injured.'

'I'm afraid it wasn't anything heroic,' he said, with a wry grin. 'I was swinging the engine on a truck and didn't let go in time when it backfired. The plaster comes off soon and then I'll be going back to my unit.'

'Oh!' To hide her disappointment she asked quickly, 'Where's that?'

He pursed his lips in a silent whistle. 'You're not a spy, are you?'

'No,' she smiled, shaking her head.

'Well, I'm not too sure,' he teased. 'They come in all shapes and sizes, and what better way to trap an unwary soldier into giving away the position of his unit than by sending a pretty girl along to chat him up?'

'If I remember correctly, you followed me, not the other way round,' Helen reminded him. She stopped as they reached a spot where the path joined the driveway. 'Your quickest way is to the right,' she told him. 'I'm leaving by the side gate. I've seen enough soldiers for one day.'

'But only for one day. You *are* going to come back? I *am* going to see you again?' His blue eyes held hers, trapped.

'It depends on how soon they remove your plaster, doesn't it?' she said, looking away and colouring.

'I can still see you, even after I rejoin the unit,' he said determinedly. 'We're stationed at Mere and that's only about five miles away.'

'Ssh!' Helen held a warning finger to her lips. 'You

shouldn't be telling me that. I might just be a spy after all,' she added impishly.

They had reached a spot where the path divided and, before he could answer, she had taken the small, twisting path to the left that she knew led to a side gate.

As she reached the first bend, she turned round. The soldier was still standing there, watching her and waving.

She hesitated, wondering if perhaps she had been rather offhand with him. He was nice – and very good-looking. It had been exciting meeting him. She wanted to see him again, but an inner caution stopped her from telling him so. Resolutely she continued along the path. Too late she realised she hadn't even asked him his name.

Chapter 3

It was almost six o'clock when Helen arrived home. After leaving Bulpitts she had gone for a long walk, her mind buzzing with thoughts of the soldier she'd met there.

'Is that you, Helen?' her mother called as she walked into the house. She came hurrying into the hall, her face beaming. 'I've got a wonderful surprise for you! Come and see who's here.'

Helen's heart pounded and she felt the blood rush to her face. She knew the young soldier had been interested in her but even in her wildest fantasies she hadn't thought he would find her so soon. She wondered if he had come back with her mother when she'd finished duty. Still, details didn't matter, only that he was here.

She felt so elated that she almost pushed past her mother in her eagerness to get into the room. Then, once inside the door, she stopped dead, feeling completely let down when she saw Donald Brady standing by the window.

For a moment she felt too choked to speak. Even when Donald planted a hearty kiss on her cheek, a wide grin on his round, full face, she could only manage a watery smile and a tremulous, 'Hello Donald.'

In his eagerness to tell her that he was joining up, Donald didn't seem to notice the coolness of her greeting or that she was only making a pretence of listening.

'And when do you go?'

'Tomorrow. Terrible rush. My papers only arrived yesterday. Barely left me time to come back here and sort out my things before I report.'

'Which regiment did you say?' she asked, desperately trying to show some enthusiasm.

'Helen, you've not been listening, have you? I'm not joining the Army. I'm going into the Air Force. I want to fly, so I'm hoping to train as a pilot.'

'Isn't that wonderful?' her mother enthused. 'Terribly brave.'

'And very dangerous,' Helen said quietly. 'Still, if that's what you want, Donald, then I'm pleased for you.'

'I've told Donald he must stay with us tonight, so will you go up and put out some towels in the guest room, Helen?'

'I'm only here for one night,' Donald protested. 'I can make do with my attic quarters at Bulpitts.'

'Out of the question,' Mrs Price insisted. 'The whole place has been taken over by the Army. Since dinner won't be ready for an hour or so, why don't you and Helen walk over to Bulpitts and sort out the things you want to take away with you?'

'I want to have a bath and get changed before dinner,' Helen said quickly, anxious to avoid going to Bulpitts with Donald. 'Perhaps Dad should drive over with him. I'm sure Donald has far too much to carry otherwise.'

'Well . . .' Mrs Price looked from one to the other in bewilderment. She had thought that Helen would have jumped at the opportunity to be alone with Donald, but she recognised the stubborn edge in her daughter's voice

21

and didn't push the matter. If Donald was disappointed then he wasn't showing it, she thought as she went into the kitchen to attend to the evening meal.

Helen filled the bath with far more than the permitted three inches of water and lay soaking in it until it was almost cold. As she dressed she studied her figure critically, twisting and turning in front of her dressing-table mirror, appraising her long, slim legs, her well-defined waist and firm, pointed breasts.

She had twirled her long hair into a knot and pinned it on top of her head before stepping into the bath. Now she loosened it so that it cascaded over her naked shoulders in a shimmering, dark cloud. Picking up her brush she began slowly and sensuously to sweep her hair back from her brow, taking the brush right from the roots to the very tips, in long, rhythmic strokes.

As static built up from the friction of her movements, a halo of fine tendrils framed her face. She leant towards the mirror, intrigued by the effect. She wondered how other people saw her and whether or not they thought her attractive.

The soldier had said she was pretty. No one had ever told her that before and she wondered if he'd really meant it. Experimentally, she combed some of the front hair into a fringe. The brown fronds partially concealed her fore-head, emphasising the dark brows arched over her big grey eyes. Tentatively, she lifted two wide swathes of hair from each side of her face, taking them to the back of her head, then brushing the rest of her hair so that it draped over her shoulders. Tilting her head to one side she studied the result and decided that she liked it.

'Donald's back. Are you almost ready, Helen?' her mother called from downstairs.

With a guilty start she let her hair fall and hurriedly pulled on a blue cotton shirt-waist dress. She could do with some new clothes, she thought, as she struggled to fasten it; this one was decidedly skimpy. Perhaps Donald had some clothing coupons to spare; he wouldn't be needing them if he was going in the RAF. She must remember to ask him.

Donald monopolised the conversation over dinner. He talked earnestly to Dr Price about the RAF and about his sister, Isabel, who had been posted to a barrage balloon site on the east coast.

Helen pretended to listen but her thoughts kept wandering back to the soldier she'd met earlier in the day and comparing him with Donald.

They were both about the same build, Donald perhaps an inch or so shorter, but there the resemblance ended. The soldier's powerful physique was lean and muscular. Donald, in flannels and a navy blazer, looked overweight and flabby.

When it came to looks, they weren't in the same league, she decided, as she remembered the soldier's handsome face, his firm jawline, and wide-set, brilliantly blue eyes. And his dark hair had been crisp and luxuriant in spite of its regulation cut, while Donald's brown hair lay as flat as a skull-cap, emphasising the broad shape of his head and the roundness of his face. His hazel eyes were much too close to his prominent nose, she thought critically, and his full lips made his mouth seem overly large and his chin insignificant. By the end of the meal, his loud, cultured voice and forced laugh were beginning to grate on her nerves.

In an effort to get Donald off the subject of the RAF, she broke into the conversation to ask him if he had any unused clothing coupons.

'I have, but I shall hand them in, of course.'

'What an awful waste!' Helen exclaimed.

'Not at all! It's the right thing to do,' he told her virtuously.

'Wouldn't you sooner give them to me . . . I'm badly in need of some?' Helen pleaded. 'I seem to have outgrown most of my clothes,' she added with an embarrassed laugh.

'Surely you'll be going into some kind of uniform yourself, so you won't be needing civilian clothes,' he said in surprise.

'Helen's going to university,' Mrs Price said quickly.

'Well she won't need new clothes to go there, will she?' Donald argued. 'I managed for three years without buying anything new,' he added smugly.

Helen pulled a face. 'In that case you must have a full book of coupons.'

'I have, and I'm handing them in!'

'Pig!'

'Helen! How *dare* you speak to Donald like that.'

Helen flushed at her father's shocked tone. She knew Donald was baiting her – probably trying to get his own back because she wasn't enthusing about his decision to join up, she thought rebelliously. Because she had always idolised him, he still expected her to hang on his every word. She suddenly felt guilty about the way she was reacting. He was, after all, off to do his bit, while she was staying at home. They'd never quarrelled before and he had always taken her part when Isabel criticised her, so she owed him some loyalty.

'Sorry Donald,' she said contritely.

'That's OK. I suppose I could spare you some of my coupons if you need them so desperately. Not all of them . . . I must hand some in.'

'Thanks, Donald.' She grinned across the table at him.

'Look, if we've all finished, why don't you and Helen go for a walk, Donald? I'm sure there are friends you want to say "goodbye" to,' Mrs Price suggested.

'I'll give you a hand with the washing-up first,' Helen said quickly. For some inexplicable reason she didn't want to spend the rest of the evening with Donald and she hoped he might go off on his own.

'No, run along. Your father will help me tonight,' Mrs Price said firmly. 'Don't be too late back.'

Their evening wasn't a success. Donald talked incessantly about the RAF. His enthusiasm was overpowering. He was in such deadly earnest that he seemed to have completely lost his sense of humour. After one or two witticisms that fell flat, Helen gave up trying and closed her ears to the boring, repetitive details. It even amused her that everyone was so impressed ... until they began to catalogue their own achievements, plans and ambitions. They were all playing such a vital part in the war effort that she began to feel uncomfortably guilty ... and envious.

As they walked home, Helen felt a sense of relief when Donald said he would be leaving very early the next morning. She was taken by surprise, however, when he stopped just inside the gateway, grabbed her shoulders, and spun her round so that she was facing him.

'Look,' he began awkwardly, 'I don't know how to say this but ... will you write to me?'

'I wouldn't have thought you'd have time to read letters. From the way you've been talking, what with the training and exams and night-flying and bombing raids, you'll be lucky if you even find time to eat and sleep,' she said, rather disparagingly.

His hands dropped from her shoulders. 'I have rather exaggerated it all, I suppose. I don't really know what to expect. In fact, I'm rather dreading it all. The thought of flying, even of just going up in a plane, scares me stiff ... that's why letters from you would mean so much.'

'So why did you volunteer for the RAF then?' Helen asked in amazement.

'I didn't have a lot of choice, did I?' Donald answered, his mouth tightening. 'With my parents working flat out at the War Office, and Isabel serving in the WAAF, I had to do something.'

'You could have gone into the Army.'

'No, it wouldn't have worked,' Donald told her grimly. 'Dad would never have let me forget that he was a Colonel. This way at least there won't be any comparisons.'

'Except with Isabel.'

'Not quite the same thing. I'm hoping to train as a pilot so I'll be operational.'

25

Remembering how stern and blustering Colonel Brady always was, Helen suddenly felt sorry for Donald. 'You'd better give me your address,' she told him.

'You mean you *will* write!' he said with relief. 'I'll have to send it on to you. Tomorrow I just report to a reception depot where we are issued with our uniforms.'

'Donald, you don't really have to risk your neck being a pilot, do you?'

'It's what I want,' he insisted doggedly, his mouth tightening stubbornly.

'Why? It's a death wish. You've only to listen to the news each day to know that. Every time there's a bombing raid over Germany more than half of our planes are shot down or reported missing.'

Donald's face hardened. 'It's what I want. As an Army conscript I wouldn't stand much chance of ever becoming a Colonel, so Dad would always have the edge on me.'

'Does that really matter?' Helen asked in surprise.

'To me, yes,' he told her grimly. 'I wouldn't want anyone but you to know that, though,' he added quickly.

'Our secret,' she promised. Standing on tiptoe, she brushed her lips against his cheek to seal the pact.

Donald caught her to him, crushing her so fiercely that his blazer buttons bruised her.

'I wish you were older Helen,' he groaned, burying his face in her hair.

Embarrassed, she tried to wriggle free. She was fond of Donald in a brotherly way. They'd grown up together, played together, shared secrets and teased each other. This new Donald, so serious and intense, made her feel uneasy.

Suddenly, she found his mouth was covering hers. She felt the sharpness of his teeth as he forced her lips apart and his tongue invaded her mouth in a ferocious kiss that left her gasping for breath.

'Promise you'll wait for me,' he rasped, his eyes glistening in the dusk as his gaze searched her face. His hand grabbed tightly at her hair, forcing her head back so that he could, once again, plunder the sweetness between her lips. She found herself pinioned in the crook of his arm, while his other hand roamed feverishly over her body, cupping and squeezing her breasts, gripping her buttocks, sliding under her cotton dress and up the length of her thighs, his fingers searching and probing.

She struggled frantically, jerking her head sideways, pushing his hand away, wriggling and twisting until she managed to free herself from his embrace. Her heart was pounding against her ribs as she stumbled towards the house.

Only when she was in her room, and the door bolted, did she allow herself to think about what had happened. Her lips were burning and swollen from the assault of his mouth, her body sore from his rough, intimate handling. She was shaking with anger that he should treat her in such a way.

She went over to the dressing-table and stared at her reflection. Her eyes were feverishly bright and there was fear in their grey depths. This was the first time any man had ever kissed her in such a way and she was filled with a burning shame.

Still trembling, she undressed and crawled into bed. For a long time she lay there, curled into a ball, frightened and humiliated by the experience.

To her relief, Donald had already gone when she came down to breakfast the next morning.

'He said not to wake you as you'd said your "goodbyes" last night,' her mother explained. 'He's left you a full book of clothing coupons,' she added. 'We must have a day out when you've decided what you want to buy.'

'Yes.' Helen pushed the book to one side, almost as if it was tainted.

'What are you going to do today?' her mother asked briskly. 'You can't sit around moping just because Donald's gone, you know. Perhaps you'd better come along to Bulpitts with me. I can find plenty there for you to do.'

Chapter 4

Adam Woodley left the medical room with a spring in his step and feeling pounds lighter. They'd taken off his plaster cast and replaced it with a khaki sling.

'You're leaving us then?' Mrs Price smiled, as she saw him clearing his bedside locker. 'Now mind you don't overdo things with that arm. It will take a little time before it's strong again.'

'I know.' He patted the breast-pocket of his tunic. 'The MO's put me on "light duties only" until I come back in three weeks for a check-up.'

'You would have had a better chance of resting your arm if they'd sent you home on leave for a couple of weeks.'

Adam's face clouded. He remembered his last leave three months earlier. His parents had been so proud to see him in uniform. They had also been delighted that he'd managed to get home in time to spend a couple of days with his younger brother Gary, who had just received his calling-up papers.

He was two years older than Gary, but they had always been close companions. At first glance they were sometimes mistaken for twins. They were both six foot tall, with broad shoulders, strong, masculine features and brilliantly blue eyes. The one striking difference in their appearance was the colour of their hair – Adam's dark like their father's, Gary's coppery-red and curly, like their mother's.

Adam knew he would never forget that first night home. It had been the end of March. After their evening meal, they had decided to go to the pub. Gary was eager to let everyone know he'd been called up and wouldn't be around for a while.

'Don't be late,' their father cautioned. 'You know how

concerned your mother gets when you're out at night in case there's an air-raid.'

'But there hasn't been one for over a week!' Gary protested. 'Anyway, I'll be in the Army in a couple of days – is she going to worry about me all the time then?'

'Probably.' His father sighed. 'She never stops worrying about our Adam, now does she?' His arm went round his wife's shoulders as he spoke and they exchanged understanding smiles.

'Take care, won't you?' Mrs Woodley said anxiously. 'Don't go lighting up a cigarette out-of-doors if there's any planes overhead, in case Jerry sees you.'

'Mum, you're a hoot!' Gary laughed. 'Do you know, Adam, she nearly breaks her neck each evening, making sure the blackout's in place at every window in the house before she turns on a single light? She's fanatical!'

'Better to be safe than sorry,' she told him sharply. 'These dark nights, the smallest chink of light is like a guiding star to those devils. Now, be off with you and take your tin hats, just in case there's a raid. And if the sirens do go, promise you'll come straight on home. You'll be safer here than in a public shelter.'

'Yes boys, do that,' Mr Woodley said quickly. 'Your mother won't rest until she knows you're home.'

They'd been in the pub with their friends for about an hour when the sirens went. Before the dismal, penetrating wail had died away, an ARP warden came in.

'A hundred or more bombers have crossed the south coast and are heading this way,' he warned. 'Best thing you lot can do is head for a shelter.'

The pub emptied rapidly, and, as Adam and Gary started to walk home, they could hear the heavy drone of the bomb-laden enemy aircraft, approaching. The probing shafts of a dozen searchlights seared the night sky, followed, almost immediately, by a piercing whistle as the first bombs came crumping down around them.

The crash of masonry, as the huge missiles found their targets, deafened them and, suddenly, the whole place was an inferno as flames leapt into the night sky, and the air became putrid with dust and smoke.

They took cover in the first shelter they could find. It was packed to capacity with entire families from the nearby houses. They found themselves wedged in between a young mother with a crying baby and an elderly woman who was shivering uncontrollably with fear.

'Let's get out of here and make for home,' Gary spluttered, coughing and choking. 'Mum'll be worried stiff.'

'Give it a few minutes,' Adam cautioned. 'Once this lot have dropped their load there will probably be a lull before the next wave arrive. We'll make a dash for it then.'

He had been wrong. There had been no respite. The Germans had concentrated their entire effort on Merseyside that night. The docks took the full toll of their impact and houses for several miles inland, on both sides of the river, also bore the brunt of their onslaught.

It had been well after midnight before the all-clear had sounded. As Adam and Gary emerged from the claustrophobic confines of the shelter, the sight that met their eyes shocked them to silence. Where once had been neat rows of houses was now a mass of burning masonry. Fire engines and ambulances were doing their best to bring the flames under control and transport the injured. ARP wardens and Home Guard were digging frantically into the rubble to try and free those who were trapped. The anguished cries of the injured and dying rent the acrid air.

Sick with apprehension as to what they might find, Adam grabbed Gary's arm and hurried him along. The closer they came to home the more anxious he felt. There was devastation wherever they looked.

Adam's worst fears were realised as they turned into their own road. Where their house had once stood was a gaping hole. As he squeezed his brother's arm, trying to

30

reassure him, he felt Gary's muscles tense, like those of an animal about to spring. Then, with a primitive howl of grief, Gary broke free and hurled himself into the smouldering rubble. Burrowing furiously with his bare hands, he threw bricks, stones, lumps of masonry, as well as smashed and charred furniture to one side. Regardless of his own safety, he scrambled and slithered into the heart of the destruction.

Two ARP wardens, yelling to make themselves heard above the rumble of falling walls and cacophony of fire engines and ambulance sirens, tried to drag Gary away. But he fought like a man demented. Tears streaming down his face, his breath rasping as dust choked him, he beat them off. As he slipped and stumbled amidst the smouldering ruins, he called out in a desperate voice to his parents, over and over again.

Realising that it was pointless trying to reason with Gary, Adam curled his right hand into a fist and swung it with tremendous force at his brother's chin. Gary's head snapped back and he slumped to the ground.

Next morning, the bodies of Mr and Mrs Woodley were dug out of the debris. Hands clasped, they had died comforting each other.

Although he had been stunned and heartbroken by the tragic death of his parents, Adam had taken charge and arranged the funeral details. He'd found temporary accommodation for them both until it was time for Gary to report to his unit.

Until now he had successfully managed to push it all to the back of his mind. Even in his letters to Gary, he never wrote of home. It was as if, by not mentioning it, it had never happened. Mrs Price's remark had brought it all flooding back. For a brief moment, he felt the need to confide in someone. He was on the point of telling her what had happened but found the memory was still too raw.

'Nowhere to go,' he said laconically. 'Both my parents were killed in an air-raid about three months ago. Home went as well. It was a direct hit.'

31

'Oh dear, so you have no one,' Mrs Price said sympathetically, her eyes full of compassion.

'I have a younger brother, but he's in the Army now. You don't know how lucky you are here. No bombs, no sirens; you'd hardly know there was a war on.'

'We have our blackouts, and rationing, and all the other inconveniences to contend with,' she reminded him. 'Still, you're quite right, we *are* lucky. Now, can you manage to carry that kit-bag with one hand or shall I find someone to help you?' she asked briskly.

'No, I can manage fine.' With his sound arm, Adam swung the unwieldy khaki sack onto his shoulder. 'I'd better go and wait for the duty-driver to arrive. Perhaps I'll see you when I come back in for my check-up. Thanks for all you've done for me.'

'Take care.'

As he reached the door Adam paused and looked back. 'Mrs Price . . . would you mind saying "goodbye" to your daughter for me?'

'Yes, of course. I didn't know you and Helen knew each other,' she said, surprised.

'We don't really,' Adam mumbled, colouring. 'We sort of met up with each other yesterday, out in the grounds. She seems a very nice girl.'

'Well, *I* think so,' Mrs Price said proudly. 'She's here today, so why don't you find her and say goodbye to her yourself?' She should be taking books around the medical ward.'

'Great!' His eyes brightened. 'I'll go and look . . . Thanks a lot.'

Adam stood in the doorway watching Helen wheel the trolley-load of books around the ward. She was even prettier than he'd remembered, he thought, as he saw her oval face light up with a warm smile as she approached each bed. And much younger. Yesterday, he'd thought she was about twenty but today, in her plain pink dress and low-heeled sandals, her hair in a plait, she looked a mere schoolgirl.

He felt very attracted to her and wanted to know her better. It was a pity he was being discharged from the hospital, or that she hadn't appeared on the scene a couple of weeks earlier.

As she looked over in his direction, he wondered if she would remember him. Her lively greeting as she came towards him, her grey eyes shining with delight, cleared his mind of any doubt.

'They've taken your plaster off. Does that mean your arm is better?'

'Sound enough for me to return to my unit,' he told her. 'I'll be back again in two weeks' time for a check-up.'

'And you're leaving right now?'

'Any minute. Just as soon as the duty-driver turns up. As I said, I'm only stationed about five miles down the road, though, so perhaps we'll meet again?'

'I hope so,' she agreed eagerly.

'Do you really mean that?' he asked, hopefully.

'Of course!'

'Perhaps I can get a lift over on the duty-truck.'

'If you do, and I'm not here, come to my home. You'll be very welcome,' she said shyly.

'I don't know where you live.'

'My father's the doctor. Anyone in the village will direct you.'

His blue eyes searched her face, trying to decide whether the invitation was anything more than a polite gesture. Was her home an open house for any lonely soldier? he wondered. As they gazed at each other and he saw the warmth in her eyes, Adam sensed that she felt the same interest in him as he did towards her. Reluctantly he looked away.

'I'd better go and see if the truck's there yet. Can you spare the time to come and see me off?'

She hesitated, looking back at the trolley she had abandoned in the centre of the ward. 'I hope that won't be in anyone's way for a few minutes,' she murmured as she walked towards the door with him.

33

'I don't even know your name,' she said as they joined the small knot of men waiting for the truck to arrive.

'It's Adam ... Adam Woodley. And yours is Helen Price. I've managed to work that out for myself!' he grinned.

They stood close together on the gravel driveway, completely absorbed in each other. When the truck arrived, Adam bent his head until his mouth hovered temptingly above hers.

For a moment she stiffened and seemed to be about to draw back. Then as their lips met, warm and gentle, delicate as the union between two butterflies, she lifted her face trustingly, as if to drink in the sweetness of his mouth.

Their kiss, though fleeting, left Adam bewitched. He wanted to draw her into his arms, crush her slim body to his own. The brief contact had stirred such deep desire in him that he was left shaken and disturbed. Abruptly, he squared his shoulders and took a pace back.

'I have to go,' he said, reluctantly. He humped his kitbag into the back of the truck and scrambled in himself.

'Take care ... and come back soon,' she whispered.

The vehicle took off immediately, scattering gravel in all directions. As it reached the turn in the drive, Adam looked back and saw Helen still standing where he'd left her. He raised a hand in farewell.

Chapter 5

The next few days passed in a golden haze for Helen. Adam's brief kiss had crystallised all the ecstasy she'd ever imagined love would bring. Her heart sang with the birds, expanded with the sun's warmth and revelled in the summer beauty of the trees and flowers.

Even her mother noticed the soft, new light in her grey eyes and the fleeting smile on her lips. Pragmatically, Mrs Price attributed Helen's buoyant mood to the fact that she was helping out at Bulpitts and therefore felt useful and fulfilled. Her maxim had always been that work brought its own rewards.

Helen spent most of her time in a world of her own, reliving every second of Adam's brief caress. The tingling sensation as his face had pressed against hers, the pressure of his firm lips, and the warmth of his hands on her arms when he had pulled her to him, filled her mind completely.

In spite of his great strength and imposing physique, Adam had been so tender and gentle, that she had been breathless to respond. It had been so different from Donald's brusque approach, which had left her feeling frightened and outraged.

Each morning and afternoon when the duty truck arrived, Helen found an excuse to be near the door just in case Adam had managed to get a lift. After three days, she gave up hoping. She resisted the impulse to ask if he had been posted somewhere else, reluctant to discover that he had simply forgotten her.

A week passed, and then, to her immense delight, Adam appeared. In his khaki battledress, his forage-cap set at a jaunty angle, so that it only half-covered his shock of dark hair, he seemed even taller and broader than she'd remembered.

For a moment they simply stood there in the sunshine, staring at each other, drinking in the pleasure of being reunited

'See you here in half an hour, Woodley, if you want a lift back,' the duty-driver called out as he swung down from the cab and headed for the Guard Room. 'Don't be late.'

'Right. Thanks for the lift.'

Hand in hand, fingers entwined, Helen and Adam moved away from the house and into the garden. Neither

35

of them spoke until they reached the secluded dell near the Silent Pool. There, with only the birds and bright, darting butterflies as witnesses, Adam drew her towards him, holding her gently, yet possessively, and tenderly kissed her upturned, oval face.

'I've missed you, Helen,' he said softly. 'Did you think I was never coming back?'

'I knew you would . . . when you could,' she breathed, dazed with happiness, the anguished waiting forgotten.

'Let's sit here for a few minutes,' he said, drawing her down onto the soft, warm grass. 'I've some good news.'

She waited expectantly, conscious of his nearness and the pounding of her own heart. It was a moment she would remember all her life, she thought – the utter tranquillity, the bird-song and gentle buzzing of insects all around them, the heady smell of meadow-sweet and warm grass.

'Remember I was put on light duties? Well,' he paused as if savouring the pleasure of telling her, 'my light duties are to come to Bulpitts with the duty-driver each morning and check out the papers of all the new intakes. That shouldn't take long, should it?' He grinned. 'Then, I have to hang around for the afternoon duty-driver to take me back to Mere.'

'Every day?' she asked, wide-eyed.

'Until my check-up in two weeks' time.'

'And then?' she asked apprehensively.

He shrugged. 'Who knows. The war may be over by then! We'll worry about that when the time comes. I may manage to hang on to this cushy little number for a bit longer. Just think, it means we'll be able to see each other every day. Are you pleased?'

'Very!' She smiled, her grey eyes softening. 'I can hardly believe it.' She frowned. 'I only hope I can escape from Mum each day!'

'You don't think she'll approve?'

'It's not that, but I am supposed to be helping out here. Still,' she smiled confidently, 'I expect I can make her understand.'

36

'I'm quite sure you'll try,' Adam grinned, hugging her closer.

'It's almost too good to be true,' she said softly, her eyes misting with happiness as she looked up into his face. 'Do your duties start today?'

'No, not until tomorrow.' He frowned. 'I have to be on parade at midday. I sneaked off just to come and tell you the good news.' He checked his wrist-watch. 'I must go or I shall miss the truck.'

'Until tomorrow, then,' she murmured, raising her lips expectantly.

As his mouth came down over hers she closed her eyes, concentrating all her senses into savouring the moment when his warm, firm lips made contact with hers.

The long, lingering kiss was breathtaking in its intensity. Helen wanted to stay there in his arms in the warm, sweet dell, close her eyes, and drift into rapturous daydreams.

Much too soon, Adam released her, scrambling to his feet, straightening his uniform and brushing it free of grass.

'Come on.' He held out his good hand, pulling her to her feet. 'I'm going to miss that truck unless we hurry.'

The occasions when Adam could get away from his work at Bulpitts became the focal point of Helen's days. At first, Mrs Price was concerned, not so much by the fact that Helen was shirking work, but because she was becoming much too friendly with just one soldier. She would have felt happier if Helen had showed no particular favouritism.

When she got to know Adam better, however, Mrs Price's fears seemed to be allayed. At least, she voiced no further objections on the frequent occasions when, bright-eyed, her cheeks flushed with excitement, Helen came to tell her she'd be 'missing' for an hour or so.

On the days when Adam's work was minimal, and they had several hours to spend in each other's company, they explored the surrounding countryside. Helen had managed to borrow a bike for him and they pedalled for miles along unsignposted roads and down winding, country lanes.

In her eagerness to share things with Adam, she took him to all her favourite haunts, places she'd known since childhood. They spent idyllic afternoons at Stourton Gardens, scrambling over the mossy boulders of Rock Arch, or struggling through brambles and overgrown bushes to the Grotto. Even though the place was neglected – since the gardeners had all been called up – it still bore traces of grandeur as intended by Capability Brown when he had first designed it.

Arms around each other, they leant on the parapet of the stone bridge, staring out across the placid waters of the lake, where vivid blue-green dragonflies skimmed over the surface, mesmerised by the reflection of flowers, trees and bushes in its mirror-like surface.

And, later, after a drink at the Spread Eagle pub, they would wander through the nearby churchyard, where proud peacocks strutted amongst the graves, or into the surrounding woods where pigeons cooed mournfully.

Their love for each other deepened daily. Often they would walk for miles, fingers linked, without exchanging a single word. It was almost as if they could communicate through the pores of their skin and the air they breathed. Occasionally, for no reason at all, except their need of even closer contact, they would pause, turn towards each other and kiss.

So great was her happiness that Helen would have liked things to go on in the same way for ever. She had never felt so content, so enveloped in an aura of love. Each day her passion seemed to heighten, a huge radiant ball inside her mind, bathing the world around her in a golden haze.

The morning Adam reported, not for duty, but to see the Medical Officer, Helen felt tense and nervous as she helped on the wards. She wanted his arm to be better but she feared that as soon as he was fit for normal duties they would see much less of each other. He might even be posted, or sent overseas.

She was hanging about in the corridor outside the MO's office when Adam came out, flexing his fingers and stretching and bending his arm.

'Better?'

'One hundred per cent!' He grinned.

'Does that mean you'll be back on regular duties?' she asked anxiously.

'More than likely.' His face clouded, 'I'll know tomorrow. I've got the rest of today free though, so can you get away?'

She nodded eagerly. 'I've already told my mother I'd be taking the rest of the day off,' she said, untying her overall as she spoke.

'I bet you've even planned where we're going,' he joked, his blue eyes creasing with laughter.

'Fordswater. It's a lovely spot and within walking distance. There's a stream there, so we can paddle!'

'Sounds great!'

'I've even packed a picnic!' She smiled triumphantly.

'Then let's go.'

It was one of the hottest days of the summer. But by the time they'd eaten the sandwiches and apples Helen had packed, the sky had darkened, as mountainous black clouds, which had been hovering on the horizon, began to gather overhead.

'Come on, we'd better make a run for it,' Adam said, as dull rumblings of thunder filled the air.

They were only halfway across the field when the storm broke. Torrential rain soaked them, moulding Helen's thin, cotton dress to her body.

'There's a barn at the far end of this field,' she panted. 'We can shelter there until the worst is over.'

The barn was dark, but dry – redolent of the new-mown hay stored there.

'You'd better take off that wet dress,' Adam suggested, 'otherwise you'll end up with pneumonia.'

'You're soaked as well!' She laughed, pushing strands of dripping hair out of her eyes.

'Yes, that's true. And this uniform smells rank when it starts to dry out,' he added as he peeled off his battledress top and shook it vigorously before spreading it out to dry. 'Look,' he went on, as he undid the buttons on his shirt and began to remove it, 'take your dress off and slip this on while it dries out.'

'What are you going to wear?'

'I won't hurt without a shirt; it's not cold.'

'If you're feeling shy, I'll go and stand by the door while you change,' he offered.

'What it lacks in length, it certainly makes up for in width!' Helen giggled as she slipped his shirt over her head and wrapped the rough khaki flannel round her.

The look on Adam's face as he turned round, confirmed her suspicions that she looked ridiculous.

'If you laugh, I'll take it off,' she warned.

'Is that a promise?'

'Well, I would – only I've practically nothing on underneath.' Her cheeks flared as he raised an eyebrow.

'Come and sit here until your dress is dry. It shouldn't take long,' he said, as he settled himself comfortably on a bale of straw.

The hay was prickly, but not as itchy as Adam's shirt. Helen fidgeted so much that in the end Adam unfastened the front buttons of the shirt, easing the scratchy fabric away from her body.

'Is that any better?'

She nodded, not trusting herself to speak. The touch of his fingers against her bare skin was electrifying. She could feel her pulse racing and was sure that he must be able to hear the pounding of her heart.

Trembling, she looked up and was immediately daunted by the naked desire in Adam's eyes.

'Helen,' he whispered hoarsely, 'my sweet Helen.'

Fear and ardour mingled within her. She longed to reach up and pull his dark, tousled head down onto her breast. An inner caution warned her that to do so might be foolhardy. The turmoil of her feelings raged every bit as fiercely as the storm outside.

A sudden violent crash of thunder, that seemed to be immediately overhead, made Helen cry out. It seemed to be a signal for Adam to hold her closer, as if to shield her from the storm.

He moved so suddenly the shirt fell open. For a long moment, neither of them spoke or moved. He stared, as if transfixed, at the exposed, pearly-white flesh of her body and she felt powerless to cover her nakedness. Then, with a groan, he lowered his head and she felt the imprint of his burning lips on her cool skin.

Gently, but thoroughly, he began to explore her panting body with his lips. She murmured with pleasure as his lips focused on the delicate pink nipples of her firm, pointed breasts, and he gently teased them erect, before moving down the length of her body.

She lay back on the soft bed of hay, every nerve-end tingling as she succumbed to the magic of his hands as they stroked and probed.

When he raised himself on one elbow and began removing his trousers, she tried to protest, but his mouth came down over her lips, silencing her in its own special way.

Gradually, she relaxed. Her breathing became more even and a warm glow suffused her limbs. She made no resistance as she felt his naked body cover her own.

For a moment they lay quite still, savouring the fusion of their flesh. Trembling, she moved one hand slowly over his broad shoulders and on down to his slim waist.

Suddenly he seized her other hand, dragging it downwards until it brushed against something hard. Firmly he wrapped her fingers around his erection and the throbbing that met her touch made her breath quicken.

Heat surged through her, as he forced her thighs apart and his probing fingers entered her body. As his hand

41

created a rhythm, her senses stirred and, she felt herself straining towards him. Then he was guiding her, letting her be the one to make the final commitment.

There was a moment of searing pain when she thought the hugeness of him would rip her in two. But then the pain was gone and ripples of mounting tension made her body heave and contort, fusing with his movements until they both reached a passionate frenzy. The culminating crescendo of sweetness left her clinging to him breathlessly, trembling and exhausted.

The storm was over, and the sun was shining again from a placid blue sky as they left the barn. Words deserted them as, hand in hand, they hurried back to Sturbury. When they reached the Guard Room at Bulpitts, they found the duty-driver waiting impatiently.

'Sorry I'm late. We got caught out by the storm and had to shelter,' Adam told him.

'Hop in.' The soldier ground out his cigarette and swung up into the cab.

There was no time for any kind of farewell. Helen stood in the driveway, waving, as the truck vanished in a scattering of gravel and a cloud of dust.

Chapter 6

The war raged on. Although most of the major cities and towns as far north as Liverpool and Humberside had been devastated, people remained undaunted. Their fight went on, their energies directed on plans to invade Europe and eventually attack Germany itself. The first foothold had already been made in Sicily and it was rumoured that the Eighth Army, under General Montgomery, planned to land at Salerno.

Even though rationing grew tighter and an increasing number of commodities became unobtainable – except on the black market – people were still cheerful and confident that the war would soon be over.

Most able-bodied men were now in the services and many of the younger women had volunteered, or were being called up. Everyone claimed that once the Eighth Army was established in southern Europe, the invasion of France would follow.

Even in Sturbury, talk seemed to focus on this one topic, with everyone speculating about the possible date. Nothing else seemed to matter. Even when Helen's exam results arrived, Dr Price managed little more than a perfunctory acknowledgement.

'At least university will keep you out of the Forces for two or three years,' Mrs Price said with relief.

'By then this dreadful war may be over,' Dr Price agreed gloomily.

'Until term starts you can go on helping at Bulpitts,' Mrs Price went on. 'Heaven knows we need every pair of hands we can find – the place is overflowing with wounded men. If casualties go on at this rate they'll have to put up some temporary huts. It's impossible to squeeze any more into the house, and they've even put some beds out in the corridors.'

'You're working that girl too hard,' Dr Price warned his wife, when Helen left the room. 'She looks absolutely washed-out.'

Mrs Price was forced to agree. She, too, had noticed the dark circles under Helen's eyes, accentuated by the paleness of her cheeks.

'I keep telling her to take a day off and get some rest, but she's become almost fanatical about work,' she told her husband. 'I don't think she's sleeping well; probably too exhausted to unwind when she gets to bed. Someone has to go to Mere tomorrow for a fresh supply of drugs, so perhaps I'll send her. At least it will be a day away from the wards.'

She didn't want to worry her husband, but she was sure it was more than just tiredness; she suspected Helen was in love. She'd noticed a change in her ever since Adam Woodley, the young soldier Helen had become so attached to, had left Bulpitts. Since then, Helen had spent every day on the wards, refusing to take any time off. It was almost as if she was afraid to be away from the place.

Her behaviour was different, too. Although she laughed and joked with the patients and nurses it was only in a very superficial way. Her air of reserve was like a protective shield that divided her from everyone around her.

Helen accepted, with alacrity the suggestion that she should collect the medical supplies. There was always the chance that, since the Guards HQ was in Mere, she might get some news of Adam. It was now five weeks since their memorable day at Fordswater, and she hadn't seen him once since then. She didn't understand it. Surely he couldn't have just dismissed it from his mind?

'We'd better go, I don't want to miss the duty truck,' she said, pushing her plate to one side.

'Finish your breakfast. There's plenty of time,' her mother told her.

'I've had all I want.'

'That's your bacon ration for the week . . . surely you're not going to waste it!' Dr Price exclaimed.

'Sorry, I just don't feel like it.'

'You do look rather washed-out,' her mother said. 'The change will do you good. Don't rush back, have a look round the shops.'

'All four of them?' Helen said scornfully.

'You still have those coupons Donald left you,' her mother went on.

'Well, I'm not likely to find very much in Mere to spend them on, now am I?'

'No, you're probably right!' Mrs Price laughed. 'We'll both have to take a day off and go to Salisbury or Bath.'

'I'm not in the mood for buying clothes,' Helen said gloomily.

44

'Then you must be ill,' her father said in alarm.

'We'll have to fit in a shopping trip before you go to university,' Mrs Price persisted. 'I'm sure none of your winter stuff will fit you.'

'I haven't grown all that much,' Helen muttered.

'No, but you have put on some weight,' her father said sharply. 'Anyway a shopping trip will do your mother good, and get her away from that hospital for a bit.'

'OK, but not today,' Helen said quickly as she pushed back her chair and began to clear the table.

'No, of course not. Today, it's Mere for you and Bulpitts for me,' Mrs Price said briskly.

The small grey-stone town was packed with soldiers and, after she had collected the medical supplies, Helen plucked up courage and went along to the Company HQ to see what she could find out about Adam Woodley.

'Special friend, was he?' the burly RSM asked her with a leering grin.

'Just someone I knew,' she said nervously. 'I thought you might be able to tell me where he's been posted.'

'I can find out from Records . . . if it's important.'

She sat reading some out-of-date magazines until he came back. 'Afraid he's on special duties,' he said impassively. 'He should be back in about two weeks time . . . that's if we're still here.'

She stared at him in dismay, then, seeing the avid curiosity on his florid face, pulled herself together.

'Thank you. You've been very helpful.'

'Anytime!' He grinned knowingly. 'Sure there's no message you want to leave for him?'

As Helen ticked off the days to Adam's return her worst fears were realised. At night, alone in her bedroom, she knew moments of sheer panic in case he didn't come back to Mere. Suppose his unit was posted overseas? So many soldiers were being killed as the Allies struggled for supremacy that she might never see him again.

Several times she tried to talk to her father about the

45

predicament she was in, but each time her courage failed her. She knew he would not only confirm her fears but hold Adam to blame, and she dreaded the row that would follow.

Her mother would be utterly devastated. She had no patience with girls who 'got into trouble'. The blame was theirs she always contended. They only had to say 'No!'.

To her shame, Helen knew she had never for one moment considered saying 'No!', but that would be very difficult to explain to either of her parents.

There was only one solution, for Adam to come back and for them to be married. Then she could tell them and it would be quite acceptable.

As she struggled to conceal her morning-sickness and the general feeling of being unwell, the hot August days dragged on. Helen was glad it was so busy at Bulpitts. She had less time to worry when she was working hard. And when her mother commented on her pallor and moodiness, she always had the excuse that she was tired.

Having made his pronouncement that Helen was working much too hard, Dr Price put the whole thing from his mind. Evacuees had almost doubled the number of patients on his list and without his chauffeur and gardener, or anyone to help in the surgery, he had far more than his fair share of work.

Helen pinned her hopes on the RSM's assurance that Adam would be back in two weeks' time, and began making discreet enquiries. One duty-driver promised to find out for her, but he was posted to another unit the very next day and she never saw him again.

'If you're looking for a date, I'm free tonight,' his replacement laughingly told her when she asked if the other driver had left any message for her.

Helen turned away, biting her lower lip. His quick jibe stung her. He obviously thought she was free and easy with her favours. And that was what other people would think once the news broke, she thought bitterly. Yet it hadn't been like that. Not for her, at any rate, though she was no longer quite so sure about Adam. Would he have gone away without a word for almost six weeks if he'd thought anything about her? Surely he could have written, even if it was only a postcard?

Each day she became more and more worried. Soon she would be forced to tell her mother. At night, as she undressed for bed, she studied herself in the mirror. Already her waist seemed to be thickening and her breasts growing larger. The veins that had once been a mere blue tracery were now pronounced. The voluminous white overall she wore at Bulpitts hid her secret well, but soon she would have to spend some of the clothing coupons Donald had given her.

Whenever her mother started talking about her going to university, Helen quickly changed the subject, since she knew it was now quite out of the question. And yet, she mused, it could provide an alibi. If she could conceal her secret until the end of September, her parents need never find out that she was pregnant. She would let them think she had gone to university, but instead she would find a room somewhere and work until the baby was born.

The idea offered considerable scope and, for a time, she began to build her hopes around it. Then commonsense prevailed as the flaws became obvious. How could she possibly disappear and live her own life? She had no money to live on until she found a job. And when she didn't register at university someone would be bound to make enquiries. And then there would be the letters from home. Her parents would be frantic with worry if they were returned unopened. Reluctantly, she abandoned the idea as being impracticable and tried to think of some other solution. She had pushed all thoughts of Adam so far to the back of her mind that when she found him waiting for her one evening as she left Bulpitts, she wondered if he were some sort of hallucination. She stared in disbelief as the tall, handsome figure began hurrying towards her, hands outstretched in greeting. As she looked up into the lean, square face she felt dazzled by the intense brilliance of his blue eyes and fainted.

Minutes later, when she came round, Adam was

supporting her with one arm, frenziedly patting her cheek and calling her name.

'Adam!' Even to her own ears, her voice seemed a long way off.

'Come on! What's happening? I didn't know I had *that* sort of effect on people!' He grinned.

Tentatively she reached up and touched his cheek, outlining his familiar profile with her fingers, as if to make sure he wasn't a figment of her imagination.

'You didn't write . . .'

His head dipped as his lips sought hers. 'Couldn't. We weren't allowed to. I was on special duties. They wouldn't even tell us where we were, not until they brought us back here this morning.'

'You've been overseas?'

He shook his head. 'Look, I shouldn't be telling you this – I've been on special guard duty at Chequers . . . the Prime Minister's place.'

'Now you're back here for good?'

'Afraid not.' He grimaced. 'I'm being sent to the south coast with the next batch from our unit, in readiness for the invasion.'

'No! Oh, Adam, please say it's not true?'

'Come on . . . what's all this? I've no choice, you know that.' He held her tightly, hugging her close. 'I'll be back again, someday. This war can't last forever.'

Her eyes were enormous smokey-grey pools of despair as she stared up into his smiling face. 'Adam . . . I'm pregnant,' she blurted.

His smile faded and she felt him tense.

'I don't know what to do, Adam,' she said, tearfully.

Masterfully, he took her arm and drew her off the roadway. 'Let's go somewhere quiet, where we can talk. What about that pool we went to the first time we met?'

They didn't speak until they were in the secluded grassy dell, but the pressure of his hand on her arm comforted her.

'Now,' he said as he lowered his long frame onto the grass beside her, 'tell me what's happened.'

She did so, haltingly, waiting anxiously for his reaction.

'Your father's a doctor, can't he . . .'

'No!' She shook her head violently. 'It's out of the question. I haven't dared tell either of my parents . . . oh, Adam, what *am* I to do?'

He ran his hands through his dark hair in a gesture of hopelessness.

'I'm not sure. Give me a day or two and I'll try and think of something,' he said bleakly.

'You may not be *here* in a day or two. You just said you're due to be sent to the south coast with the next batch from your unit.'

'Well, have *you* any suggestions then?' he asked sharply, his eyes narrowing. 'You've known about it for weeks, and you haven't managed to think of a way out.'

'Only one that would really work,' she said in a small, tight voice. She waited hopefully, wanting him to be the one to say it, not her.

Her heart pounded as she saw the stern look on his handsome face. She had dreamed of him proposing, a sweet, tender moment when he would bare his soul, and tell her how much he loved her. She'd lived the scene over and over, even to the point of choosing the exact words she would use as she accepted.

Now, as she looked into Adam's eyes and sensed his utter bewilderment, her dream collapsed like a pricked balloon. He was so obviously overwhelmed by the problem she'd posed.

Impulsively, she put her arms around his neck and pulled his head down. His lips were hard, cool and unresponsive as she pressed her own to them. Feeling hurt, she drew back.

As if emerging from a trance, his hand shot out and held her face. For a moment his gaze raked over her, then with a groan his mouth savagely possessed hers, crushing her lips against her teeth, leaving her gasping for breath.

They were both breathing heavily when he released

her. 'I've dreamed of us being together again,' he muttered thickly. 'I hoped you'd still be waiting for me, I had no idea anything was wrong, of course . . . what can we do?'

Her heart sank. Trembling and tight-lipped she shook her head, tears prickling behind her eyelids. If she was the one to say those fateful words she would always feel she'd trapped him.

'Please, Helen,' he begged. 'You've been in my thoughts the whole time I've been away, but this news has knocked me sideways. I know it's all my fault and that I should have taken precautions.' He passed a hand through his hair in a bewildered way. 'I feel a complete rotter. If there's anything we can do to put things right then tell me. I just can't think straight. You do have something in mind . . . I can tell.'

'We could get married,' she whispered.

She felt his body stiffen, almost as if warding off a blow. She closed her eyes and breathed slowly and deeply, willing herself not to panic when he refused. Then his breath was hot on her cheek as he pulled her into his arms. 'Helen, my wonderful darling! Why didn't *I* think of that!'

The despair and frustration of the past weeks began to evaporate like snow when the sun shines on it. Anxiously, she looked into his eyes and then relaxed as she saw her own happiness and relief echoed there.

The magic of the Silent Pool enveloped them. With a sigh of contentment she pulled his head down until their lips touched. This time Adam was aroused and responsive. His lips paid homage, adroitly travelling from her lips to her eyes, before sensously seeking out the sensitive areas of her throat and shoulders. Blissfully she clung to him, desire flooding through her entire body.

With immense will-power, she raised his head. Avoiding his lips which still searched hungrily for her own, she said, 'We still have to tell my parents.'

His face clouded. 'You don't think they'll approve?'

'I don't know.' She frowned uneasily. 'They're both set on me going to university.'

'And you?'

She looked up quickly, studying his face for signs of his real feelings. She wondered if in his heart he hoped she would say she did want to go to university. Yet he must know that was impossible . . . unless. She was filled with misgivings; surely he wouldn't want her to consider something so terrible?

He stood up, extending a hand to pull her to her feet. 'I want you to have our baby more than anything else in the world,' he told her gently as he held her close. 'So why don't we go and tell your parents right away?'

Her elation was immediately dampened at the thought of the shock it would be to them both.

'We'll just tell them we want to get married, not . . . not about the baby.'

Tenderly he tilted her face so that she was forced to look at him. 'If that's how you want it,' he promised, 'but I think they'll wonder why we're in such a hurry and I think we owe them the truth.'

'Later, perhaps,' she whispered as they clung to each other, 'not right away, Adam . . .'

Chapter 7

'Is that it?' Dr Price's grey eyebrows shot up in surprise as the Registrar carefully blotted their signatures and shook hands with Adam and Helen.

'Yes. I'm now Mrs Woodley,' Helen breathed blissfully, linking her arm through Adam's and smiling up into his face. Proudly she held out her left hand, displaying its shining gold band for her father's inspection.

'It's the starkest wedding ceremony I've ever attended,'

Dr Price said. He cast a disparaging glance around the sparsely furnished office, with its threadbare red carpet, a vase of wilted roses on the desk the only form of decoration.

'Well, never mind dear. It all went very smoothly,' Mrs Price said placatingly. She stroked the backs of her white gloves, and then nervously moved her handbag onto her other arm.

'But it doesn't feel like a family wedding,' Dr Price muttered gloomily as he held open the door for them to leave. 'We're twenty miles from home; we know no one – we might have been negotiating a bank loan for all the atmosphere there is.'

'No fuss, no dressing up, no speeches, no waste of time ... I would have thought you would have approved,' Aunt Julia said tartly.

'I'm so glad you're pleased with the way we've done things, Aunt Julia,' Helen said quickly. 'And you do look very smart in your uniform,' she added warmly.

'Certainly better than seeing you dressed up in one of your exotic outfits and peculiar hats, I suppose,' Dr Price muttered drily. 'Although that might have made the occasion seem more real. At least we'd be able to look through the wedding album and have a good laugh. As it is, there isn't even a photographer here.'

'I've brought my camera though,' Aunt Julia retorted, 'so we can take our own.'

'You'd better let me take them,' Dr Price said, holding out his hand for the camera. 'Your snaps are usually pretty disastrous.'

'Rubbish! You can take some in a minute, but there must be at least one family group with you on it,' she insisted.

'Well, get on with it then,' Dr Price snapped, as he stood with the rest of the group.

'I really don't understand why you are being so disagreeable,' Mrs Price said sharply, frowning at her husband. 'There's no call to be so disparaging. Normally you abhor big weddings and having to dress up in top hat and tails.'

'Other people's perhaps, but when it's your only daughter . . .'

'For heavens sake!' Aunt Julia exclaimed. 'There's a war on!'

'Helen could still have been married in the village church instead of this hole-and-corner affair. Our friends and neighbours could all have been there to see her, even if we couldn't muster up enough rations to wine and dine them afterwards.'

'And I could have borrowed a white wedding-dress from the WVS I suppose,' Helen said scornfully. 'No thanks! I'd sooner wear my own clothes, even if it has to be an ordinary dress.'

'Ordinary is a most apt description,' her father said cuttingly. 'Why didn't you at least buy something new . . .'

'Clothes are rationed – or had you forgotten?' Aunt Julia cut in triumphantly. 'Anyway, what's wrong with what she's wearing? I can see the paragraph now in the local paper. "The bride wore a full-skirted cream dress, with a hand-embroidered fitted bodice trimmed with cream lace."'

'There's a whole book of coupons lying on top of the Bureau that Donald Brady left for Helen . . .' Dr Price went on, ignoring the interruption from his sister-in-law.

'Helen will need those to buy everyday things, like a new coat for the winter,' Mrs Price said quietly. 'Under the circumstances I think she's been very sensible having a quiet wedding and not wasting precious coupons on a dress she'd only be able to wear once. Anyway,' she added brightly, 'it's not over yet. Now the legal bit's been dealt with, let's all relax and enjoy ourselves. I'm told that they still do a first-class lunch at The Crown, so now's our chance to find out.'

The Crown was one of the oldest hotels in Salchester. A three-storeyed grey-stone building facing onto the square, its imposing façade gave it an air of subdued luxury as well as solid respectability.

It was like entering another world as they walked through the heavy, carved-oak doors. Their feet sank into the deep-pile red Wilton that stretched down the wide, endless corridors, and the general air of opulence made rationing and shortages seem like a grey dream. It was like stepping back a decade, to the days when war had been far from people's minds and the hotel had been the meeting-place for wealthy landowners and their wives, in town for market day or the races. It was where affluent tourists visiting the famous cathedral stayed.

The moment they entered the Crown Hotel, Adam felt out of place. Everywhere he turned there were majors, captains, colonels, as well as a general or two, intermingled with high ranking Naval and Air Force officers. Even some of the women present were in uniform, with pips or crowns on their shoulders and gold braid indicating their rank.

As they were being shown to their table, heads turned in surprise at the sight of an ordinary soldier sitting down to eat in the same dining-room as themselves. Adam's khaki battledress, even though it bore the shoulder-badges of a Guards regiment, stood out in marked contrast to the well-tailored officers' uniforms. And, although he had ignored regulations and worn his own black shoes instead of the clumping boots which were standard issue, he still felt clumsy and ill-at-ease.

Dr Price was not in the least perturbed by the raised eyebrows. Adam's embarrassment heightened when he saw the speculative gleam in his father-in-law's eyes as he looked around the room. He knew how sharp and censorious Dr Price could be when he chose. He had experienced a sample of his scathing tongue when he and Helen had told him they wanted to be married.

'Married! At your age,' he had rasped. 'Utter nonsense. I suppose you both think you're in love? Let me inform you it's nothing of the sort. Put it down to animal magnetism, chemical attraction, immaturity, childish infatuation, or whatever you wish to call it.'

Stubbornly, Helen had stuck to her guns, although she had been trembling with fury at her father's derisory remarks.

Listening to the two of them, Adam had been filled with rage that there was so little he could say or do. He knew instinctively that Helen was handling the whole thing badly. Quiet reasoning, he was sure, would be much more effective with Dr Price than obstinate defiance.

Helen had won the day, and forced her father into giving his permission, but Adam was sure he still bore a grudge and it made him nervous and cautious in Dr Price's company.

He relaxed slightly when Dr Price turned to his sister-in-law and remarked, 'You must feel quite at home, Julia, with all these uniforms around. Probably half of the people here can't even recognise what yours is and are wondering what strange regiment you belong to. Good job we have Adam in a truly British uniform or we might find ourselves being mistaken for enemy spies!'

For Helen's sake, Adam tried to enjoy himself, but he felt nervous and on edge. Aunt Julia was doing her best to keep the party lively, but the note of discord raised by Dr Price in the Registrar's office still hung in the air, a spectre at the feast.

The meal was superb, with luxury foods which, though unrationed, were generally unobtainable. Canteloupe melon, filled with rum, was followed by grilled river trout. For the main course there was venison, and, for dessert, strawberries topped with fresh cream.

As they sipped vintage champagne between courses, the atmosphere became more relaxed, but Adam still felt an outsider and wished Gary had been there to support him.

As soon as the wedding date had been fixed, he'd written to Gary, inviting him to the wedding, only to get a letter the next morning which read: 'Just spent 48 hours embarkation leave in London. See you when I get back.' Now it might be months, or even years, before Gary and Helen would meet.

As the meal finally came to an end, he hoped Dr Price wouldn't make a speech. All he wanted was for the three of them to disappear so that he could spend every second that remained of his leave alone with Helen. The longer he was in Dr Price's company the more he sensed that he not only didn't approve of Helen getting married so young, but he didn't endorse her choice of husband either.

'I'm not at all the sort of son-in-law your father would have wished to have,' he murmured to Helen later that evening when they were finally alone in the huge bedroom, with its massive four-poster and dark, walnut furniture.

'Rubbish. Anyway, he'll soon get used to you. How could anyone help but love you,' she teased, running her fingers through his thick hair and drawing his head closer so that she could feast her mouth on his.

'That's not the point,' he told her, pulling back and walking across to the window. He drew aside the thickly lined curtains and stared out across the blacked-out city to where the cathedral spire pointed a sharp, admonishing finger skywards.

'I think he is disappointed. I have no career prospects, you know. I am sure he would have been a lot happier if you'd married someone from your own social stratum . . .'

'Social stratum . . . what's that? We live in a democracy; you are fighting for your country; we are all fighting for survival. Without people like you there would be no future for my father or any of his wealthy friends and patients,' she declared indignantly.

'That may be . . .'

'Adam!' The sharpness of her tone made him wince. 'What are we doing arguing about such matters on our wedding night!'

'You're right!' He whisked shut the heavy curtains, quickly checking to see there were no gaps that would allow any light to escape before switching on the bedside lights and holding out his hands to Helen.

'Come on, Mrs Woodley,' he invited, 'we've less than forty-eight hours to get to know each other.'

From that moment their honeymoon was idyllic, though the few precious hours seemed to pass in a flash.

They made love, they dreamed and planned the future they would have together when the war was finally over. And, on the last morning they talked about the baby Helen was expecting.

'Do you want a boy or girl?' she asked.

'Well. . .' he considered the question carefully,' . . . a girl if she's going to look like you, with thick brown hair and dove-grey eyes.'

'And if it's a boy then he must look like you, with brilliantly blue eyes and an unruly mop of dark hair, and when he grows up he'll have a firm jawline, just like this one,' she told him as her fingers moved caressingly over his chin.

'No.' He captured her hand, imprisoning it in his own. 'If it's a boy, I'd want him to look like my brother Gary.'

'Well, you said he had blue eyes.'

'So he has, but his hair isn't like mine. It's a rich, coppery colour, just like our mother's was. I wish he'd been able to come to our wedding. You'd like him. He's great fun . . .'

'Quite your favourite person . . .'

'Next to you!'

'Perhaps the baby won't be like any of us. Look how different Mum and Aunt Julia are – and they're sisters. There's only three years age difference, yet Mum seems years and years older than Aunt Julia. I think it might have something to do with their build. Aunt Julia's so slim and trim that she makes Mum look quite matronly.'

'They're alike in other ways; both efficient organisers.'

'True. Mum seems completely different when she's at Bulpitts. I've never seen her so brisk and bustling. I actually think she enjoys working there. Dad doesn't approve, of course. He'd sooner have her at home, running around after him. He hates having to dispense his own medicines. It's a wonder he doesn't give his patients a prescription and tell them they'll have to go to the chemists in Winton and have it made up there.'

'Now that you're going to be at home, perhaps you could act as his dispenser. Easier work than you're doing at Bulpitts.'

Helen shook her head emphatically. 'If I was that close to him all day, he'd guess about the baby in no time.'

'When are you going to tell your parents?' Adam asked.

They were still in bed, replete from a gourmet breakfast which had been served in their room.

'Not until I have to,' Helen told him, as she replaced her empty cup on the tray. 'Wasn't that absolutely delicious?' she said with a satisfied sigh. 'I'm sure we've just eaten a week's ration of bacon each. I wonder how they do it?'

'Black market, probably.'

'Mmm. You could be right,' she murmured, popping the final piece of hot buttered toast into her mouth and wiping her fingers on a serviette. 'If you've got money you seem to be able to buy most of life's luxuries, even in wartime.'

'That's another reason why you must tell your parents as soon as you get home.'

She looked at him, bewildered. 'Are we still on the same wavelength? I'm talking about how people manage to get extra rations.'

'So was I. As soon as a doctor officially pronounces you pregnant, you'll be entitled to extra rations, won't you?'

'I can't tell anyone yet!' She giggled. 'No one would believe me. How could I possibly know so soon!'

'There are tests, surely?'

'You think I should go straight home from my honeymoon and announce that I'm pregnant!'

58

'Why not?'

'Everyone would know that I'd had to get married,' she replied in shocked tones.

'They'll be able to work it out for themselves in a few months' time,' he told her drily as his hand rested gently on the smooth, rounded contours of her stomach.

'No they won't,' she said defiantly. 'I don't intend saying anything for another couple of months. When the baby arrives I intend to tell everyone he's premature.'

'And what if the baby decides to be premature anyway?'

'He won't be,' she said confidently.

'I still think you should tell your parents. At least let your father keep a professional eye on you.'

'No!' Stubbornly, Helen shook her head, her grey eyes determined. 'I'd feel terrible having to face them on my own. At the moment neither of them suspect a thing. I want you to be there when I tell them . . .'

'That mightn't be possible,' Adam said firmly. 'I mightn't be home again before we go overseas.'

'Then I'll tell them at Christmas.' She traced the outline of his mouth with her index finger, before sealing the pact with a tender kiss.

'You're simply evading the issue; they'll guess for themselves long before then.'

'Well, if they do, I won't have to be the one to tell them, will I?' Her hands cupped his chin, drawing his face closer until once more their lips met.

He sighed as he pulled away from her. Reluctantly he threw back the bedclothes. 'I must go. I have to report back before midday.'

She reached and caught his arm, pulling him down beside her. 'Not yet . . . one last cuddle.'

His mouth settled hungrily on hers, transporting them both back into a timeless, enchanted abyss.

Chapter 8

'Mrs Woodley, do you know where I can find Matron?'

For a moment, Helen stared blankly at the orderly. Although she'd now been married for six weeks, she still found it strange to hear herself being addressed as Mrs Woodley.

Her parents treated her marriage as if it had never happened. They rarely referred to it and there was not a single trace of Adam, apart from a framed photograph. It was one Aunt Julia had taken on their wedding-day and showed them both standing in a lop-sided manner, with a portion of Adam's head missing from the top of the picture. Helen treasured the photograph since that, and their marriage certificate, were the only things she had as confirmation of that brief civil ceremony.

Except, of course, the gradual thickening of her waist and the waves of sickness that assailed her if she sprang out of bed too quickly in the morning.

After their brief honeymoon, Adam had returned to his unit and, although he wrote to her two or three times a week, there had been no opportunity for them to meet. He was still 'somewhere near the south coast', confined to camp and waiting to be sent overseas. And, from what she read in the newspapers and heard on the wireless, Helen knew that most likely that meant Italy.

She dreaded it happening, for although the campaign there was having some tremendous successes, the casualty rate, both on land and at sea, was very high. Jimmy, the Price's gardener, had been killed when the troopship he was on had been torpedoed just off Salerno. The news of his death had brought the war much nearer home, for Jimmy had worked for them from the day he left school until he received his calling-up papers. He had the true countryman's empathy with the soil and the things he grew. Helen's father had constantly talked about how Jimmy would soon have the garden right once he came back, and it was hard to believe he would never return.

For Helen, life was as changing as the autumn tints around her. She felt restless, moody and apprehensive about the future. Her mother tried to persuade her to start training as a nurse but, knowing she had no possible chance of completing such an undertaking, Helen refused. She was tempted to give her reasons but drew back, unwilling to see the look of astonishment and dismay in her mother's eyes. Tenaciously, she stuck to her plan to say nothing until Christmas and then let them think she was only four months pregnant.

'It wouldn't be so very different from helping out at Bulpitts,' her mother persisted.

'Maybe, but it's not worth starting something I'm not likely to finish,' Helen told her stubbornly. 'I'm not dedicated like you. If the war ended suddenly and Adam came home, then I'd want to be free to be with him.'

'That's understandable,' her mother argued, 'but the way things are dragging on the war might last for another couple of years. And Adam won't be discharged immediately it ends, you know. It may be weeks, or months even, before he is released. By then you could be fully qualified and you could go on working for a time. The money would help you get a home together. You have to think about these things now. Getting married brings responsibilities. It's not all moonlight and roses. That's why your father was so against you rushing things.'

Finally, because she had no wish to antagonise her mother, Helen agreed to train, not for her SRN but for a Civil Nursing Reserve certificate. The training was less stringent and qualifications easier to attain.

Although not completely satisfied, Mrs Price accepted the compromise with good grace. 'It will be a sound basis and eventually you can go in for your SRN,' she commented, when Helen made her decision.

Because they were so short-staffed at Bulpitts it was arranged that she could stay there for her initial six months' training. After that she would have to move on to a larger hospital.

It seemed the perfect solution. Instead of merely going around the wards, in her everyday clothes as a 'helper', Helen now wore a blue print dress, a starched white apron and cap.

'Can't say I like you in that uniform; it makes you look fat,' her mother told her critically.

'It's because it's so stiff,' Helen told her, colouring. 'When it's been washed a few times it will be better.'

'Perhaps you're right. Anyway, what you look like doesn't really matter. It's what you can do that counts. I've just had news that they are going to extend Bulpitts. Another thirty beds, and twenty of those are to be for women.'

'It's not possible! The place is overflowing as it is.'

'The Army is going to put up huts in the grounds.'

Within days, the Pioneer Corps had moved in and a state of chaos reigned. It was short-lived. When they moved out, a spider's web of new wards, linked to the main house by long narrow corridors, had been erected. Almost immediately they began to fill up and Helen found herself worked off her feet making up beds for the new arrivals.

The first women patients to arrive were from the ATS and she quickly found they demanded more attention and were much more difficult than the men.

At the end of her first day on the women's ward, Helen felt completely exhausted. Just as she was going off duty a nurse came hurrying into the staff room.

'Helen, your name was Price before you were married, wasn't it?' she asked.

'Yes. Why?'

'One of the new arrivals is asking for you.'

Helen's thoughts flew immediately to Adam. Her heart started hammering and her legs felt like jelly. Then, just as swiftly, she regained her composure. He wouldn't ask for Helen Price. He, above all others, would know she called herself Helen Woodley.

'Do you know who it is?'

The nurse shrugged. 'I didn't ask. She's an ATS.'

Filled with curiosity, Helen returned to the women's ward. When she pulled back the curtains around the newcomer's bed, she stopped in surprise. Lying propped against the pillows was Katy Wilson, one of the girls from St Margaret's.

For a split second they simply stared at each other, then Helen's arms encircled her friend, hugging her and bombarding her with questions.

'Go easy! I've got a broken collar-bone.'

'Sorry! Just shows you the kind of nurse I am!' Helen smiled. 'When did this happen?'

'About a week ago. It's been X-rayed and set. I'm hoping that when the MO does his rounds in the morning he'll say I'm a walking case. I hate lying in bed.'

'Great. If you are up and about we'll be able to see a lot of each other.'

'When I heard the matron's name I guessed it was your mother and I thought she'd probably enlisted you onto the staff. The nurse seemed to think your name was Woodley!'

'It is!' Helen held out her left hand with its shining new band of gold.

'No! I don't *believe* it! You never had any time for boys. Miss Prim-and-Proper if ever there was one. What happened?'

Helen flushed. 'We met, we fell in love, we married. Just like that!'

'And where is he now? When am I going to meet him? Is he a doctor here?' Katy asked excitedly.

'No, he's a soldier. In the Guards.'

Katy's green eyes narrowed. 'Come on,' she said softly, 'You know I could always tell when you weren't telling the truth. What's the real story behind those wedding bells. Is he madly rich?'

'No.' Helen shook her dark head slowly. 'As far as I know he hasn't a bean to his name apart from his Army pay.'

'What rank is he? A Captain, a Major . . .'

'No, he's a Guardsman,' Helen said shortly.

Katy whistled silently and looked mischieviously at Helen. 'The truth, Helen,' she wheedled. 'You're preggers, aren't you!'

Helen felt the colour rush to her face. 'I think you should be resting, Katy,' she said primly, avoiding her friends searching gaze. 'I've got to go now. See you in the morning.'

Katy grinned and waved mockingly. 'Take care, Mrs Woodley . . . in your condition.'

Helen hesitated for a split second, then turned back to Katy. The colour that had suffused her cheeks when Katy had started teasing her was gone. Her face was now white and drawn, grim lines etched her gentle mouth and there was a haunted look in her grey eyes.

'Katy, stop joking and listen,' she said in a low voice. 'You're right, I am pregnant and I did have to get married. Adam is on the south coast somewhere, waiting to go overseas. No one knows I am expecting a baby and I don't intend telling anyone until Christmas. Can I trust you not to give my secret away?'

'Helen, I really had no idea. I was just spoofing.' Katy's green eyes softened and she reached out and covered Helen's hand with her own. 'I won't breathe a word . . . honest! Though how you hope to keep it secret when your father's a doctor beats me.'

'He'll never notice.'

'I wouldn't bet on it,' Katy said darkly.

'That's a chance I have to take,' Helen answered stiffly. 'Can I count on you though, Katy?'

'Swear it! Only I want to hear the whole story. You owe me that.'

'OK. Tomorrow. Or when you are well enough to move out of that bed and we can go somewhere private.

There's too many ears around here.' She bent and kissed Katy on the forehead. 'I'll see you in the morning.'

Having Katy as a confidante did wonders for Helen's morale. Katy found it all highly romantic, but she was adamant that Helen ought to confide in her mother. This Helen stubbornly refused to do.

'You're mad,' Katy told her. 'Your mother would make sure then that you were only given light duties.'

'I'm as strong as an ox,' Helen told her. 'I don't need special concessions.'

'I bet Adam wouldn't agree with you,' Katy insisted.

Apart from this one bone of contention, the two girls enjoyed each other's company. Katy was not confined to bed so, whenever Helen was off duty during the day, the two of them would go off together. The kaleidoscope of autumn, the golds, yellows, oranges, browns and dark greens, made walking a joy. And when the October days were cold or dull they went to Helen's home.

'Before Katy is sent back to her unit, I wondered if she'd like to come and stay for a weekend,' Mrs Price suggested. 'I've had a letter from Margaret Brady saying the Colonel hasn't been too well and she's anxious for him to have a check-up. Apparently, he's averse to seeing doctors . . . except one. I thought if I could persuade him to go up to London he could give the Colonel a check-up and have a break at the same time.'

'That's a splendid idea,' Helen smiled. 'Knowing his professional services are needed is probably about the only thing that would persuade Dad to take a break, even for a weekend.'

'I think a trip up to London would do us both good,' Mrs Price admitted. 'I was wondering about asking Aunt Julia to come and stay with you for the weekend . . .'

'There's really no need,' Helen said quickly. 'Katy and I will manage OK.'

'Well, if you're sure. I thought you mightn't like being alone in the house overnight.'

'I won't be if you arrange a sleeping-out pass for Katy.'

Katy was as delighted as Helen and plans went ahead for the following weekend. On the Friday night, after they'd seen Dr and Mrs Price off, they had supper on their knees in front of a roaring log fire and settled down to play all their favourite records. They talked until well after midnight, reminiscing about schooldays, and fantasising about the future once the war was over.

'We'll have a lie-in in the morning,' Helen said, yawning when finally they made their way up to bed. 'I've left a note pinned on the surgery door to say Dad's away until Monday and I've got a phone by my bed in case anyone calls.'

'Right, nurse!' Katy grinned. 'If I do wake up first then I'll bring you a cup of tea in bed.'

'Great! I'll make sure I sleep late!' Helen laughed.

True to her word she was still asleep when the bedside phone rang at half-past nine the next morning. For a moment, still dazed by sleep, she thought the familiar voice on the line must be Adam's and her heart raced. Then, as her mind cleared, she realized it was Donald Brady.

'Sorry! Have I woken you? I waited until I thought it was a reasonable hour . . . it's after nine-thirty, you know.'

'I've got a friend staying and we had a late night.' she explained.

'Yes . . . yes, I know. Your parents told me.' He hesitated, as if unsure what to say next.

Helen waited impatiently, irritated that he had woken her if all he wanted was to chat. The sound of the phone had disturbed Katy who appeared, yawning, tousled from sleep, clutching a green and blue flowered dressing-gown around her.

'It's Donald . . . Donald Brady,' Helen whispered, shielding the mouthpiece with one hand.

'The one whose parents own Bulpitts?'

Helen nodded absently, her attention taken by what Donald was saying.

66

'Helen . . . I saw your parents last night . . . they were all just sitting down to dinner when I left . . . About half an hour later it happened . . .'

'What happened . . . what are you trying to tell me?'

'Look, Helen. This is difficult to say on the phone . . . Are you on your own?'

'I told you, I've got a friend staying with me . . . why?'

'Could you fetch her?'

'Whatever for! You've never met Katy.'

'I . . . I think she should be there when I tell you . . .'

The distress in Donald's voice suddenly registered with Helen. She stiffened, wondering what was coming next. Her thoughts raced. Had he heard something about Adam? she wondered.

'What is it you're trying to tell me, Donald?'

'Helen . . . look . . . I don't know how to say this. Perhaps it would be better if I spoke to Katy.'

'Katy's here in the room but I'd rather you told me,' she said cautiously. A sixth sense told her that whatever it was Donald had to say it was something unpleasant.

'OK.' He gave a deep sigh, then rushed on, 'It's about your parents. They were having dinner with my mother and father when our house was bombed. It was a direct hit. No one . . . none of them . . . they were all killed.'

There was a silence, so taut that it was as if an invisible bridge linked them, then it shattered like broken glass as Donald's voice came down the line, calling her name urgently.

Helen found herself unable to answer. Dumbly she passed the receiver over to Katy and, in a stupor, listened as Katy cross-questioned Donald in a cool, staccato voice.

Katy was the epitome of practicality for the next few hours. She phoned Julia Freeman and told her precisely what had happened. Aunt Julia promised to come straight over, as soon as she had found someone to take over her ambulance duties.

Unable to phone Adam direct, Katy asked the police to relay a message to his unit and, within a couple of hours, he phoned to let them know he had been given compassionate leave and was on his way home.

Aunt Julia and Donald made the funeral arrangements. The four bodies were brought back from London for burial in the local churchyard.

It was a brief, touching ceremony, attended by most of the villagers of Sturbury. Donald and Isabel were there, too, but Katy had been posted back to her unit. Helen bore up bravely, with Adam's help, but it was as if she was living through a nightmare; none of it seemed to have any real meaning for her.

When it was all over, Donald and Isabel returned to London. Adam was loathe to leave Helen, but they both knew that if he didn't return to his unit it would be tantamount to desertion.

Helen had other problems to face, too. Immediately after the funeral, her father's solicitor disclosed that Dr Price had been heavily in debt and the house was mortgaged up to the hilt. His advice was she should sell it with the practice and he undertook to find a buyer.

'It means you will be left with nowhere to live, of course,' he went on sympathetically, 'but Miss Freeman is agreeable to you making your home with her as a temporary measure.'

Helen felt dazed by the news, but Aunt Julia didn't seem in the least surprised.

'I told them years ago that they couldn't go on as they were,' she said cryptically. 'Far too many servants, and sending you to such an expensive school, was bound to drain their resources. Your father only had about eight paying patients and most of them were much too healthy for his own good.'

'His surgery was always packed,' Helen protested.

'Yes, with villagers who traded a cabbage or a rabbit in return for a bottle of medicine. None of them could afford to pay him. And if they had tried to do so he would probably have handed the money back to them with a shilling of his own added to it.'

'Did mother know about this?' Helen asked be-wildered.

'Of course she did. She was as soft-hearted as he was. More food went out of that house to people in the village than was ever eaten at their table.'

'How do you know about all this?'

'She was my sister, Helen. We were very close. That's why I hope you'll move in with me . . . at least until after your baby is born. It's what your mother would have wished.'

'You know about that, too!' Helen gasped, staring at her open-mouthed.

'Of course I do. Your mother guesed right away, that's why she didn't oppose you getting married!'

'And did Dad know as well?'

Aunt Julia shook her head. 'I don't think so, not unless your mother told him when they went up to London.'

'I do wish she'd said she knew,' Helen sighed. 'It would have made things so much easier.'

'Mmm!' Aunt Julia picked up her cigarette-case, took out a cigarette, then snapped the case shut. 'I won't offer you one and start you on my bad habit,' she said, with a tight smile. 'Your parents were against me smoking so I never did when they were around. Cowardice really . . . a bit like you not telling them about the baby. Anyway,' she added, as she struck a match, 'now that is out in the open, and there are no secrets between us, you'd better come and live here at Willow Cottage until this war is over and you and Adam get a home of your own.'

To take her mind off her personal worries, Helen decided to go on working at Bulpitts. The new matron was young, stern and hardworking, and the atmosphere changed over-night. Helen told her she was pregnant. Now that her parents were dead it no longer seemed to matter who knew. Matron's only comment as she noted down when the baby was due, was, 'Right, I'll put you on light duties.'

Although Aunt Julia made her welcome, Willow Cottage wasn't home for Helen. She had never liked cats and Aunt Julia's two sleek Siamese seemed to resent the intrusion of a stranger, spitting and clawing at her whenever she went anywhere near them. Finally, she wrote to Adam and asked him if he would find her somewhere to stay near where he was stationed, at least until he was sent overseas.

Chapter 9

Adam Woodley lowered his kit-bag onto the floor and looked around the hotel bedroom critically. He hoped Helen would like it. Compared to the opulence of the bedroom at The Crown in Salchester, where they'd spent their brief honeymoon, he had to admit it was pretty stark.

The heavy blackout curtains at the window looking out onto Sussex Square, gave the room a sombre air. On the cream walls hung one picture of a sea scene. The double bed had a plain, wooden headboard that matched the oak bedroom suite. Two armchairs, a round, oak coffee-table set between them, stood on the beige floral carpet.

He looked at his wrist-watch; he'd have to hurry or he wouldn't get to Waterloo Station in time for Helen's train.

He'd been surprised and delighted when she had suggested they should spend his Christmas leave in London. He had thought it would be the last place she would want to visit after what had happened to her parents there less than six weeks before. But she had been adamant, insisting that Aunt Julia needed Willow Cottage to herself over the holiday.

He'd known it wouldn't be easy to find somewhere to stay. Despite the risk of bombings, the blackout and rationing, everybody seemed to want to spend Christmas in London. And American soldiers, with pay-packets twice the size of those of British servicemen, seemed to have taken over every available room. He'd been lucky; someone in camp had put him on to the Regent Court Hotel and there'd been a room available.

At Waterloo Station he elbowed his way through the crowds to the platform where the train from Salchester and the West Country had just pulled in. He scanned the people emerging from it, but Helen was not on it. Concerned, he went to check the time of the next train. As he did so, he heard his name called on the tannoy, asking him to report to the station-master's office.

Filled with a sense of foreboding, Adam sprinted along the crowded platform. A hundred thoughts raced through his head. It was almost an anti-climax when he was handed a slip of paper with Helen's phone number on it.

The phone was answered as soon as he was put through, as if someone had been sitting waiting for his call.

'Is that you, Adam?'

'Yes, who's that?'

'Helen's aunt . . . Julia Freeman.'

'Where's Helen? She was supposed to be coming to London . . .'

'I know, that's why I left a message for you to phone. Helen's not coming . . . she . . . she's had a miscarriage . . .'

'Is she all right? Can I speak to her?'

'They've taken her to Salchester Hospital. I'm afraid you can't see her until tomorrow . . . and you must phone first.'

'Is it very serious?'

'There are complications. Are you going to stay in London until the morning or come on down here?'

Adam looked at his watch. It was almost eight-thirty, so it would be nearly midnight before he reached Sturbury. 'Perhaps I'd better leave it till the morning,' he told her. 'I'll phone you again first thing.'

71

Adam left the phone-box in a daze, and made his way back to the hotel, his mind churning with worry about Helen. He stopped at the reception desk and asked for his bill so that he could pay in advance and catch the first train next morning. When the receptionist heard the name Woodley, she told him, 'I've just taken a telephone call for you.'

'My wife . . . she's worse?'

The woman looked puzzled. 'I don't know anything about that.' She picked up a slip of paper on which she'd written the message and began reading it aloud. 'Regret to inform you Gary Woodley has been reported killed in action.'

The words echoed in Adam's brain like a nursery rhyme chant. Over and over they drummed, until he thought his head would burst. Clamping his hands over his ears he heard himself shouting aloud, 'No! No! No!'

'Here, you all right? Would you like a nip of something. Bit of a shock is it?'

'What?' he stared at her uncomprehendingly.

'That message I've just given you . . . upset you like? Someone close was it?'

'My brother.' He turned away from the desk, hands clenched, unable to stand the pity in her eyes. 'Think I'll just go for a walk . . . sort myself out . . .' Choked with emotion he made for the door.

The streets were in complete darkness. The thin crescent of moon that had been shining when he had set out to meet Helen, was now hidden behind low cloud. Within a few minutes Adam was completely lost. Uncaring, sick with grief, he wandered wherever his feet took him, until finally he felt so exhausted he knew he must have a drink. He had no idea where he was, except that he must be a long way both from his hotel and from the centre of London. The houses were smaller, packed together: long terraces in narrow streets. Great gaps between buildings and mounds of rubble indicated where bombs had devastated homes and shops. Finding a pub in the blackout wasn't easy.

After several abortive attempts Adam was lucky. A door opened as he turned the handle and, when he pushed aside the heavy blackout curtain that hung over it, he could smell cigarette smoke and hear the friendly chink of glasses and the buzz of voices.

After the darkness outside, the sudden light dazzled him. He stumbled to the bar, ordered a whisky, and drained it at a gulp. Banging the empty glass down on the counter he ordered another. The neat spirit seared a burning path down his throat to his stomach, but spread warmth and strength back into his limbs. After his third whisky he ordered a beer.

When the barmaid, a plump peroxide-blonde with roguish green eyes and an impudent smile, came and leant her elbows on the counter, he promptly offered to buy her a drink.

'And I'll have another whisky . . . make it a double.'

'What are you celebrating?' she asked as she clicked her glass against his.

'Being alive,' he said morosely.

To his surprise he found himself telling her about Gary. The words came gushing out like wine from a newly uncorked bottle. So much whisky on an empty stomach had completely banished his normal reserve.

Dora was a good listener. She said very little, but her sympathetic nods and understanding murmurs were all he needed. When she finally put the towels over the barrels and called, 'Time', Adam was almost out on his feet.

'Come on. You need some food.' She turned out the lights and guided him towards the stairway at the back of the bar. 'If I let you go out like that you'll be picked up by the MPs, end up on a charge and give this pub a bad name.'

She half pushed him up the narrow stairs to the sitting-room above and helped him across to the settee.

'Sit there while I rustle up something for us,' she told him.

It was a low-ceilinged room, stuffy and crammed with heavy furniture. Every available surface was cluttered with ornaments and photographs.

Adam slumped back against a pile of gaudy cushions. When Dora returned ten minutes later with a plate of sandwiches and two mugs of steaming black coffee, he was already asleep.

'Come on,' she said, relentlessly shaking him awake. 'You've got to eat.'

'Do you look after all your customers like this?' he said, yawning, as he struggled to sit upright.

'Only the good-looking ones. My ma'll skin me alive if she gets back and finds you here. Good job she's gone over to see her sister and won't be back until the morning.'

'You mean you have to sleep here all on your own?' Adam asked in surprise.

She smiled up at him provocatively. 'Does it worry you?'

'Well . . . you don't look all that old.'

'I'm twenty!'

'Same age as my brother Gary . . . he's just been killed.'

'I know. You've talked of nothing else all night.'

'Sorry.'

'That's all right. I know how you feel. My boyfriend was killed in action about three months ago. We was going to be married next time he came on leave.'

'I'm sorry!' Adam's hand squeezed hers reassuringly.

'It's this bleeding war, ain't it?' Her fingers idly traced the veins on the back of his hand as she spoke.

Suddenly Dora's arms were around his neck, her lips warm and soft as they found his, while her body, hot and voluptuous, pressed urgently against him.

With a moan he gathered her close, savaging her mouth. She responded hungrily, returning his kisses with a passion that matched his own.

74

As his hand pushed her skirt aside and slid up her leg, she grabbed his wrist, forcing him to stop.

'Please,' he begged hoarsely.

'Not here,' she protested.

Together they groped their way across the landing to her bedroom.

Feverishly he tore off his clothes, then, without waiting for her to finish undressing, pushed her down on the bed and threw himself on top of her.

Their coupling bordered on rape. As he furiously pounded into her, his thoughts were dark and hideous. It wasn't Dora's soft, vulnerable body but the whole world he was wrestling with. Anger, fury, hatred and lust went into every thrust until he was completely spent and could only collapse beside her.

He had heard neither her soft moans nor her cries of anguish. He was unaware of the scalding tears that streamed from her tight-closed eyes and trickled down her cheeks to mingle with his sweat.

When he awoke next morning he was alone. He stared around the cluttered bedroom, trying to remember where he was. Slowly, with increasing depression, he recalled the events of the previous night. Overcome with shame and remorse he dressed and went down into the pub. The bar that had been warm and friendly the previous night, now smelled acrid with cigarette smoke and stale beer.

Dora was cleaning. She stopped as he came into the room and leant against the corner of the bar.

'You off then?'

He nodded. 'About last night . . .'

'Forget it.' She shrugged helplessly, a crooked smile curving her generous mouth. 'I suppose you won't be coming back?'

He shook his head. 'I'm catching the next train to Sturbury. Look, about last night . . .'

Lightly she placed her hand over his mouth. 'Don't say anything more. Don't explain . . . or apologise. I couldn't bear that. It was something we both needed. Look after yourself.'

'I'm sorry we should meet and part like this,' Adam said gently. 'I wish things had been different . . .'

She gave a low laugh. 'What – for us two! Don't try kidding me. I'm not really your type, now am I? I only wish I were. You're a lovely sort of feller.' Swiftly she planted a kiss on his cheek.

Adam felt abashed at having treated her as he had done. He wanted to say something, as much to ease his own conscience as to appease her feelings.

He wondered if he ought to offer her some money, then his face burned at the realisation of what an added insult such a gesture would be. Feeling helpless, he walked out into the pale winter sunshine and made his way towards the nearest bus-stop.

Chapter 10

For several weeks after losing the baby, Helen felt listless. The weather was cold and bleak so she spent most of her time huddled over the fire at Willow Cottage, brooding and waiting for Adam to phone.

Her need for him filled every waking moment. She ached to be in his arms, to have him comfort her and reassure her that he still loved her even though there was now no baby.

She read his letters over and over again, but they brought scant consolation and didn't ease the desperate pain inside her. She had been devastated when she heard that his brother had been killed at the same time as she had lost her baby. Knowing how much he had cared about Gary, it seemed so hard that she and Adam should be apart at a time when they both needed each other so much. She sat numbly, waiting to hear that he had found somewhere for her to stay and that she could be with him until he was sent overseas.

It was Aunt Julia who eventually brought her out of her black despair by insisting she should go back to work.

'There are men losing their arms and legs from gangrene, and dying because they're so short of nurses, and all you're doing is sitting around feeling sorry for yourself,' she told Helen sharply.

Shocked into action, Helen went back to Bulpitts and once again became immersed in hospital life. She still worried about Adam. As spring turned into summer, the uncertainty about where he was troubled her. There were no letters from him in the weeks after D-Day, and she became convinced he'd finally gone overseas.

When Paris was freed at the end of August she had listened avidly to every news bulletin on the wireless, hoping to pick up some clue about where Adam's unit was likely to be. She went to the cinema in Winton three nights in a row, just to see the Pathé News because it showed British Guards marching through Paris and she thought she might catch a glimpse of Adam amongst them.

Like so many others, Helen thought that liberating France would mean an immediate end to the war, but instead it seemed only to create new horrors. The newspapers were full of horrendous stories of the sick and suffering people the troops encountered as they travelled through Europe, and of the atrocities they were finding at the countless prisoner of war camps as they advanced into Germany. She had no way of knowing whether Adam was involved in any of this or not. The letters she now received were always censored, so Adam wasn't even explicit about where he was or what he was doing.

When they were first married Adam had written warm, passionate letters, filled with hope and plans for their future together. As time passed, his letters had become more pragmatic. Now, after almost a year and a half, apart from *Dear Helen* and *All my love, Adam* there was nothing to lessen the ache in her heart; no words to bridge the terrible separation.

When she wrote to him, knowing that some other eye would read every word she'd written cramped her style, too. As time passed, her letters also became tight and formal.

On her nineteenth birthday, when the only card she received was the one left on the kitchen-table by Aunt Julia, she arrived at Bulpitts with a lump in her throat. She knew that when any of the other nurses had a birthday they organized an impromptu party and that she could have done the same. Even though she generally treated both fellow staff and patients with cool reserve, they would have joined in, yet she had said nothing.

New nurses tended to laugh behind her back because she was so reserved. At the same time, they treated her with grudging respect, admiring the way she turned aside invitations and mild flirtations without any of the men resenting her attitude.

Aunt Julia was forever trying to persuade her to have some sort of social life.

'You don't suppose Adam refuses to go for a drink in the NAAFI, or mess, or wherever it is they relax, just because you're not there, do you?'

'It just doesn't appeal to me.' Helen shrugged.

'There's no need to become a recluse or a martyr,' Aunt Julia told her drily. 'When Adam comes home you want to establish right from the start that you intend keeping your own friends and interests.' Her face relaxed into a smile. 'Maybe that's why I never got married. I couldn't bring myself to sacrifice my independence. Mind you,' she added tartly, 'you might feel the same way yourself when you've lived with Adam for two or three years and discovered just how selfish men can be.' She sighed. 'Take a lesson from your own parents. If your mother had been firmer with your father over financial matters then you might not have ended up penniless. And,' she added darkly, 'I would say you are lucky that it is just penniless and not in debt.'

Helen had quickly changed the subject. She knew she was on dangerous ground. The home she'd grown up in and loved so dearly, was now occupied by strangers. Other children scampered in the garden and people talked about 'young Dr Peterson' instead of Dr Price as they had done before.

She was grateful to Aunt Julia for letting her make her home at Willow Cottage, but she yearned for Adam to come home so that they could have a place of their own.

In moments of despondency, when the war news was particularly depressing, or when she hadn't heard from Adam for several weeks, Helen sometimes wondered if she should have listened to her father and not rushed into marriage. She and Adam had spent so little time together that he was still almost a stranger, and it was daunting to think they would spend the rest of their lives together. Yet how well did you ever know anyone? she thought, sadly.

The picture Aunt Julia had painted of her father, philanthropic to the point of being careless about his own financial welfare, hardly fitted her own memory of him.

Discovering that he had mishandled his affairs so badly that he had been heavily in debt, had come as a great shock. She had always looked up to him and thought him to be a man of great integrity, and she wondered how he would have resolved his problems had he not been killed.

It was only very occasionally Helen found herself dwelling on such matters. Generally she was much too busy. The Allies continued to advance across Europe, war still raged in the Far East, and sick and wounded soldiers constantly arrived at Bulpitts. No sooner was a bed empty than someone else was brought in to fill it.

She kept telling herself that it must all end soon. It was

almost a year since D-Day, and the Allies were pushing deeper and deeper into Germany. In March they had taken Cologne, so surely the Germans must know they were beaten and Hitler must realise there was no point in holding out any longer?

It was a beautiful May day. Before sitting down to enter up reports and records in the day book, Helen walked down the ward, opening windows to let in the light spring breeze, that brought with it the scent of lilac and the promise of summer.

'Helen, it's over . . . the war's over!'

Phyllis Lane, the Ward Sister, face beaming, hazel eyes dancing with excitement, came hurrying up to her.

'Over . . . what do you mean?' Pen poised in mid-air, Helen stared in disbelief.

'The Germans have surrendered . . . it's victory!'

'Are you quite sure?' Helen looked doubtful.

'Of *course* I'm sure. Winston Churchill made the announcement himself. I heard it on the wireless, and Matron's had a phone call from Army HQ confirming it.' She struck a pose and, pitching her voice as low as it would go, announced dramatically, 'The German war is now at an end . . .'

'I can't believe it . . .'

'Neither can I! I wonder how long it will be before they start sending the men home and demobbing them?'

'If it's anything like the time when they reached Paris last year, we'll need a lot of patience. We all thought then that the war was over – and look what happened.'

'That was just a breakthrough. This time it's completely over. German forces in Italy, Germany, Holland and Denmark, have all surrendered unconditionally.'

'In the Far East as well?'

'No.' A note of caution crept into Phyllis Lane's voice. 'Only in Europe. The Japs are still holding out.'

'Then our boys might not come straight home. Leastways not all of them,' Helen said slowly.

Phyllis Lane's hazel eyes clouded. 'You think they might send some of them on out to the Far East? Hell, they can't do that, not after what they've gone through in Europe.'

'I don't see why not. If they need reinforcements, it makes sense to send troops who are already battle-trained.'

'My God, you're a cool one! How long has your Adam been over there?'

'Almost eighteen months.'

'And all you can think of is that they might ship him straight out to the Far East!'

'I may as well be realistic. Not much point getting all excited and then for it to come to nothing, now is there,' Helen stated, shrugging, her grey eyes hard as flint.

Phyllis Lane looked deflated. 'I'll never understand you,' she said.

Helen bent her head over the day book and started to write. 'I've been disappointed too many times in the past,' she said, and though her tone was even there was an undercurrent of bitterness in her voice.

'Well, *you* may not be ready to celebrate, but *I'm* going to tell the whole ward – the entire hospital if it comes to that,' Sister Lane declared. 'I'm so happy I want to shout it from the roof-tops.'

'Do you think it's right to raise their hopes?'

'Helen, what's wrong with you! You're not normal! Of course I'm going to tell them. It will do them more good than all the pills and medicines we keep pushing down their throats. It means they're one day nearer to getting back home to their families.'

'Even that won't do some of them much good,' Helen retorted bitterly. 'From what they tell me, most of them have been sacked or are too badly injured to ever work again. So what sort of future will they have being pushed about in a wheelchair, or hobbling around on crutches?'

'Shut up, Helen, for goodness' sake. You're too morbid for words. The war is over – *isn't* that enough to make even you rejoice?'

'It's not over, not completely,' Helen argued stubbornly.

'Until the Japs surrender and all our boys are home from the Far East, it isn't over.'

Once the news broke, everyone in the hospital seemed to be in celebratory mood. The shortages, the fatigue, the cold and heat, the searing pain, the hours of misery and frustration, of black despair and discomfort, were all forgotten.

Even those soldiers who had been so badly maimed or injured that they could never hope to resume a normal life again, seemed optimistic that everything would soon be back to normal and their harrowing experiences would be just a hazy dream.

By the evening, after hearing on the wireless that the King and Queen, the two princesses, and the Prime Minister, Winston Churchill, had appeared on the balcony at Buckingham Palace, to wave to the cheering crowds who thronged the Mall, even Helen felt light-hearted, and laughed and joked as she attended to routine duties.

The thought of Adam coming back into her life scared her and she wondered just how soon it would be before he was demobbed. Some said it was to be 'first in, first out' so there was just the chance that he would be home by midsummer.

Helen had no idea where they would live. She hoped Aunt Julia would let them stay on at Willow Cottage until they found a home of their own.

So much would depend on what sort of job Adam managed to get. Helen had saved every penny of her Army allowance and had even managed to add some of her nursing pay to it, but, even so, it wouldn't go very far, since they didn't own a single item of furniture. She supposed she should have kept some of the furniture from her parents' home, but she hadn't done so because she wanted to have a completely fresh start.

Chapter 11

Helen read Adam's letter through twice, unable to believe that he was coming home at last. All the fears and frustrations she had bottled up for so long, came to the fore. She felt choked and tears streamed down her cheeks as a sense of panic swept through her, leaving her weak and trembling.

She wondered if he would think she had changed. Would he even recognise her! She sighed, remembering how young and carefree she'd been in those far-off days. She was no longer the fresh-faced eighteen-year-old with her hair in a plait. Tragedy, heartache and nursing sick men, many of whom had died from their injuries, had matured her. She certainly felt older, and she was sure such traumas had left their mark.

Folding the letter, she slipped it back in its envelope and placed it on top of the bundle in her dressing-table drawer. Leaning forward she studied her face in the mirror and fresh doubts churned in her mind about how Adam would feel when he saw her. She *had* changed. Frowning, she traced the dark shadows under her grey eyes and the hard, tight lines around her mouth.

I look more like thirty-five than twenty, she thought critically. Even my figure has altered. She was more rounded, more mature. She had never regained her youthful slimness after her miscarriage. At the time she had felt far too depressed to worry about such a triviality. Now, with Adam on his way home, she was aware of how she had neglected herself and was worried in case he was disappointed when they met.

She reread his letter again to check when he was due to arrive. The line 'probably within a couple of days of this letter' caught her eye and sent fresh alarm signals pulsing through her. There was no time for even a crash diet!

Opening her wardrobe she riffled through the clothes hanging there, panic mounting as she realised she had nothing special to wear. She spent so much time in uniform that she had bought nothing new for ages, not since Paris was liberated when, believing Adam would be home almost any day, she had spent her carefully hoarded coupons on a new dress. That was now almost two years ago.

She had refused to build her hopes after VE Day, because she half expected Adam to be sent to the Far East. Instead, he had remained with the Rhine Army of Occupation. He was still in Germany the following August when the Allies had dropped atomic bombs on Hiroshima and Nagasaki.

The horrifying reports and newspaper pictures of the devastation and suffering had sickened her, even though it had brought an immediate end to the war.

Even after Japan had capitulated, Adam had still not returned home, so Helen had worn her new dress whenever she was off-duty just to cheer herself up.

Although their letters were no longer censored, they never regained their initial warmth. Each time Helen wrote she tried to tell Adam how much she wanted him home, but she could never find the right words and ended up penning her usual bland note. A page of nothingness, the sort of letter she could just as well have written to a cousin or a casual aquaintance.

Adam's letters to her were just as colourless. She longed desperately for him to tell her how much he wanted to see her and how he was counting the days until he was home with her at last. Each time a letter with BAOR franking on the envelope arrived, she would delay opening it, deluding herself that this time it really would be that sort of letter.

She had even done that with the letter she had just opened. Aunt Julia had brought it upstairs while she was dressing for work. Helen had propped it up on the dressing-table, fantasised about what it would say, then left it there when she had gone down to breakfast. She had gone off to Bulpitts and forgotten all about it, and it was not until she had gone upstairs to put a hot-water bottle in her bed that night, that she had noticed it was still lying there on the dressing-table.

As she slit it open, she expected it to be Adam's routine note, so at first the words didn't register. When she checked the postmark, she was filled with a mixture of excitement and panic. It had been written over a week ago, so he could arrive at almost any time.

Where would he sleep? She giggled a little hysterically. Surely Aunt Julia wouldn't expect him to sleep on his own in the small box room up under the eaves of Willow Cottage? Yet they could hardly share her single bed!

A loud knocking at the front door startled her and she froze momentarily. Then, her heart pounding, she raced to answer it, stumbling and slipping on the narrow twisting stairs in her haste.

'Adam,' she whispered to the tall figure standing on the step. 'Adam is it really you?'

'Helen!' He dropped the kit-bag from his shoulder and held out his arms to embrace her. Shuddering, she leant against him, finding comfort against his solid chest and strong arms.

'Oh Adam, Adam . . .' Tears trickled down her cheeks, as a deep feeling of relief flowed through her veins, leaving her weak but happy.

With child-like simplicity she raised her face invitingly. His lips were cool from the night air, firm, yet gentle. As their pressure increased she felt waves of desire burn through her body, from her fingertips to her toes.

Adam's hold on her tightened and he groaned as he tore himself away, then immediately kissed her again, as if afraid she might vanish.

'Come on inside,' she murmured in a dazed whisper.

Keeping one arm around her waist, Adam picked up his kit-bag from the front step and put it inside the hall.

'You don't still have blackout do you?' he asked in surprise as she closed the front door before switching on the hall light.

'No!' She laughed nervously. 'Not for ages now. It's just habit.' She led him into the cosy sitting-room where Aunt Julia was sitting in a comfortable armchair by a crackling log fire.

'Adam!' she gasped in surprise. 'I had no idea you were on your way home . . . welcome back!'

'Thank you. It's good to be here.'

'Have you come far?'

'From Germany – and I'm ravenous. I couldn't get anything on the train from London. In fact, I've only had a snack since first thing this morning.'

Helen moved quickly towards the door. 'I'll get you something to eat . . . you two have a chat.'

'Nonsense! You're the ones who have a lot to say to each other,' Aunt Julia declared. 'You come and sit down with Adam, and leave the kitchen to me.'

'All right.' Helen suddenly felt shy and tongue-tied. In the light of the sitting-room Adam seemed almost a stranger. He had removed his greatcoat and cap and seemed much more powerfully built than she remembered. His long, muscular legs emphasised his slim hips and she noticed how his khaki battledress top strained across his broad shoulders and chest.

She studied his face. His shock of dark hair was as thick as ever and his eyes as intensely blue as she remembered them, but he looked older and there was a leanness that gave his cheek-bones a new prominence.

Adam stood motionless for a few seconds, feasting his eyes on Helen, then, almost roughly, he clasped her to him and held her face between his hands. Burning with passion, his lips fused with hers, gently at first, then with increasing pressure, until she felt she was being sucked into an inferno. Her knees weakened and she leant against him, feeling the heat from his body burn into her. Gently she restrained him, twisting her head sideways so that his lips slid from her mouth to her ear where they nuzzled the lobe, sending shivers of delight through her. Again she curbed his ardour, holding his face tight between her own hands, the sharpness of stubble under her fingertips making her acutely conscious of his masculinity.

'Later Adam, later,' she murmured, as her gaze met his. 'Aunt Julia will be back in a moment.'

He released her without speaking and sat down on the settee, patting the cushion beside him as Aunt Julia came bustling back with a bowl of hot soup and some sandwiches. While Adam tucked in, Helen made coffee for them all and brought in a plate of home-made cakes.

His hunger eased, Adam began to relate some of his experiences: the months of delay on the south coast when all leave was cancelled and they expected each day to be sent overseas; the build-up to D-Day; the crossing to France and the long summer of fighting. When Paris had been liberated, towards the end of August, he had thought it would soon be over and he would be going home again. Instead, he told them, that was the time when, for him, the war had really begun. As the Army began to advance across Europe it had been every man for himself. Living conditions had been haphazard. They had slept in barns, disused farmhouses, or even in the back of their trucks. Army rations were supplemented by whatever they could find or scrounge.

'When we liberated villages in Belgium or West Germany we often felt so sorry for the children that we gave them our own rations. To see those kids' faces light up when you gave them a bar of chocolate, or a tin of fruit, was incredible,' Adam said, smiling as he reminisced.

On VE Day he had been in Celle and was still there when the Japs capitulated after the Hiroshima bomb was dropped.

'There were a lot of Americans stationed there, too,' he told them, 'and they went absolutely wild with joy. They even packed their kit ready for home! I warned them they were being optimistic and, of course, I was right.'

'Are you home for good now?' Aunt Julia asked.

'Well, no . . . not exactly.' Adam moved uncomfortably in his seat, looking apprehensively at Helen.

'You mean you're only on leave?' Helen asked in dismay.

'Sort of.' He hesitated again, as if unsure whether or not to say more.

'Well, I'm off to bed,' Aunt Julia announced diplomatically. 'It's good to have you safely home, Adam. I'm afraid you'll have to share Helen's single bed tonight. Tomorrow we must make some better arrangement.'

'We'll manage, Aunt Julia,' Helen assured her. 'Goodnight.'

They sat in companionable silence, Adam's arm around Helen, her head resting against his chest, listening to the creaking of the stairs and the floorboards overhead, until Aunt Julia settled into bed. Then Adam reached out and switched off the lamp on the table beside him.

Helen waited, feeling as nervous as if she was on her very first date. Her mouth felt dry and her heart was thudding so loudly against her rib cage that she was sure Adam must hear it.

When he tenderly scooped her up in his arms, laid her on the sheepskin rug in front of the fire's glowing embers and began to unbutton the front of her dress, she offered no resistance.

The warmth of his breath on her exposed neck rekindled the desire she had felt earlier in the evening. And when his lips began gently to explore the whole length of her throat, finally coming to rest in the warm hollow between her breasts, she murmured with delight.

As his fingers fumbled with the fastenings on her dress, she eagerly undid them for him. Her need was as great as his and now her shyness was gone. Eagerly, she unbuttoned his khaki shirt, feeling the heat from his broad chest burning beneath her hands.

She moaned with ecstasy as his mouth travelled over her

88

naked flesh. The exquisite pleasure as he paused to salute each erect nipple before moving further down her body, sent shudders of sensual excitement flooding through her.

Her desire increased as Adam grasped her body tightly to his own, flattening the rounded swell of her breasts against his hard chest, firmly prising her legs apart with one of his own. Then his hands slid down her back, cupping her towards him in a firm decisive hold so that their bodies united of their own volition. She could hear her own breath rasping as she matched her rhythm with his powerful strokes and the exhilaration built up to a crescendo of passion that left her gasping. Waves of blackness obliterated even the glowing embers of the fire as Adam rolled from her and collapsed at her side.

Her happiness was complete when, with supreme effort, he raised himself on one arm and gently kissed her on the mouth.

Chapter 12

Adam's leave flew by. They spent much of it walking in the countryside around Sturbury. The autumn days, though short, were warm and colourful. The trees and hedgerows, an ever-changing panorama of vivid golds, reds, oranges and browns, delighted their eyes and filled Helen's heart with joy. She felt that sharing the beauty of the glorious landscape with Adam was a way of celebrating that he had been one of the lucky ones who had come through the war unscathed, when so many had been killed or injured.

Often, when she woke before him, Helen would hear Adam mumbling in his sleep and realise how much the memories of war haunted him. Powerless to help, she would lay cool fingers on his brow, or gently stroke his face, hoping to erase from his mind whatever was troubling him. Although he never spoke of it, she sensed he still mourned the loss of his brother, Gary.

Even her lightest touch seemed to wake him. She would feel him tense and his eyes would snap open. For a brief second he would lie motionless, like an animal before it springs. Then, as he remembered where he was, he would roll over and gather her close to him.

Although neither of them could readily express their feelings in words, Helen found their love-making fulfilled all her dreams and expectations. Adam's infinite tenderness came as a pleasurable revelation. She responded to his every touch, deriving and giving so much pleasure that every moment brought immeasurable joy.

Their passion remained unabated, their love-making exciting. There was only one cloud that hung over the three weeks Adam was at home and that was his future.

They talked endlessly about whether or not he should stay in the Army. Helen was against him doing so because she couldn't bear the thought of separation. Adam argued that since he had no job to come out to, and only limited prospects, it was the most sensible thing to do.

'There are all sorts of schemes available,' Helen insisted. 'You could even apply for a university course . . .'

'I have done and been turned down,' he told her. 'I muffed my School Certificate when I was sixteen, so I didn't stand the ghost of a chance.'

'You could apply for an apprenticeship . . .'

'For what? I'm not all that clever with my hands.'

'What about the police?'

'If I have to be in uniform then I'd sooner stay in the Guards.'

'You mean apply for a commission and make a career of it?'

'I haven't the educational qualifications needed to become an officer. The highest rank I'll ever reach will be sergeant.'

The argument went on incessantly. Helen felt bewildered by his attitude. On Adam's last night at home, long after he was asleep, she lay awake, cradling him in her arms, her face wet with tears, trying to understand his reasoning. It wasn't as though he even liked the Army all that much, she thought, bemused.

While he had been on leave she had tried desperately to think of some other kind of work he could do, something that wouldn't take him away from home. He had turned down every suggestion she'd made. Aunt Julia had put forward the idea of a small farm, even offering to let him use what little capital she had, but he was not to be persuaded.

'You're worrying needlessly,' he assured Helen when she tried to tell him she couldn't bear the thought of separation. 'Once I'm in the regular Army you'll be able to live in married quarters. It's not all that different from living in a village. Everyone knows everybody else. You'll soon make friends. You don't think I'd be considering it if I thought we were going to be apart all the time, do you?'

'But we will be! When you go back to Germany I'm going to be left behind,' she had argued.

'Only for a short time. Once I've signed on I'll be sent back to England, to the Guards Depot, for special training. Wait until you see me in my uniform! The Guards *are* rather special, you know. Sentry duty at Buckingham Palace and Windsor Castle – and then there's all sorts of ceremonial parades, like Trooping the Colour, as well as acting as Guard of Honour when foreign dignitaries visit.'

'They're still part of the Army so you could be sent anywhere where there's trouble,' Helen said stubbornly.

'But there won't be any more trouble, will there? The war is over.'

'There may be another. Anyway, you could be sent to Europe, the Middle East or the Far East, as part of the peace-keeping force.'

'And if I am then you'll be able to come with me. Just think of it – you'll be able to see the world and it won't cost you a penny!'

Since nothing she said made any difference, Helen finally

gave up trying to change Adam's mind. She only hoped he had got his facts right and that when his training was over she would be able to join him.

A month after he had gone back to Germany she was still waiting for a date and, although his letters made light of the delay, she sensed that he was growing just as impatient and frustrated as she was.

She was glad she still had her job at Bulpitts. At least her days were so fully occupied that she had no time to brood. At night she was so tired that she was usually asleep within minutes of her head touching the pillow.

As Christmas approached, the festivities at the hospital kept her busy. Those well enough to go home to their families were given special leave and the nursing staff were determined to make Christmas as happy an occasion as possible for those who remained.

The enormous Christmas tree was beautifully decorated and there were presents for each patient. Aunt Julia organized carol singers as well as a rota of visitors. Now the war was over she had given up her Civil Defence work and was enjoying a busy social life. She tried to involve Helen, but, unless the parties were actually being held at Willow Cottage, Helen did not take part. She preferred to spend what little spare time she had writing to Adam.

It was mid-January 1946 before Adam wrote to say he would be returning to England the first week in March. Helen was overjoyed and would have given in her notice at Bulpitts right away if it had not been for Aunt Julia's cautioning.

'Wait and see if you can join him before you do that,' her aunt advised. 'It might be weeks before he's posted, so you may as well go on working until then.'

It had proved to be sound advice. Adam's intensive training lasted for six weeks and, at the end of it, when he came home, it was just for a long weekend leave before being sent away on another course.

'After this I'll be made lance-sergeant and get my permanent posting,' he told her, 'and then I can apply for married quarters.'

This time Helen did give in her notice.

'We're closing the place down, anyway,' Matron told her, 'so it saves me having to tell you there's no job for you here after the beginning of June.'

'What's happening to all the patients?'

'They'll be dispersed. Those well enough to go home will be discharged, the rest will be moved to some other military hospital.'

'And Bulpitts?'

'Hand it back, I suppose.' Matron shrugged. 'Not really my concern. As you probably know, the people who leased it to the Army were killed quite early on in the war. Their son has been a prisoner of war but he is due home again and I heard he wants it back.'

Helen found herself thinking of Donald for the first time in years. She knew he had been shot down, but so much had happened that she had lost touch. She wondered where Isabel was and what sort of war she'd had. The days when they had played together seemed to belong to another era. She must invite them to come and visit once she and Adam had their own place.

The thought of having a home of her own at last excited Helen, yet filled her with trepidation. She had no experience at all of running a home or cooking; Aunt Julia took care of all that at Willow Cottage.

'We'll be living on tea and toast unless you teach me how to cook,' Helen told her that evening when she got home from work.

'You've left it a bit late, haven't you?' her Aunt said drily. 'When is Adam due to join his unit?'

'About the end of May.'

'Well . . .' her aunt looked doubtful, 'it's pretty short notice. You'd better make a start by cooking the supper tonight.'

'What!'

'You said you wanted to learn, so here's your chance!' Aunt Julia smiled.

'Not tonight! I've had a killing day at Bulpitts.'

'When you have a place of your own you'll have to prepare lunch and breakfast as well as an evening meal. *And* wash up afterwards. Marriage isn't just moonlight and roses, or walking hand-in-hand and daydreaming. You've got to deal with the practicalities as well. Cooking and cleaning are just part of them.'

Helen shook her head in bewilderment at her aunt's change of attitude. 'You never said any of this before!'

'You've never asked for advice so I've never given it. I've always treated you as a guest in my home. Don't worry though, you'll soon pick it up,' Aunt Julia told her confidently.

'I'd better make a start then, hadn't I?' Helen said quietly, as she lifted her chin proudly to meet the challenge in the older woman's light-blue eyes.

Chapter 13

'What a fantastic birthday present!'

Her grey eyes shining like molten silver, Helen took the key Adam held out to her and then flung her arms around his neck and hugged him.

'This is the most wonderful present I've ever had,' she exclaimed, her voice husky with joy. 'A home of my own at last!' Then her smile faded and a hot flush suffused her cheeks. She dropped her arms from Adam's neck and went over to Aunt Julia. Dropping to her knees and clasping her arms around her aunt's waist, she looked up into her eyes and whispered, 'I didn't mean to sound ungrateful. Willow Cottage has been a wonderful home for the past three years . . .'

'Hush! hush!' Tears filled Julia Freeman's eyes as she patted Helen's shoulder. 'I understand, my dear, and I'm so happy for you. Remember though, there's always a home for you here should you ever need one.'

'You will come and visit us?'

'Of course I will! Just as soon as you're settled in.'

Bubbling with excitement, Helen turned back to Adam. 'Is it nice? Will I like it?'

'I hope so, because you can't change it! Everything is standard issue, even the furniture.' He pulled a typed document from his pocket and handed it to her. 'Here's the inventory. Check it thoroughly when we go in because the Army will expect to find every item on that list still there when we move out, right down to the last teaspoon. We pay for any shortages or breakages.'

'Well, I suppose that's fair.'

'It's the system,' Adam said drily.

'When can we move in?'

'Just as soon as you like . . . you've got the key right there in your hand.'

Her grey eyes still shining, Helen turned back to her aunt. 'Would you mind very much if we left tomorrow?'

'I'd be wondering what was wrong if you didn't,' Aunt Julia assured her. 'Just as long as you don't go today and miss out on the party!'

'Party . . . what party?' Adam asked in surprise.

'Just a few family friends. Being twenty-one is rather special, you know! Most of the people who are coming have known Helen all her life. And, what's more, it's giving her a chance to try out her cooking.'

'Aunt Julia has been giving me a crash course,' Helen explained. 'This party is my passing-out test.'

Helen was so excited she hardly slept. She was up at first light packing her clothes and personal belongings so that they could leave the moment breakfast was over.

They caught an early-morning train to London, then took the suburban line to Brookwood, the nearest station for Pirbright. From there it was only a short walk to the Guards Depot.

As they walked past regimented rows of red-brick houses, with tiny gardens in front, Helen wondered if she would ever get used to living there.

Number eight, Redwood Square, looked so identical to the houses on either side that she checked the number twice to make sure it was the right house, before fitting the key in the lock.

The door opened onto a small lobby with the stairs going straight up from it. To the right was a long, narrow room with a window at each end. The one at the far end looked out onto a sloping garden fringed with tall fir trees.

Helen walked down the room, her hands touching the wooden arms of the three-piece suite which stood on a mottled blue and black carpet that almost matched the slubbed curtains.

The dining-room area was furnished with a rugged pine table and four matching wooden chairs. A door on the left led to the kitchen, stocked with everything from saucepans and a frying-pan to blue-and-white cups and saucers, and even basic cleaning materials.

Helen walked back to the lounge area and stood for a moment, gazing out at the communal front garden where two small boys were kicking a ball around.

'Do you want to see the bedrooms?' Adam asked.

She nodded and preceded him up the stairs. The bathroom was straight ahead. The small landing had three bedrooms opening off it. None of the beds were made up, but on each mattress were two pillows and a pile of neatly-folded blankets and bedlinen.

Although it was a hot July day, Helen suppressed a shiver. She crossed to the window, opening it wide, conscious of how the tall firs shadowed it.

'Are we allowed to change things?' she asked, pulling the blue slub curtains back as far as possible, in an attempt to let some sun into the room. 'It feels damp in here.'

'Probably the general bareness of the place makes it feel cold,' Adam commented. 'You're used to velvet drapes, wallpaper on the walls and pictures and ornaments and nick-nacks everywhere.'

'It's this awful blue colour they've used.'

'You can't repaint the walls, or put wallpaper on them or anything like that,' Adam warned her. 'You can put up pictures as long as you don't mark the walls. It's so different from your aunt's place that it's bound to feel strange. You'll get used to it after a day or two.'

'I don't think I will, not until I've added our own bits and pieces . . . and we haven't got many of those.'

'Let's live in it and get the feel of the place first before we make any changes,' Adam suggested.

'It's much bigger than I thought it would be. Three bedrooms . . . we only really need one!'

'Sergeants who move out of barracks and into married quarters are usually family men!' He grinned. 'Perhaps we'll soon be needing an extra bedroom ourselves.'

'Oh, Adam, I hope so,' she whispered, as his arms went round her and their lips met, blotting out everything except her joy that they were finally together.

'Come on, Mrs Woodley,' Adam teased gently, 'your husband is starving.' He looked at his watch 'It's gone three and we've had nothing to eat since breakfast-time. Let's pop across to the NAAFI shop and see what they've got. There's absolutely nothing here . . . not even a packet of tea! From now on it's all up to you: shopping, washing, cooking . . . the lot!'

As he hugged her, his enthusiasm bolstered her flagging spirits. She rested her head on his shoulder with a deep sigh. 'It's a bit like a dream,' she whispered. 'I still can't believe I'm here and this is really going to be our home.'

Helen took some time to settle down into married quarters. Her natural reserve made her shy with her neighbours. Their outspoken frankness about their own lives startled her. They all had young families and seemed rather amazed when they heard she had no children, although she had been married almost four years.

'Stop worrying about it,' Adam told her when she became anxious and depressed because there was still no sign of a baby. 'You'll probably end up having twins, or even triplets!' He grinned.

'Just one would do,' Helen said wistfully. 'I feel so odd, so different from all the other women. Every time I meet any of them they always have a baby in their arms or they're clutching a toddler by the hand while I . . . I have nothing, no one.'

'You've got me – and no one could need more looking after than I do!' Adam teased, letting his hand slide sensuously up and down her spine. Drawing her into his arms, his lips found hers and since she still loved him to distraction it ended any further serious discussion. From that point on nothing else mattered except releasing their pent-up passion.

By the time Aunt Julia came to visit, towards the end of September, Helen had managed to transform the barrack-like shell – with the help of plants, pictures, colourful cushions and rugs – into an attractive home. She knew most of the wives from the surrounding houses but her special friends were Sheila Wilson and Nesta Evans.

Sheila was a diminutive brunette with hazel eyes, married to a massive sandy-haired Scottish sergeant, Jock Wilson. They had two children – Patsy, an adorable three-year-old miniature of her mother, and Jamie, a robust tousle-headed seven-year-old with scabbed knees and a cheeky, freckled face.

Nesta was slim and as dark-haired and dark-eyed as her husband, Taffy Evans. Their two boys, David, aged six and Llewellyn, who was almost eight, were both football crazy and spent most of their free time kicking a ball around, either in their own back garden or out on the front lawns. Their two-year-old daughter, Delia, had huge brown eyes and a mop of dark brown curls. She was inseparable from Patsy Wilson, and the two little girls liked nothing better than to visit Helen. They would play happily for hours in her garden or sitting-room, usually entertaining her as well as themselves.

Aunt Julia was pleasurably surprised at how well Helen

had settled into her new life. Helen took her to London to watch the Changing of the Guard and felt inordinately proud of the part Adam played in the colourful ceremony.

They attended a Regimental Dinner in the Sergeants' Mess and Aunt Julia was very impressed by the smart turn-out of the wives in their elegant evening dresses.

'They certainly do things in style.' She smiled as they sat down at one of the long tables laid with gleaming silver and sparkling glasses and decorated with bowls of fresh flowers.

'That was an excellent meal. You must be enjoying your new life very much,' she commented afterwards as she sipped her coffee.

'The only drawback,' Helen grumbled, 'is that Adam is away so often. He's only just back from three weeks in Thetford and soon he'll be off again to Otterburn for two or three weeks on a training exercise. Even when he *is* at home he often spends several days at a time on guard duty in London or Windsor. There always seems to be some special occasion or other. You must come to London with me next year when he takes part in Trooping the Colour.'

Before she went home, Aunt Julia promised to come and stay with them over Christmas. When the time came, however, it was so bitterly cold she refused to make the journey.

Helen agreed to go and visit her early in the New Year but blizzards had blocked the roads and railway lines so she decided to leave it until the weather improved. It was something to look forward to through the long bleak winter that was made worse by a coal shortage and electricity cuts.

Helen remembered how lovely spring could be in Sturbury and hoped Adam would manage to get leave so that they could visit while the daffodils were out and the orchards in blossom. She missed the lush meadows and flower-filled hedgerows. Although the countryside around Pirbright was pretty, it didn't have the same appeal for her as Sturbury.

Aunt Julia always made Helen welcome at Willow Cottage and kept her up-to-date with local events, but, as time passed, Helen found they had less and less appeal. Most of her childhood friends had left the village. Isabel, now married, was in Australia and even Donald, although he had taken over Bulpitts, was away in Canada on an extended working holiday and the house was shuttered and neglected.

In addition, Helen found that her new life and friends in Pirbright seemed to be taking up more and more of her time. She had become involved in the social life there, the Sunday lunches in the Mess and the parties that always seemed to be held on the slightest pretext. There was even a party organised when Princess Elizabeth and Prince Philip announced their betrothal. As soon as the wedding date was announced, plans of how they would celebrate that spiked every conversation.

Although she was caught up in all these activities, Helen still felt that her life lacked something. When it was announced that Princess Elizabeth was expecting a baby, Helen felt quite desperate. It seemed so unfair; Princess Elizabeth had been married no time at all. Helen even began to wonder if her own miscarriage had left her unable to have children. Just a few months later, however, she finally became pregnant herself and her joy knew no bounds.

For several months she guarded her secret, not even telling Adam, until it became impossible to conceal her thickening waist any longer.

Their excitement was dampened a little when Adam told her he was being sent to Cyprus for two months early in the New Year.

'I shall be away in March when the baby's due,' he grumbled.

'Never mind, I've plenty of friends nearby. Sheila and Nesta will be on their own as well so we can all keep each other company.'

'Jock and Taffy won't be away. I'm being sent on my own. It's a special assignment.'

Helen was immediately alarmed. Although Cyprus was quiet at the moment, she was afraid it meant that trouble was expected.

But Adam was quick to deny it. 'I didn't want to say anything until I was quite sure, but I think it's going to lead to promotion,' he told her. 'If I've read the signs right, I shall be promoted to full Sergeant once this trip is over. And that means a bigger pay packet.'

'Does it mean we'll move from here?'

'Hope not. Mind you, the entire Battalion is due for a posting sometime in 1949.'

'Must we go?'

'No choice. That's the Army.'

The news worried Helen. She even mentioned it when she wrote to Aunt Julia to tell her about the baby. By return came an invitation to stay at Willow Cottage just whenever she wanted to and for as long as she liked.

Helen had an easy pregnancy. By Christmas she was so huge that Sheila and Nesta were adamant she'd got her dates all wrong. Over coffee each morning they discussed it at length until she was almost convinced herself.

Although the three boys seemed to ignore totally the imminent addition to their immediate circle, Delia and Patsy, now five and six, waited with growing impatience for the baby's arrival. They had both been given dolls' prams at Christmas and argued constantly as to which of them would be first to take the new baby out in it.

Gently but firmly, Helen explained that the baby wasn't a toy and that it already had its own pram. In the end she promised that the first time she wheeled the new baby out they could come as well, with their prams.

'You must be mad to agree to something like that!' Nesta laughed. 'They'll hold you to it, you know. Can you imagine walking through the estate with those two in tow? It will be like a procession!'

'Our Patsy won't forget,' Sheila Wilson assured them. 'She keeps asking her Dad why can't we have another baby. I wish she'd stop putting ideas into his head! Three kids are enough to look after. Now she's at school, and I can go shopping on my own, I'm just beginning to feel human again. You stick at one, Helen, that's the perfect number and don't let anyone tell you different.'

When Ruth was born, and she had to cope single-handed, Helen was inclined to agree with Sheila. The baby was small, dark-haired, grey-eyed and adorable, but very demanding.

Ruth was seven weeks old when Adam returned from Cyprus, and he was enslaved from the first moment he set eyes on her.

'She's a perfect replica of her mother and I couldn't ask for more,' he assured Helen the first time he held her in his arms.

'It's like seeing you as a baby all over again,' Aunt Julia told Helen when she came to Pirbright for the christening.

It seemed to Helen that the Fates were smiling on her. Ruth thrived and Adam delighted in every new stage of her development, eager to nurse her whenever he was at home.

They didn't even move from Pirbright as had been forecast. Strikes seemed to be the order of the day and the Guards were sent to help unload meat at London Docks.

Secure in her home, Helen's world revolved around Adam and the baby. She shut her ears and eyes to every-thing else, whether it was national news or local gossip.

Over coffee, she would listen to Sheila and Nesta's hair-raising tales of rows, break-ups, intrigue and scandal amongst the other families in married quarters, as if it was no part of her world. She always knew where Adam was and, anyway, he just wasn't that type. Her cup of happiness was full. They were still deeply in love and he was devoted to Ruth.

Ruth was not quite eighteen months old when Helen found herself pregnant again. Adam was now a Training Sergeant, permanently based at Pirbright, training the eighteen- to twenty-two-year-old conscripts who, though they only served for two years, often chose to be drafted into the Guards and, when they did, their training had to match up to that of the rest of the Regiment.

Adam found the work monotonous, but Helen welcomed the opportunity for them to remain at Pirbright, even though she knew it couldn't last. Jock Wilson and Taffy Evans had been out in Malaya for well over a year and Adam was due to go out there just as soon as his latest intake of conscripts were sufficiently trained in jungle warfare.

Again, luck was with them. The Guards were withdrawn from the Far East before he went out to join them and so he was still at home when the new baby, a boy, was born at the end of February. They called him Mark. He had Adam's vivid blue eyes, and thick crop of dark hair and Helen felt that at last they were a complete family.

Mark was nowhere near as placid as Ruth had been. By the time he was ten months old the two year age gap between him and Ruth seemed to lessen, for by then he could walk and was into every kind of mischief. He was so sturdy that he kept up with his sister in just about everything.

The following February, just a few days before Adam was due to be sent to Palestine, King George VI died, and, instead, Adam found himself part of the escort for the King's funeral parade. No sooner was that over than full-scale rehearsals began for the Coronation, which was to take place the following year.

Helen wanted to take Ruth and Mark up to London to watch the Coronation but Adam was against her doing so.

'You can't possibly take the children there,' he protested. 'The crowds will be massive; they won't be able to see a thing.'

'Can't you find us a good viewing point? I wanted the children to see you taking part,' she pleaded. 'They are always so excited when they see you marching through the streets when we are out for a walk. Remember how Mark saluted the last time you gave your squad an "Eyes right" as they passed us.'

'You mean it's you who wants to see me,' he teased, his blue eyes gleaming. 'At their age they're not likely to know what it's all about, now are they? It's not as though I could stop and speak to them. Bring them to London next time I'm doing a Palace Guard; that should impress them.'

Reluctantly, she agreed to stay home and watch the ceremony on television. There was to be a party in the Mess for the children, and the houses and streets were gay with bunting, so at least there would be some sense of occasion.

When Ruth started school, Mark was so bored and lonely on his own that Helen decided to send him to a playgroup. For the first month Helen revelled in her new-found freedom because it coincided with Adam being on leave. Once or twice they arranged for Nesta to collect Mark at midday, so that they could go to Guildford to do some shopping, and have lunch out.

They still enjoyed each other's company and as she dressed for these special days, Helen felt as excited as if she was on her first date. She had quickly regained her figure after Mark's birth and had found that the 'new look' styles which were all the rage suited her. The mid-calf skirts and nipped-in waistline, showed her tall, slim figure to advantage and made her feel elegant. She had even bought a pair of stiletto-heeled shoes to go with the new outfits – although she didn't risk wearing them except when she was out with Adam and could hang on to his arm.

Adam teased her about her smug little smile as she straightened his tie and brushed the shoulders of his tweed sports jacket, before linking her arm through his. But she knew from the appreciative gleam in his vivid blue eyes that he was still as much in love with her as she was with him.

Sometimes, as she listened to Nesta and Sheila gossiping

about the break-ups, and the husbands who were unfaithful, she marvelled at her own good fortune. A
husband with whom she was still in love, and who
wanted only her, two happy, healthy children, a comfortable home and no money problems. It seemed almost too
good to be true.

Even though Helen knew that sooner or later Adam
would go overseas, when he was posted to Cyprus in
1955 she felt her world had been torn apart.

'It's not just the separation, it's the danger you'll be in.'
She sobbed as she clung to him on their last night
together.

'Come on, I know how to look after myself,' he
reassured her. 'I'm just as likely to have an accident here
in England as over there. The way some of these young
crows aim when we're out on the shooting range, it's a
wonder I haven't been maimed long before this.'

'It's not the same,' she protested tearfully.

'Look what happened to one of the Guardsmen on
sentry duty outside Buckingham Palace last year,' Adam
went on, 'he was bitten by one of the Queen's corgis and
had to be treated for a septic leg wound.'

'But at least he stayed here in England,' she argued.
'His family could see him and be with him. Ruth and
Mark are going to miss you as well as me.'

'Only if you let them. You've got to be strong, Helen.
We've had a fairly settled life here at Pirbright. We've
been luckier than most of the others.'

'As Depot Training Sergeant you had to stay in England.'

'Exactly! A cushy number by other people's standards.'

'How long will this posting last?'

'I don't know yet. There's trouble out there, otherwise I
would have been able to take you and the children with
me. Perhaps in two or three months time . . .' his voice
trailed off as her mouth sought his, seeking their own
special kind of solace in the few hours they had left.

Chapter 14

'I feel as if I'm being deserted,' Helen sighed as she refilled Nesta's coffee cup. 'First Sheila and now you. I almost wish I could persuade Adam to do the same as Taffy and leave the Army.'

'My Elwyn's a lot older than Adam. He was a regular soldier when the war started so he's done his twenty-one years,' Nesta pointed out. 'And that's long enough for anyone to serve,' she added forcefully.

'And he's already fixed up with a job. That was lucky!'

'I only hope it works out,' Nesta said anxiously. 'He's putting his gratuity into a garage along with his youngest brother. It means jobs for our two boys as well.'

'A real family business!'

Nesta made a face. 'Sounds grand, but I don't know how they'll all get on working together. My Elwyn's more used to giving orders than taking them and it's his brother who knows about cars, not him. At least we're not all living together, so I suppose that's something.'

'I hope you'll be happy. I wonder if we'll ever meet up again?'

'Of course we will, cariad!' Nesta's Welsh accent became stronger with emotion. 'You'll come to visit us . . . promise now! We've been friends for nearly twelve years; we can't just lose touch with each other. Good friends are hard to find, you know.'

'You and Sheila were the first people I really got to know when we arrived in married quarters,' Helen said reflectively. 'I wonder where she is now?'

'Still living with her mother the last time I heard,' Nesta said, shaking her head sadly. 'It was sad about her and Jock breaking up like that.'

'Yes, but I can understand it. He *was* cheating on her.'

'I know, but I think she should have turned a blind eye to his antics; most wives do, don't they?'

'Oh, come on, Nesta. He was even getting other sergeants to cover up for him by saying he was on duty, when in fact he was out on the town with other women. What wife is going to stand for that?' Helen said sharply. It was a situation she had never had to deal with herself and she just couldn't understand how other wives found themselves in such a predicament. If Adam had deceived her with someone else then, much as she loved him, she would not have tolerated such behaviour.

'Plenty do. We talked about it often enough. I don't think you ever believed half the stories we told you, though.'

'It's the children I feel so sorry for when families break up,' Helen said gloomily.

'True, but Sheila's are both teenagers now and will soon be old enough to stand on their own feet. Army kids are pretty resilient . . . they have to be. All the moving around, new places, different faces, strange schools . . . they grow up faster than most children and they're used to not having their dad around.'

'I suppose you're right.'

'You've been lucky, Helen. Adam's only had a couple of short spells overseas; the rest of the time he's been here at Pirbright.'

'True, though I sometimes think Adam gets bored being Training Sergeant – but it's suited me not having to keep moving.'

'Adam gets plenty of variety. He gets a better life than you,' Nesta assured her. 'He's away for three or four months each year on exercises and he gets the occasional trip to Cyprus or Rhodesia.'

'Up until now I've been perfectly happy, but I feel restless now you're going. Most of the wives who've moved here recently seem to be a different generation. All they think about is parties and dances. After you've gone

I think I'll become a recluse and no one will ever come inside my house,' Helen said with a tight little laugh.

'Except the mosquitoes!' Nesta smiled.

'I don't think even I could manage to keep them out,' Helen agreed. 'They're always around. I've even been bitten by the damn things in winter. I think Pirbright must be a breeding ground for them.'

'Which just goes to prove how unutterably boring it can be here . . . you even notice things like mosquitoes!'

'So you'll be glad to get away?'

'No! I'm being bitchy because I know I'm going to miss this place something terrible,' Nesta admitted. 'Sunday lunch in the Mess, especially on Mothering Sunday when we are all given flowers, the Summer Ball, Down Sunday at Epsom each year, the theatre trips and Christmas parties! They have been part of my life for so long that without them there will be nothing to look forward to.'

'But you always used to grumble about having to go because we always met the same people!' Helen exclaimed in amazement.

'That was part of the fun. Remember when the kiddies were small, and we were hard up, how we used to swap clothes — even ball gowns!'

'Yes, and then change the trimmings on them so that no one would recognise them . . . or so we hoped!'

'We had some great times.' Nesta sighed. 'There was always plenty of good food and drink . . .'

'Come to the next Troop Ball as our guests,' Helen interrupted eagerly. 'It would be something for all of us to look forward to. Promise?'

Helen found she wasn't the only one to feel unsettled after Nesta and her family had left. Ruth was lost without Delia. They had grown up together and since Patsy Wilson had moved away they had become inseparable. For several weeks Ruth made no attempt to mix with any of the other girls, but just wandered around on her own or spent her evenings shut away in her bedroom playing records. She became so moody that Helen breathed a sigh of relief when she started joining in again and going to the youth club.

But not for long. Gradually, Helen noticed a change in Ruth's entire attitude. Her school reports were poor and several times Helen caught her smoking. When she asked Adam to give Ruth a talking-to, he seemed to think she was taking it all too seriously.

'Stop being so protective,' he warned, looking up from his newspaper. 'She's only experimenting. If you try to stop her or punish her for doing these things she will either do them all the more or something far worse. Be patient; it's just a phase she's going through.'

'She's setting Mark a bad example.'

'Rubbish. At his age all he's interested in is football and cricket. Oh, and going to gym. I understand he's one of the best they have.'

'Who told you that?' Helen asked in surprise. 'Michael Blake never said Mark showed any special ability.'

'Well, he wouldn't would he? It's just a job to him. It was his wife, Margery, who mentioned it. She stood in for him when he sprained his ankle a few weeks back. She used to teach athletics in a girls' school . . .'

'And she made a point of telling you that Mark was good?'

'Well, you know what it's like when you take on something for the first time; you're full of enthusiasm.'

'And where did you see her?'

'She'd dropped into the Mess bar for Happy Hour.'

'With Michael?'

'No, she was just having a drink on her own. Michael was resting his foot. We had a long chat . . . she's quite a remarkable woman.'

'I'm sure.' Abruptly Helen put down her knitting and went into the kitchen. She stood for a long time staring into space, willing herself to be calm.

I'm reading far more into this than I should, she kept telling herself over and over again. Why shouldn't Adam

109

have a conversation with Margery Blake if she was in the Mess? They were talking about Mark, nothing more. If Adam knew she was standing in for her husband then it was only natural that he should ask about Mark's progress. He was very proud of him.

As she put the kettle on, she tried to remember if Adam had been on duty the last time Mark had gone to gym. He worked such erratic hours that she always assumed that if he wasn't at home then he was working. She never thought of him being in the Mess drinking, not unless he was off duty and said that was where he was going.

There was probably a perfectly logical explanation, and all she had to do was walk back into the other room and ask him. But she couldn't bring herself to do it. Instead she thought how Sheila had been misled. When it had all come out into the open, Jock hadn't even been in camp half the time he claimed he was on duty, but up in London with other women.

Helen knew she was being ridiculous, torturing herself with such thoughts. She had no reason to doubt Adam for one minute. He had always been an exemplary husband. Their love for each other had, if anything, deepened over the years.

Unable to put Margery Blake out of her mind she went upstairs and took a long, critical look at herself in the wardrobe mirror. She might not have Margery's corn-coloured hair, or her lithe, muscular body, but she was wearing pretty well for thirty-six. She was still slim and trim and there wasn't a trace of grey in her dark hair. She studied her face for signs of any lines around her eyes or mouth and even managed to smile at her reflection because there were none.

Her ego boosted, she went downstairs. Instead of making coffee she hunted out half a bottle of sherry and carried it back into the sitting-room, together with two glasses.

'Have I forgotten something . . . a birthday . . . an anniversary?' Adam frowned as he took the glass from her.

'No! Can't we have a drink together without it being a special occasion?'

'We can, but it's out of character,' Adam said drily. 'There must be a reason. You must be trying to soften me up for some purpose or the other.'

'No,' Helen told him quietly, as she touched her glass against his, 'just a drink to us . . . we're the last of the old-timers. Only two more years and you'll have done your twenty-one years. Time to start planning what comes next.'

'You've become disenchanted with life here, haven't you?' Adam said quietly.

'Yes, I think I have, in a way.'

'Anything to do with Taffy and Nesta leaving?'

'It began when Jock and Sheila split up.'

Adam's hand reached out and took hers, squeezing it reassuringly. 'Two years will pass quickly enough.'

'I know. But what then? Where will we go . . . we've no home and I don't suppose we'll be able to manage on just your pension.'

'Is that what's worrying you?' he asked, his voice full of concern.

'Amongst other things,' she said evasively.

'Come over here,' he patted the settee beside him.

His arm went around her, holding her close to his broad, solid chest, and her anxiety dispelled. As she looked up into his strong, square face, and saw the mixture of love and concern in his intense blue gaze, she felt almost ashamed of harbouring doubts about him.

She buried her fingers in his shock of dark hair, pulling his head down until their mouths met. The firmness of his lips, the sharp rasp of his chin against her cheek, the warmth of his breath, stirred her senses as much as they had always done. She could tell she still excited him, even before he grabbed her hand, guiding it down his body to prove what she was doing to him.

'I knew you had some devilish scheme in mind when you poured me that glass of sherry,' he murmured.

With a small sigh of contentment she relaxed against him, revelling in the heat from his muscular body, which she could feel even through his shirt. With trembling fingers she began to undo the buttons, running her finger tips over his chest.

'Two can play at that game,' he breathed, as his hand slid up underneath her sweater and deftly unfastened her bra. In a quick, decisive moment he freed her breasts and bent his head towards them. She shuddered as the delicious sensation of his tongue teasing her nipples erect sent waves of urgency rippling through her.

Without releasing his hold he gently lowered himself on to the sheepskin rug in front of the fire, taking her with him. Memories of their first-ever encounter, in the barn at Fordswater when she was just eighteen, came rushing back into her mind. And, just as she had then, she abandoned herself to his passion, rejoicing in his power over her, wanting only to please him.

Chapter 15

'Why don't you dance with Ruth? I feel exhausted,' Helen exclaimed as Adam, looking extremely handsome in his dark blue and red Mess Dress and frilled white shirt, held out a hand to lead her back onto the dance floor.

It was the first time they had ever had the chance to take Ruth and Mark to a 'do' in the Mess. Usually children were not allowed in the Mess but because one of the sergeants was holding his wedding reception there, the rule had been relaxed. And, since Adam would be leaving the Army the following March, Helen had been delighted that they had the opportunity to take Ruth and Mark with them.

'They'll probably remember this more than anything else about Army life,' Helen reflected.

In her full-length pale-blue dress, her long, dark hair in

a chignon, Ruth looked so very grown-up it was hard to believe that she wouldn't be fourteen until after Christmas. Only her innocent grey eyes and her shy smile, confirmed her youthfulness.

Ruth had been an adorable baby and had grown into a quiet but lovable child. There had been one short period after Delia Evans had moved away when she had been unmanageable, but that had soon passed. She was clever as well as pretty. Her school reports were glowing now and Helen was already planning that she should go on to university when the time came. Ruth would make a wonderful teacher. She had infinite patience as well as the ability to communicate. Without her help Mark would be a dunce. When he wasn't watching television he much preferred listening to his Beatles' records rather than reading a book or doing his homework.

Helen felt a wave of love and pride as she watched them. She only hoped their luck held when Adam left the Army next year and that he would be able to find a job he liked to help supplement his Army pension.

It was at times like this Helen found herself wishing she had gone to university when she'd had the chance. If only she had some training or qualifications she could have been the one to go out to work. Then Adam could have taken his time in deciding what he wanted to do, instead of accepting the first job that came along.

She thought about the letter she'd had from Nesta Evans. Taffy had found it hard to adjust to civilian life. His brother, though a good motor mechanic, was not very organised and this had proved to be a sore point. Already the partnership had been dissolved and Taffy was working as a security guard. It meant that Nesta was on her own most nights, which was worse than when her husband had been in the Army.

Helen dreaded something like that happening to Adam. He was forty-three, but he was outstandingly fit and bursting with health. Looking at him, Helen felt she knew what was meant by 'the prime of life' and it seemed ridiculous that his Army career should be ending.

'Where's Mark?' Adam asked as he and Ruth returned to the table, flushed from their exertions. 'This young lady is tireless. She wants to go on dancing, but I'm exhausted. I thought Mark might like to partner her.'

'You sit down with Mum; I'll go and look for him,' Ruth said, grinning.

'Helen, are you all right?' Adam asked anxiously the moment they were on their own. 'You're looking awfully pale.'

'I feel a bit faint. Probably the heat in here . . . and all the noise,' Helen replied.

'And the chasing round getting all of us kitted out for this event. I must say Mark looks good in his dinner jacket. Quite grown-up.'

'You might make a point of telling him so,' Helen smiled. 'He made a terrible fuss about getting "dressed up" as he put it. I asked him what he would do if he had to wear full Mess dress like you.'

'And what did he say to that?' Adam asked, laughing.

'He said that would be different.'

'Yes, he's still keen to join the Army, isn't he?'

'He's talking about becoming a boy-soldier when he's sixteen.' A shadow passed over Helen's face as she spoke.

Quickly Adam's hand covered hers, giving it a reassuring squeeze. 'Another couple of months and we'll be out of barracks and he'll forget all about the Army. Something else will take his interest, you'll see.'

'I hope so!' Helen said fervently.

'Just stop worrying about Mark and look after yourself more,' Adam told her.

His blue eyes were dark with worry as they scrutinised her face. She flushed under their intense searching. She knew she was looking tired; she felt it. Some days it seemed as if she didn't have enough energy to get through all the chores.

She was putting on weight, too, although she tried very hard to watch her diet. Sadly, she sighed, then smiled tremulously as she saw the concern on Adam's face.

'I'm getting middle-aged,' she said with a forced laugh. 'Maturing early . . . it's the sheltered life I lead.'

'At thirty-seven!'

'I was joking,' she said quickly, taken aback by the alarm in his voice.

'I should hope so. You aren't on top form, I'll give you that. I wish you'd have a check-up.'

'OK I will, I promise. I'll make an appointment tomorrow.'

Adam leaned closer and his lips brushed her cheek. 'Make sure you keep that promise,' he said softly. 'Now,' he stood up and pulled her to her feet, 'I'm going to have this dance if I have to carry you round the floor.'

Helen kept her word and went for a check-up, even though she thought there was probably very little the doctor could do for her, other than tell her to go on a diet and perhaps give her a tonic.

'I wondered if it might be the change,' she said rather diffidently, when he asked her what was wrong. 'I believe some women do start early. I'm certainly putting on weight . . . it could be middle-aged spread.'

He looked at her over the top of his glasses, then checked her record sheet on the desk in front of him.

'You're still in your thirties?'

'Late thirties . . . yes. Thirty-seven to be exact.'

After he examined her, he pursed his lips and shook his head. 'Did you say your husband was leaving the Army?' he asked.

'Yes . . . in about three months.'

'Hmmm.' He stared at her, unblinking for a few seconds. 'What are your plans then?' he asked.

'Nothing decided really. We hope to buy a house . . . or perhaps a business of some kind . . . we once talked about taking a pub and I'd be able to help . . .'

'I shouldn't plan on that,' he told her quickly.

'Something's wrong, isn't it?' she said, with an inward tremor. 'And just when we planned to start a new life,' she added sadly.

'You've already done that,' he told her jocularly. 'The reason you're feeling "out of sorts" as you put it, and why you seem to be putting on weight, is because you are pregnant!'

'Pregnant! I can't be . . . you must be mistaken!' she gasped.

'I'd say at least four months, possibly a little more. And you haven't suspected?'

'It never entered my head. Ruth's nearly fourteen and Mark will be twelve in a couple of months' time. What will they say!'

'They'll probably be tickled pink.'

'Adam will be . . .'

'Over the moon,' the doctor assured her. 'Everything will work out fine. Now don't worry.'

He was right, of course. Once over the initial shock, Helen quite liked the idea of having another baby. Ruth was ecstatic, and even Mark accepted the news without objection.

Adam's main concern was how would they manage financially when he left the Army, since his pension wouldn't be enough for them all to live on.

'We'll cope,' Helen assured him. 'It does mean you will have to get a job right away, of course. I won't be able to go out to work for years . . . probably not until the baby is old enough to go to school.'

'By that time you shouldn't need to work. Ruth will be nineteen and Mark seventeen so they should both be earning by then.'

'Not if they manage to get to university.'

'Well, we'll have to wait and see about that. It mightn't be possible . . . not now . . . not with a new baby.'

'The baby isn't going to stop them!' Helen exclaimed, white-faced, her grey eyes darkening with determination.

'We'll just have to wait and see,' Adam repeated. 'Neither of them may get enough "A" levels.'

'No,' Helen admitted reluctantly, 'but if they do, then I want them to have the chance,' she persisted.

116

'Let's not waste time worrying about it now,' Adam said firmly. 'Our immediate problem is a job for me. I'm away for the next two weeks at the shooting range, but once I get back from that . . .'

'Must you go? Couldn't someone else take your place?'

'Afraid not. Weapon-training is the responsibility of the Senior Training Sergeant. It will be the last time I'm away . . .'

'I still wish you weren't going.'

'I'll only be in Norfolk! You'll have Ruth and Mark to look after you. Now that they know about the baby they won't let you lift a finger, you'll see. While I'm away, why don't the three of you work out where you'd like to live? That should keep you busy until I get home again.'

It was like planning a holiday, Helen thought as the three of them spread out the maps each evening and pored over them, arguing whether it should be town, country or somewhere near the coast. Mark was keen on being able to go swimming in the sea and longed for them to have a boat. Ruth was more concerned about whether there was a good shopping centre nearby. Mark pointed out that if Ruth was going to university he didn't see what these things mattered since she would hardly ever be at home.

'I will be home in the holidays, silly!' Ruth argued.

As they made lists, Helen was far more practical. She knew they had to consider some place where Adam would be able to find work. She didn't want to live in a big town, not with a new baby, but neither did she want anywhere that was too isolated.

They finally short-listed half-a-dozen places and Helen folded up the maps and put them away.

'I think we've spent enough time on this,' she told them both.

'Dad'll be the one who has the final choice, anyway,' Ruth said flatly.

'Perhaps he'll decide to stay on in the Army after all,' Mark said hopefully.

'I don't think he's even considered it,' Helen said. 'Anyway, he's too old to keep his job as Training Sergeant.'

'He could always do something else,' Mark persisted.

'Well, he might be able to become a Recruiting Officer, I suppose,' she said thoughtfully.

'Where would he be sent then?' Mark asked.

'Almost anywhere in the country, though probably to one of the larger towns or cities, of course.'

'Perhaps London,' Ruth suggested.

'I wouldn't want to live there,' Helen said quickly.

'Would he be able to choose?' Mark asked.

'I don't know. I've never thought about it until now. Perhaps we'd better wait until your dad gets back from Norfolk. He mightn't go along with such an idea.'

'Then again he might,' Mark insisted. 'After all, he does like the Army . . .'

'You mean *you* do,' Ruth interrupted him. 'I don't think we should mention the recruiting job to Dad, not now that he has decided to leave the Army and find some other kind of work.'

'That's enough.' Helen said firmly. 'Mark, take these maps back upstairs.'

'OK. Just a minute – there's someone knocking.'

Ruth was already opening the door and Helen looked up in surprise, as Captain Bishop, Adam's Commanding Officer, and Bill Blackstaff, the RSM, both in uniform, came into the room. She saw at a glance that both men looked uneasy.

'Has something happened?' she asked in alarm.

'We've bad news,' Captain Bishop said gruffly. 'It's about your husband . . .' he hesitated, looking at the RSM.

'There's been an accident on the range,' Bill Blackstaff said in a level voice. 'Adam was demonstrating the use of hand-grenades . . . you know the drill. The lads practise with dummies until they've learned how to take the pin out. Then they have to use a live one . . .'

'Oh no! Oh my God!' Helen clung to the table, white-faced and trembling. It was the sort of mishap she had always dreaded might happen.

Captain Bishop moved quickly, reaching out to steady her as she swayed.

'I'm all right,' Helen said quietly. She felt for a chair and sat bolt upright on the edge of it, still holding onto the table. 'Please go on,' she said in a low, tight voice.

The two men exchanged glances before Captain Bishop took up the story. 'They had just started using live grenades. The first two or three were operated quite smoothly, then one chap fumbled with his, dropped it . . . right at your husband's feet . . .'

'And it exploded.'

He nodded.

'And Adam?' she whispered.

'He took the full force . . . it was instantaneous . . .'

Helen stared from one man to the other. Their faces swam before her, merged into one, then gradually receded further and further away into a black void. From somewhere far off she could hear a woman crying, a shrill keening sound that splintered the silence and then echoed away into blackness.

Chapter 16

'According to the rule book, we can let you stay on in this house for another three months. That should give you time to make other arrangements.'

Helen stared at Captain Street, the Families' Officer, in dismay. For a moment she wondered if she had heard correctly. It was only a week since Adam's funeral and it seemed that already the Army's relentless machinery was in motion.

'I do appreciate that in your case three months may be rather difficult, so we might manage to give you an extension . . .' As his voice trailed away he looked at her from under hooded lids, as he tapped his well-tailored khaki-clad leg with his drill stick.

Helen's hands involuntarily went to her swollen body as if to protect her unborn child.

'Have you any family . . . somewhere you and your children can go?'

Helen shook her head. There was only Aunt Julia and she was now in her sixties, too old and set in her ways to have her home invaded by a young family.

'Where did you live when you were first married?' Captain Street persisted. 'We might be able to get you a council house there.'

'It was wartime, and Adam was already in the Army, so we didn't have a home of our own when we were first married,' Helen told him.

'I see.' He pulled on his lower lip thoughtfully. 'And where did you live as a child . . . that might be worth a try.'

'Sturbury. It's a village. There are only six council houses there so I don't think I stand much chance of getting one of those.'

'I see.'

She stood up, squaring her shoulders, a hand pressed to the small of her back to ease the ache. 'I'll think of something, Captain Street,' she said, determinedly.

Relieved, he picked up his cap and gloves from the table and gave her a thin smile. 'Good! Good! That's what I like to hear. Come to me if you have any problems.' He raised his drill stick in a salute as he departed.

Helen smiled fixedly until she had closed the door, then she went back into the sitting-room, collapsed into an armchair and was overcome by a paroxsym of violent sobbing. It was the first time she had cried since she had been told Adam was dead.

Afterwards, she felt completely drained, then, as her mind cleared, she sat late into the night, trying to plan their future.

As the hands of the clock crept towards midnight, and the sheets of paper on which she had been trying to work out some kind of budget covered the table, she knew there was nothing for it but to see if Aunt Julia could help. It was the hardest phone call she had ever had to make.

'If you could just let us stay with you for a few weeks . . . a month perhaps . . .'

'Stay as long as you wish, my dear. I've always told you that my home is yours. When will you arrive?'

'I don't know . . . I'm still confused . . .'

'Shall I come and help you pack?' Aunt Julia offered.

'No . . . no. I can manage. Ruth and Mark will help.'

'I'm afraid you and Ruth will have to share a bedroom,' Aunt Julia said apologetically. 'And Mark will have to sleep in the boxroom. It's very small . . . still, if it's only temporary then I don't suppose he'll mind too much.'

'Aunt Julia, it's only fair to tell you now . . . there's something you don't know.'

'Oh, what's that?'

'I . . . I'm expecting a baby.'

The silence on the line seemed interminable. Helen tried desperately to think of something else to say, but the words caught in her throat. From a long way off she heard her Aunt's voice ask rather queruously, 'Helen, I did hear you rightly . . . you did say a baby?'

'Yes, in about three months' time.'

'Oh, my dear! Well, in that case, I suppose the sooner you come and settle in the better. I had no idea . . . oh, you poor child. This news *has* come as a shock.'

'I was wondering if it might be better if I stayed on here until after the baby was born.'

'You must do whatever you think is best.'

'If Ruth and Mark could come to you when it's time for me to go into hospital . . .'

'Yes, of course, if that would help.'

At first Ruth was distressed to think her mother would be left to go into hospital on her own.

'I'll be all right,' Helen assured her. 'I'll worry less if I

121

know you are with Aunt Julia than I would do if I had to leave you and Mark here to look after yourselves.'

'But you'll have no visitors!'

'I'll only be there for a few days.'

'But all our things . . . moving and that,' Mark protested. 'You won't feel like doing it when you come out of hospital.'

'I shall do it all beforehand,' Helen explained. 'Look, we'll begin sorting things out right away. We can send all our books, ornaments and personal possessions on ahead to Aunt Julia's. Then, when I'm ready to go into hospital, you two can pack your clothes and go on ahead and I'll follow with the baby.'

'What about handing over the quarters? You'll never feel up to coping with the inspection!'

'Don't worry. I don't intend to comply. It's not as though we are ever going to need other quarters. I'll post the key back after I get to Aunt Julia's and they can send me a bill for any loss or damage when they check the inventory.'

Once she had made her plan, Helen stuck to it with grim determination. Her timing was perfect. Ruth and Mark had just phoned from Aunt Julia's to let her know they had arrived safely, when her pains started. Calmly, she phoned for a taxi to take her to hospital.

Lucy, weighing six pounds, three ounces, arrived in the early hours of the following morning. When she was discharged, Helen took a taxi back to married quarters.

'Could you help me collect some cases?' she asked the driver when they pulled up outside.

When he had taken them out to the cab she slammed the front door shut and followed him, without even a backward glance.

'Where to now?' the cabby asked in surprise.

'Waterloo Station.'

'Cor, you leaving him then?' he asked, pushing his cap back on his head.

'No. There's no one to leave . . . only the Army.'

He stared at her for a minute, then gradually began to comprehend. He put the cab in gear and his eyes, as they met hers in the driving mirror, were full of understanding.

Aunt Julia was relieved to see her. She fussed over the baby, worrying unnecessarily about whether there was going to be room in the bedroom for the cot, and if they would be able to get a pram into the hall.

'We haven't even got a cot or a pram,' Helen told her.

'Where's she going to sleep . . . and how will you take her out!' Aunt Julia exclaimed.

'For the moment, I'll use the carrycot.'

'Oh, poor little mite!' Aunt Julia said sadly.

'Rubbish! It's lovely and comfortable. She slept in it all the way from London.'

'Well, I suppose you know best. These modern ideas . . .'

It quickly became apparent to Helen that living at Willow Cottage wasn't going to work out. Years of being on her own had made Aunt Julia very set in her ways. Helen tried not to upset her aunt's routine, but it wasn't easy. Ruth and Mark were irritated by her criticisms of their clothes, they both missed their friends, and Mark resented always being told to turn down the sound whenever he played his Beatles' records.

'It's only for a few weeks, just until the money side of things is settled,' Helen told them. 'Once I know how much pension we are entitled to, then I can start looking for somewhere for us to live.'

'Why can't we look *now*?' Mark argued.

'Because at the moment I don't know what we can afford.'

In an attempt to give Aunt Julia time on her own, Helen took them out on long walks. Ruth and Mark enjoyed visiting the places she had known as a child, and listening to her anecdotes about them.

It was on one of these expeditions, when she was

showing them Bulpitts, and telling them about her time as a nurse there during the war, when it was a military hospital, that they met Donald Brady.

She had been unlatching the side gate when a voice said, rather sternly, 'This is private property, you know.'

She looked in astonishment at the burly, red-faced man in a tweed jacket, riding breeches and high-legged brown leather boots who was addressing her.

As her gaze met that of the man with the angry, close-set hazel eyes, she recognised him immediately. Even though his hair had receded at the temples, it still crowned his head like a flat, brown skull-cap. Once he realised who she was he seemed overjoyed to see her, and his severe expression dissolved into a beaming smile.

'I was going to show Ruth and Mark the Silent Pool . . . I never thought about trespassing,' she apologised.

'Well, you wouldn't be trespassing, now would you!' Donald grinned. 'Why don't you let them go and find it for themselves, while we go back to the house for coffee? I usually stop for one about this time of the morning. It will give us a chance to catch up with each other's news.'

'When the war ended, and I came home from the POW camp,' Donald told her as they sat in the huge kitchen, 'I spent a few years in Canada. Then I decided that since Bulpitts was now mine I might as well farm as do anything else.'

'What about Isabel? Aunt Julia told me she had married and was living in Australia.'

'That's right. I hear from her at Christmas . . . and on my birthday. She's got three boys . . . seems happy enough.'

'And you . . . you're married?'

Donald shook his head. 'The girl I'd set my heart on married someone else.' His look spoke volumes and she felt herself colouring.

'And you?' he said enquiringly. 'I see you have two very fine children . . .'

'Three!' she indicated the carrycot at her feet.

Donald looked down in surprise to where Lucy lay sound asleep. 'Good heavens! I thought that was a picnic hamper. There's not a sound coming from her!'

'She'll be awake soon and then you'll change your opinion,' Helen laughed.

'How old is she?'

'Just over three weeks.'

'Three weeks . . . but you said Adam was dead . . .' his hand went out and covered hers. 'Helen, what happened?'

She shook her head, fighting back the tears. 'Adam was killed in an accident almost four months ago.'

'So he never saw her?'

She shook her head, unable to speak. It was the first time she had spoken about Adam's death to anyone outside the family and it was as if she was ripping away a protective covering from an open wound.

Donald's hand grasped hers again, his hazel eyes full of concern.

'And you're staying at Willow Cottage . . . all of you?'

'Until we find something to rent. You haven't got a spare cottage, have you, Donald?'

He shook his head. 'I haven't got a spare cottage but there's plenty of room here . . .'

'No, I was only joking!' Abruptly she pulled her hand away. 'I . . . I've got things planned,' she said quickly.

Donald looked at her in silence for a moment, then he said with slow deliberation, 'This is a big house, Helen. I rattle around it living here as I do all on my own. You are more than welcome to come and stay . . . for just as long as you like. Think about it. It must be very cramped living at Willow Cottage. You can't be very comfortable.'

'We can manage.'

'Your other two are practically grown up; they need space, their own rooms,' he went on persuasively as if she had not spoken. 'Give it some thought. Move in when you like, there's enough room for your furniture . . .'

'We don't have any . . . we lived in furnished quarters.'

'Couldn't be better then, now could it? Here's Ruth and Mark coming. What about asking them?'

'No . . . please, Donald. Give me time to think about it,' she pleaded.

Aunt Julia's look of delight when Helen mentioned Donald's offer decided the issue. Ruth and Mark were thrilled at the prospect.

'Think he'll let me drive his tractor?' Mark asked eagerly.

'I'd sooner learn to ride one of the horses,' Ruth said with a sigh.

'Wonder if I'll be able to go fishing in that lake?' Mark said wistfully. 'Dad would have loved Bulpitts.'

'He did quite like it. It was where we met,' Helen explained. 'I told you it was a military hospital during the war. Well, your father was a patient here and I was one of the nurses.'

'How romantic!' Ruth's grey eyes became dreamy.

'So how do you know Donald Brady then?' Mark asked.

'He lived at Bulpitts before the war and I lived in the village. We used to play together . . .'

'Oh, so *that's* why he said we could all go and live there,' Ruth said flatly. 'I though he'd fallen madly in love with you the moment he saw you . . . it's not really as romantic as I'd thought.'

'There's nothing romantic about it at all,' Helen told her sharply. 'If we go there to live then it will be a business arrangement . . . as Donald's housekeeper.'

'Housekeeper!' Mark and Ruth looked at her in horror. 'You mean you're going to work for him?'

'How else will we earn our keep?' she asked quietly.

'I thought you were going to live with each other. I'm sure he's crazy about you, Mum,' Ruth insisted. 'I can tell from the way he looks at you.'

'You can stop that ridiculous talk right away,' Helen snapped. 'If we move into Bulpitts it will be as a working arrangement and nothing else.'

Donald looked as disappointed as Ruth when Helen told him her intention.

'If that's the way it has to be then I must accept your terms,' he said quietly. 'I hope one day you'll really want to make it your home.'

She turned away quickly, unable to stand the hurt look in his eyes when he was being so kind to her. His words had brought back to her unpleasant memories of the night before he had joined the RAF, and she knew her feelings for him remained unchanged. Apart from that, no one could ever take Adam's place. Theirs had been the perfect marriage and her love for him was as strong now as when he'd been alive.

Chapter 17

The arrangement at Bulpitts worked surprisingly well. Ruth and Mark enjoyed being there from the moment they moved in and even little Lucy thrived, growing plump and brown as the summer advanced.

She would lie in her pram on the sloping green lawn, gurgling happily at the trailing fronds of the willow tree as they waved and danced in front of her.

Donald was captivated by Lucy. He made frequent detours so that he could pass her pram and stop to talk to her.

Watching them together, Helen felt a lump in her throat. If only Adam had lived to see his new daughter; if only Lucy could have known a father's love.

She knew that could be easily overcome. Right from the start, Donald made it very clear that he was more than ready to marry her, but she turned down his frequent suggestions with unswerving firmness, making it quite clear that no one could ever replace Adam.

Remaining true to Adam's memory was her tribute to him, because their marriage had been so unsurpassable.

Their relationship had been so special – something she couldn't express in words but which burned deep inside her, filling her heart with tenderness whenever she thought about him. Helen felt sure that, had she been the one to die first, Adam would never have married again.

She had tried to explain all this to Donald when he had said with his characteristic bluntness, 'It would look better if we got married now that you're living at Bulpitts, Helen.'

'Married!'

'I've always wanted you, Helen. And now I feel my patience has paid off . . . it was obviously meant to be,' he told her arrogantly.

Anger because he had the audacity to assume she would say, 'Yes', welled up in her. As she stared at the round, florid face with its large full-lipped mouth and prominent bony nose, she remembered with repugnance the first time he had kissed her and knew he hadn't changed at all. It took all her self-control to suppress the shudder his words invoked and hold back the scathing answer that burned on her lips. In her present position, to antagonise Donald was a luxury she dare not indulge in.

With icy coldness she told him firmly that she wouldn't marry again . . . ever.

'Let me know if you change your mind.' Donald smiled complacently.

'I won't, so if you feel uncomfortable, or embarrassed about us living here, then say so,' she told him defiantly, her heart in her mouth in case he did decide to turn them out. The thought of them all having to cram back into Willow Cottage, even for a short time, was daunting. Nevertheless, she intended to set matters straight, right from the start.

'No, let's leave things the way they are. I won't pester you . . . I promise.' He gave his characteristic loud laugh. 'I'm too clever for that. I shall go on waiting, just as patiently as I've done all these years. One day you'll change your mind and when you do . . .' His laugh boomed out again, and his close-set hazel eyes glittered.

Although they had their own separate sitting-rooms, most of the time they lived as a family. They took their meals either in the enormous kitchen or in the oak-panelled dining-room that looked out onto the lawns at the front of the house. Donald automatically sat at the head of the long, polished dining-table, playing the family man as if it was his natural role.

As the months passed, Helen became more and more aware that in so many ways Donald acted as father to her three children. He taught Ruth to ride and on her sixteenth birthday bought her a black gelding. He encouraged Mark to enjoy the farm, allowed him to drive the tractor and took him fishing. He spent a lot of time with Lucy, nursing her when she was fretful, playing with her when she was lively. He also spent hours patiently encouraging her to walk and talk.

Seeing them together, watching the trusting way Lucy held his hand, and the way her face creased into a smile whenever Donald came near, Helen often wondered whether she had, after all, made the right decision. Having decided to live at Bulpitts, perhaps it would have been more honest, and better for the children, had she married Donald.

Such thoughts usually troubled her at night, when she tossed and turned, unable to sleep, even though she was tired. Then she would ask Adam for guidance. It was a habit grown out of years of separation. Usually she fell asleep before her problem was solved, but, next morning, when she awoke, the solution would be there, just as if she had discussed it with him.

For the first few months after they went to live at Bulpitts, Helen refused to let Donald take them out as a family, in case people drew the wrong conclusions. But he was patient and persuasive and eventually won her round. He started by taking Ruth and Mark to local county shows and agricultural events. And, seeing how much they enjoyed such outings, Helen eventually agreed to go along as well.

Ruth was doing exceptionally well at school, renewing Helen's hopes that she would go on to university. Donald's encouragement had a lot to do with it. Ruth seemed anxious to please him. He seemed to be able to stimulate her competitiveness and make her work. When Donald pushed she rose to the challenge, but if Helen tried to persuade her to turn down an outing, or spend less time playing with Lucy and more time studying, Ruth accused her of nagging.

Mark, though happy to be living on a farm, still hankered to join the Army.

'Why don't you try and get into university and then go into the Army as an officer,' Donald suggested, but Mark was not to be talked round. He recognised Donald's ploy as being a delaying tactic.

'Or join the Army Cadet Corps,' Donald suggested. 'They train, go to camp, and do most of the things a regular soldier does. It's a good way of finding out if Army life is really what you want.'

'I've lived in barracks ever since I was born,' Mark pointed out. 'I know all about the Army, and I'm quite certain it's the life I want. I'll never be really happy doing anything else.'

At fifteen, Mark was already tall and had his father's powerful build. His hair was dark and thick, like Adam's had been. His eyes though were a much deeper blue and lacked the intenseness Helen remembered so well.

Lucy, golden-haired and adorable, was undoubtedly the catalyst for them all. Delicately built with fair skin and huge blue eyes she had completely captured Donald's heart. For her third birthday, he bought her a Shetland pony and after breakfast each morning he took her out on it. For the rest of the day, she would pedal after him on her tricycle, following him all around the farm, not wanting to let him out of her sight for a moment. When he was ploughing, harrowing or spraying, she would climb up on the gate to watch, happy and contented as long as he waved to her each time he circled the field.

Lucy was sitting astride the huge iron gate that divided Bulpitts from Home Field, the morning the accident happened.

Helen, busy in the kitchen preparing lunch, heard her screaming and ran outside to find out what was wrong. Lucy came running towards her, tears streaming down her face, choking with sobs.

When she finally understood what Lucy was saying, Helen's heart thudded with fear. When she reached the meadow, Helen found Donald pinned beneath the tractor.

He was unconscious and there was not even a flicker of movement from his still figure. She tried to feel for his heart but the heavy machinery lying across his body made it impossible. She rubbed his hands and called his name, but not a muscle of his face moved. Blood was oozing from a gash on his forehead and his eyes seemed glazed. She felt for his pulse, but there was not even a tremor of movement in his thick wrist.

Grasping Lucy's hand she raced back to the house to get help. She phoned for the fire brigade as well as an ambulance, because she was sure cutting gear would be needed to free him. While she waited, she telephoned to ask if Ruth and Mark could come home from school to look after Lucy so that she could go to the hospital with Donald.

As it turned out, that wasn't necessary. Donald had died instantaneously. The blow to his head had knocked him unconscious and, when the tractor had turned over, his chest had been crushed by the weight of it.

Shocked though she was by the news, Helen was relieved to learn he hadn't suffered. She was, however, filled with remorse as she thought of how she had taken all Donald had offered and given nothing in return.

After the funeral, the Bradys' family lawyer explained that Bulpitts had only been left in trust to Donald. In the event of his death it went to Isabel. Knowing she would not be coming from Australia for the funeral, the lawyer had already asked her for instructions and had been told she wanted Bulpitts to be sold.

Helen stared at him aghast, knowing that once more her own future was in jeopardy.

'There is a provision for you in the will, however,' the lawyer told her. 'Mr Brady recently acquired a small farm just a few miles away. He bought it as investment property. His long-term plan was that, in due course, your son Mark might wish to farm on his own. Fortuitously the lease expires next quarter-day and, since the tenant has not applied for an extension, it would seem he intends moving on. Under the terms of Mr Brady's will the farm is left to you, in trust, until your son is twenty-one, so you could move in as soon as it is vacant, should you so wish.'

'I really don't know what to say,' Helen said wearily. 'I need somewhere to live . . . but it would be a pity not to use the farm . . .'

'Mr Brady has left you, personally, a small legacy. You could use that to buy stock. Or, of course, you could rent the farm out and find other accommodation for yourself and your family.'

'I don't know enough about the everyday running of a farm,' Helen said in bewilderment. 'And Mark is only a schoolboy. Anyway,' she said, sighing, 'his heart is set on joining the Army.'

'I can probably find a good all-round man to help out,' the lawyer offered. 'Your son is familiar with farm equipment . . .' He hesitated, as Helen, remembering Donald's accident, shuddered and shook her head violently.

'I was referring to milking machines . . . equipment of that kind,' he said hastily.

'Yes . . . yes, of course.' With an effort Helen pulled herself together. Could she take on a farm, looking after animals, haymaking, gathering in corn, raising chickens, taking pigs to market? With the right help, she decided, it would be worth trying. It meant independence for her and for the children. Anything was better than going back to live with Aunt Julia.

After the spaciousness of Bulpitts, Hill Farm seemed

cramped and inconvenient at first. Helen valiantly hid her dismay and, whenever Ruth and Mark began to criticise the place, reminded them that they should be grateful Donald had left them a home of their own.

Jim Baines, who had been hired to help out, was a willing, though rather plodding, worker, so Mark did the milking before he left for school in the morning, leaving Helen to see the milk through the cooler and put in churns, ready for collection by the local dairy.

Helen herself fed the hens and ducks while Jim Baines saw to the cattle and then attended to some of the field work. He refused to do any of the ploughing or to drive the tractor, so most of this work was contracted out to a neighbouring farmer. The rest Mark managed to do at the weekends or during his school holidays.

Remembering Donald's accident, Helen hated Mark using the tractor, for fear of an accident, and would usually take Lucy along to the field where he was working on some pretext or the other.

Ruth showed no interest in the farm at all. Far from resenting this, Helen was secretly pleased, since it meant that Ruth was spending more and more time studying.

Helen had become obsessive about Ruth going to university and achieving what she herself had failed to do. It was the one thing she felt would make everything worthwhile. She was so confident that Ruth had done well in her 'A' levels that after the exams were over she encouraged her to go on a school trip to Brecon, as a reward for all her hard work.

Chapter 18

Ruth's trip to Brecon was a turning point in all their lives. Her insistence on marrying Hugh Edwards, although she had only known him for a couple of weeks, shocked and saddened Helen. And her outspoken condemnation of the life they had led since leaving married quarters disturbed her deeply.

Sitting downstairs, long after the others had gone to bed, Helen pondered on Ruth's outburst and also on the way Mark had reacted.

At the time of Adam's death, it had never entered her head to discuss with them the changes she was making. She had simply done what she thought was for the best. And, looking back, she didn't see how else she could have acted.

Homeless, and with a new baby, Donald's offer of accommodation had seemed the perfect solution. They certainly couldn't have gone on living at Willow Cottage for any length of time; it had been far too cramped, and it had seemed unfair to put such a strain on Aunt Julia.

Perhaps if Donald hadn't been killed and they had been able to go on living at Bulpitts instead of having to move to Hill Farm, Ruth and Mark would have felt differently about things.

She wondered what would have happened if Ruth hadn't met Hugh Edwards, and how long they could have gone on living as a family without some dramatic outburst.

She felt a deep-seated guilt because Ruth wanted to leave home. It was almost as if it was some sort of retribution; history repeating itself. She thought guiltily about the agonies her own parents must have gone through when she had been equally determined to marry Adam.

The circumstances were different, of course. In wartime everyone snatched their happiness when and where they could. And she had been pregnant. Yet she couldn't help wondering if her own mother had felt as depressed and helpless as she did now, because she had insisted on letting her heart rule her head.

She was so deep in retrospection that she didn't hear Mark come downstairs. She looked up, startled to find him in the room, a dressing-gown over his striped pyjamas, his hair tousled and his eyes screwed up against the light.

'Mark! Why aren't you in bed . . .'

'I could ask you the same question. Do you know the time, Mum?'

'Around midnight . . . I wanted to think things through.'

'It's half-past one!'

'You go on back to bed, dear. I'll be up in a few minutes.'

'Not much point if you're not going to be able to sleep, is there? Why don't we talk about it?'

'About Ruth?'

'If that's what's troubling you,' he said as he sat down on the floor beside her chair.

As Helen reached out to ruffle Mark's shock of dark hair, he caught her hand and held it firmly between his own. The strength of his grasp confused her. As she looked down into the serious blue eyes set in the strong, square face, it was like looking at the Adam she had known when she was eighteen.

'Why are you so upset about Ruth wanting to get married?' Mark persisted. 'Hugh seems a decent sort.'

'You don't understand . . . she is just a child.'

'No she isn't. She's eighteen. She's old enough to drive a car and vote, so why can't she get married?'

'But why does she want to leave home, Mark? I've always tried to be a good mother to you all; where have I failed?'

'You haven't failed. We've grown up just that little bit quicker than most kids. Dad being in the Army probably had something to do with it.'

Helen looked at him in surprise. 'Someone else once said that to me,' she said quietly. 'Perhaps it is true. But we're not an Army family now.'

'And we haven't got Dad,' he added, his voice gruff with emotion. 'Ruth's probably looking for someone to replace him. Think it lucky she didn't go for someone old enough to be her father! Girls like Ruth often do.'

Helen bit her lips to stop them trembling. How did Mark know things like that? she thought aghast.

'If you stop her marrying Hugh Edwards,' Mark went on, 'then she'll probably elope with him. And if she does that we may not see her again for ages, not until the rift heals.'

'What do you think your father would have said about all this, Mark?'

'I think he would have agreed to them getting married.'

'But Ruth is so young . . .'

'Hugh isn't though,' Mark cut her short. 'Look,' he said, standing up and reaching out a hand to pull Helen to her feet, 'why don't you sleep on it, Mum? It will all make sense in the morning.'

As he leant down and kissed her cheek, she raised her hand to caress his firm jawline. 'You sound just like your father.' She smiled. 'That was the sort of thing he always used to say when there was a problem and we couldn't find a solution.'

She saw him flush with embarrassment. Then with a grin he said, 'Well, what about taking my advice? I *am* the man of the house, you know.'

Comforted by Mark's concern, and hopeful that it would all look different in the morning, Helen went to bed and slept soundly until the noises from the farmyard and the early-morning birdsong woke her.

Helen was in the kitchen preparing breakfast when Ruth came downstairs next morning. Dressed in jeans and a blue and pink checked shirt, she looked subdued and very young. Her eyes met her mother's hesitantly, almost as if expecting an outburst.

'Is Hugh ready for breakfast?' Helen asked quietly.

'I don't know. Shall I go and call him?'

'Tell Lucy to do it. You lay the table. Mark will be in from milking any minute now.'

As she spoke, Mark came into the kitchen, Hugh with him.

'Good morning.' Hugh smiled briefly at Helen, then, walking over to Ruth, placed his hands on her shoulders and stood looking down into her eyes, before kissing her lightly on the lips.

Lucy watched, round-eyed. Then she ran over to Hugh and raised her face, 'Kiss!'

Laughing, he swung her high into the air, while she squealed excitedly, then kissed her on both cheeks.

When they had finished breakfast, Helen looked across at Hugh challengingly. 'I'll agree to you and Ruth being married . . . on one condition,' she stated.

'Mum!' Ruth was out of her chair, hugging Helen, her grey eyes shining.

'Hold it . . . you haven't heard my condition.'

Ruth's arms dropped to her side. 'It's not about me going to university is it, Mum? Honestly, it wouldn't work. I really don't want to . . .'

'It has nothing to do with university,' Helen said quietly. 'I've had my say about that. I won't drag it up again.'

'What is the condition, Mrs Woodley?'

Hugh's dark eyes met hers. He looked ready for a battle and she smiled to herself, wondering just what he thought she had in mind.

'That you and Ruth have a white wedding.'

There was a hushed silence in the kitchen after Helen had spoken. Ruth and Hugh exchanged glances, Mark's brows drew together in a puzzled frown and Lucy crept up to slip her hand in Helen's, conscious that something was being decided but unable to understand what was going on.

'You mean in church? A long dress and bridesmaids and everything?' Ruth said in an awed voice.

'One bridesmaid . . . Lucy.'

'That will cost a lot of money . . . we can't afford it!'

'I can. I've been saving up to help pay your way through university. It's not needed for that now, so we'll spend it on your wedding,' Helen said firmly.

'Oh, Mum! Does that mean you approve?'

Helen barely hesitated before nodding. 'On reflection, yes. You have Mark to thank for my change of mind.'

'Mark!' Ruth looked bewildered.

'He made me see that I wanted you to go to university because that was what I thought I should have done.'

'And you want Ruth to have a church wedding because that was something else you should have done?' Hugh asked softly.

Helen felt the colour staining her cheeks as she looked him square in the face. 'Perhaps. I also think it might help you both to realise the seriousness of the occasion,' she added cuttingly.

For a moment it looked as if the battle between the three of them was about to break out all over again. Quickly Mark summed up the situation and intervened.

'And I'm going to be the one to give you away, Ruth!' He grinned. 'Can you see me in top hat and tails?'

'You can't, you're not old enough,' Ruth told him.

'There's no one else . . . except Jim Baines.'

'Who is Jim Baines?' Hugh asked.

'The elderly chap who helps out around the place,' Helen told him.

'Perhaps we should let Mark do the honours then,' Hugh told Ruth. 'The journey to London might prove a bit too much for an old man like that.'

'London . . . who mentioned London?' Helen asked, perplexed.

'I've agreed to your condition, Mrs Woodley. Now I've one of my own to make,' Hugh informed her gravely. 'If we are to be married in church, then it will be in the Guards' Chapel at Wellington Barracks.'

'Oh Hugh . . . I'd love that!'

Ruth's cry of delight brought the discussion to a close.

138

Helen knew she was getting her own way, but on Hugh's terms. It would probably always be like that, she thought resignedly. She rather liked the fact that he had agreed to compromise without in any way losing face. It was the sort of thing Adam would have done.

Now that the die was cast, Helen entered whole-heartedly into all the plans for the wedding. There were a thousand and one things to be arranged. Hugh undertook to make all the arrangements for the service and Helen was happy to leave that in his hands. She had quite enough to do getting Ruth's wedding-dress and Lucy's bridesmaid's dress ready in time, as well as hiring a grey morning suit for Mark.

Buying an outfit for herself was also more difficult than she had thought. She did so want to look right. In the end, she decided on a matching dress and coat in deep cream slub silk. And, to wear with it, she eventually found the perfect hat, wide-brimmed and in a dramatic shade of deep pink.

'Hugh's parents are staying in London and meeting you at the Guards' Chapel just before the ceremony starts. That means I won't meet them until after I'm married to Hugh,' Ruth said in a worried voice. 'That seems all wrong, Mum, doesn't it?'

'Talk to Hugh about it,' Helen advised. 'Perhaps you could both spend a couple of days at his home before the wedding.'

'There isn't time. Hugh wants to save his leave for our honeymoon.'

'Then the only other thing we can do is to ask them to come and stay here for a few days before the wedding.'

'Oh, Mum! I'm nervous enough as it is without having strangers around the place,' Ruth wailed. 'They mightn't even like me!'

Ruth was trying on her wedding-dress as she spoke and Helen felt a lump in her throat. Ruth looked so radiant. The tight-fitting bodice was cut just low enough in the neckline to reveal the tantalising curve of her firm breasts, before billowing out in a froth of lace and tulle. The shoulder-length lace veil, held in place on her dark brown hair with a circlet of tiny white roses, framed her oval face like a halo. Her big grey eyes shone with happiness and her mouth curved in a smile of sheer contentment. How could anyone not like Ruth? Helen thought proudly. Hugh was fortunate to be getting such a lovely bride.

She wished Adam could have been there to see her. Hugh had been right; she had wanted this ceremony because it was something she had forgone. Tears stung her lids as she remembered the grim registry office where she and Adam had been married, and her father's derogatory remarks at the time. Perhaps he had only been expressing the hurt inside him at seeing her make the greatest commitment of her life in such a tawdry fashion.

She pushed the thought away. It hadn't mattered; she and Adam had enjoyed a wonderful marriage. No one could have found a better husband, or a more faithful one. She hoped Ruth would be as lucky.

Ruth's wedding was a picture-book one. A coach-load of friends and relatives came from Sturbury, including Aunt Julia, who was wearing a flowered hat that was far more elaborate than Helen's. Hugh found a moment to introduce his parents to Helen, before taking his place in the front pew alongside a fellow Guardsman, to wait for his bride to arrive.

The Chapel at Wellington Barracks had not long been restored after being hit by a V1 flying bomb in 1944. As she sat admiring the magnificent apse and rich mosaics, which were the only part of the original building to survive, Helen felt the tension within her subside. For the first time since Ruth had returned from Brecon, she felt at peace.

When Ruth entered on Mark's arm, she seemed a little over-awed by so much grandeur. Helen, watching proudly as they made their way slowly down the blue-carpeted aisle, saw her nervousness vanish as soon as she took her place at Hugh's side. Her own heart thudded with past memories as she saw Hugh turn and smile into Ruth's eyes.

In her magnificent white dress and flowing veil, Ruth made a radiant bride. As she stood beside Hugh, who looked resplendent in his red and blue Guards' uniform, Helen found it hard to control her tears. Surreptitiously, she dabbed at the corners of her eyes with a lace-edged hanky and tried to focus her complete attention on the service.

Mark, looking very grown-up in his grey morning suit, took his duties very seriously. His voice seemed to acquire a new depth and authority as he solemnly gave Ruth away.

Lucy looked adorable in a dress of palest blue, a matching cap on her golden curls. She behaved perfectly, sitting motionless on the crimson velvet stool provided for her throughout the long ceremony. She even remembered to take Ruth's bouquet at the right moment.

The sun was brilliant, the sky over London cloudless, when they all moved outside to have photographs taken. The vibrant colours of the Guards' uniforms added to the splendour of the occasion. Passers-by in the road outside stopped to look through the railings and watch the colourful spectacle. Listening to the cameras clicking repeatedly, as guests were re-grouped for more and more pictures, Helen thought wryly of the single picture taken by Aunt Julia that was the only momento she had of her own wedding day.

As they walked across the Parade Square to the Mess where the reception was to be held, Helen found that being back in Army surroundings filled her with nostalgia.

Mark was in his element. He wandered around, immersing himself in the atmosphere, like someone returning home after a long absence. Watching him, Helen knew in her heart that she must resign herself to him enlisting. It was obviously the life he wanted.

Mellowed by the excellent food and witty speeches, the two families began to mix more freely. Helen liked Hugh's parents. They were older than her and she could see that Hugh's mother was worried because Ruth was so young.

'I was married at eighteen, too,' Helen assured her with a smile.

'But the Army is a hard life. Hugh's away overseas or on exercises such a lot. A young girl will find it very lonely.' The older woman sighed, shaking her grey head sadly.

'Ruth knows all about Army life. Her father was in the Guards,' Helen said quietly. 'We lived in married quarters until about three years ago. Adam, my husband, was killed . . .' she stopped, unable to go on.

'My dear, I'm so sorry.' Mrs Edwards patted Helen's hand. 'I didn't mean to bring up unhappy memories, not at a time like this . . .' she stopped in confusion.

'It's all right,' Helen said quietly with a tremulous smile.

When Ruth and Hugh left for their honeymoon, Helen found Mrs Edwards by her side. 'Hugh will take good care of her,' she said softly in her lilting Welsh accent.

Helen smiled and nodded, returning the pressure of the older woman's hand, too choked to speak.

As she stood holding Lucy's hand as the car taking Ruth and Hugh on the first stage of their honeymoon pulled away, Helen felt Mark's strong arm on her shoulders.

'We'd better be getting home, hadn't we?' he said firmly. 'I shan't be going into the Army now, Mum. One soldier in the family is enough. I'm going to try and make something of the farm.'

Chapter 19

'Mum, can Hugh and I come to stay?'

'Of course, dear. When will you be arriving?'

'We're at the station, now. Any chance of a lift?'

'Oh, Ruth! You could have given me some warning!'

Helen replaced the receiver as the line went dead. She took a quick look in the hall mirror, pushing her hair into shape, wishing she had got up early and washed it that morning as she'd meant to do. Ruth might have let her know they were coming, she thought, as she outlined her mouth with a pink lipstick. She hated being caught unprepared.

She called out to Lucy to let her know where she was going. Lucy was engrossed watching television, and, knowing Mark would soon be in from milking, Helen decided to let her stay where she was.

Ruth and Hugh were waiting in the station forecourt, Ruth wearing a red mini-skirt and white blouse, Hugh in grey slacks and an open-neck short-sleeved blue shirt.

'What kept you?' Ruth asked as she settled into the passenger seat beside Helen, leaving Hugh to sit on his own in the back of the car.

'Nothing kept me,' Helen told her sharply. 'I came the moment I put the phone down. If you'd warned me you were coming . . .'

'Here we go,' Ruth interrupted. 'Nag, nag, nag!' She turned to Hugh, 'What did I tell you!' She turned back to her mother and said, 'Blame him; it was his idea to come.'

'I'm not blaming anyone,' Helen told her. 'I'm always pleased to see you, you know that. It's just that I'm not prepared and you know I like to have everything ready. I'm not even sure if there's enough dinner to go round!'

'There'd better be,' Ruth laughed. 'We've had nothing since breakfast-time. We're both starving. We missed out on lunch we were so busy packing.'

'Packing?' Helen asked in surprise. 'You've only brought a weekend case with you.'

'I've been posted.' Hugh said. His eyes met hers in the driving mirror, darkly intense.

Helen's heart thudded wildly. 'You . . . you don't mean . . .'

'Yes,' Hugh said tersely. 'Northern Ireland.'

'I was afraid when they announced that troops were being sent over there that you might have to go,' Helen murmured, struggling to keep the emotion out of her voice.

She had heard on the news about the riots in Londonderry

and the need to send in extra troops and she'd hoped it wouldn't be the Guards. It seemed ludicrous to think of them going over there to deal with terrorists when only recently they had been on duty at Caernarvon Castle for the lavish spectacular of the investiture of Prince Charles as Prince of Wales. She and Lucy had sat glued to the TV set, straining to pick Hugh out from the hundreds of red-coated Guardsmen, but finding it impossible since their bearskins almost totally concealed their features.

'They should never have allowed the Apprentice Boys' Parade to go ahead,' she added sadly.

'That's what brought things to a head in the Bogside,' Hugh agreed, 'but it has been building up for some time.'

'When are you being sent over there?'

'Next Tuesday.'

'Next Tuesday! It's Friday now . . . that's only four days away.'

'That means you only have to put up with us for a couple of days,' Ruth quipped. 'We'll have to go back on Sunday because there's still a lot of packing to be done. The Army collects the boxes on Monday and we hand over the quarter first thing Tuesday morning.'

'You're going as well then, Ruth?'

'Of course. It's a two-year posting – the chance I've been waiting for.'

'You'll be over there at Christmas!'

'That's right.' Ruth grinned. 'Do you think Father Christmas will be able to find us?'

'I hope so. I shouldn't think Hugh would get leave that soon,' Helen said lightly, sensing the strain underlying Ruth's banter.

She had changed so much since her marriage that it worried Helen. The softness had gone from her grey eyes, and her gentle, sensitive mouth was now so much firmer. Helen had wanted her to come back home while Hugh had been on tour first in Hong Kong and later in Oman, but Ruth had insisted on staying on at Chelsea Barracks.

Hugh, too, seemed older and more cynical. Helen felt

144

she knew so little about him. She had been shocked when his mother had died just three months after the wedding. Mr Edwards had never fully recovered and four months later had suffered a massive stroke, which left him in a coma until he died three weeks later.

Over the next few days Helen's uneasiness about them increased. Ruth seemed to be on the defensive all the time, too ready to argue, and to pick on Hugh whenever he was in the wrong. But if he made the slightest criticism of anything she did, then she rounded on him and quickly asserted her rights.

There were times when Helen thought Hugh was actually afraid of Ruth. Yet, when they were on their own, they seemed close enough, strolling hand in hand, or with their arms around each other's waist.

It was Ruth's bossiness, her perverseness, and her sudden flare-ups, that worried Helen. It was almost as if Ruth didn't know how to share her life with someone else, Helen mused as she listened to them arguing fiercely. At times, Ruth even seemed to be deliberately trying to provoke Hugh, Helen thought, watching the scowl on his face when Ruth contradicted him.

Watching them together, Helen was convinced that Ruth's attitude would lead to trouble and she tried to find a way to talk to her alone and tactfully point this out. On the Saturday evening she suggested that Ruth went with her to visit Aunt Julia.

'I'm sure Hugh would sooner stay here with Mark than come with us,' she said with a smile.

'If I have to suffer Aunt Julia, then I don't see why he shouldn't,' Ruth protested.

'Suffer her!' Helen's voice was sharp with annoyance.

Ruth laughed a little awkwardly. 'You know what I mean, Mum.'

'No, I don't. She's a sweet old lady and she's always been very kind to you.'

'Oh, I know that. Don't take everything so literally,' Ruth snapped. 'She does go on a bit though about Dad and she likes to delve into the past and talk about when you were a girl and all that.'

'She only has her memories now,' Helen defended. 'She's crippled with arthritis so she isn't able to get out and about very much these days. Looking back is one of the few pleasures left to her.'

'Oh all right. I suppose I ought to go and say "Cheerio" to her before we leave for Ireland. Do you want to go right now?'

'I must put Lucy to bed first.'

'Hugh can do that. Come on, I want to be back before half-eight. There's a programme I want to watch.'

'Hugh can't put Lucy to bed!' Helen exclaimed.

''Course he can. All he has to do is tell her to go upstairs and remember to clean her teeth. Don't worry, he'll pop up later and tuck her in and kiss her goodnight.'

'I want a story,' Lucy protested.

'OK. You shall have a story,' Ruth snapped. 'Hugh tells wonderful stories . . . or he'll read to you, whichever you like. Come on Mum, don't let's stand here arguing all night.'

'Well . . .' Helen looked bemused.

'It's all right,' Hugh assured her. 'Lucy will be OK. You two go on.'

The speech Helen had carefully memorised, and worked herself up to give, fell flat. Ruth was in no mood to listen. The moment they were on their own she turned the tables and launched into a full-scale attack.

'Why do you always take Hugh's side whenever we have an argument, Mum?' she asked angrily as they left the house.

'Take Hugh's side . . . what are you talking about!'

'Come off it, you know what I mean. The minute I criticise him, or disagree with him over anything, you fly to his defence.'

'Well, he *is* a guest . . .'

'Rubbish! He's one of the family. We're married, re-member.'

Her tone inflamed Helen. Forgoing the gentle, tactful approach she said angrily, 'I don't know what's got into you, Ruth. You've become bossy . . . aggressive . . . you seem to be looking for a row all the time.'

'No, I'm not.'

'From where I stand it certainly looks that way,' Helen said heatedly. 'You've changed.'

'I've learned to speak up for myself. I wouldn't survive long in married quarters if I didn't . . . you should know that.'

'I never found it necessary to contradict your father every time he said something.'

'I don't argue with Hugh . . . except when it's necessary – and when I know I'm in the right and he isn't. I'm not just going to agree with him for the sake of peace and quiet like you used to do with Dad. You needn't bother denying it. I've seen you back down time and time again when you should have taken a stand.'

'I don't know *what* you're talking about,' Helen denied hotly.

'Oh yes you do, Mum. Things are different today. Marriage is a partnership. I don't accept Hugh's word as law. I have a perfect right to my own opinion about things.'

'Of course you do, dear.'

'And I expect Hugh to do his share of the chores. I don't go along with the way you treated Dad. I have no intention of waiting on Hugh hand and foot. When Dad was at home, our whole life had to revolve round him. He had the best chair, chose what we all watched on telly, and where we should go if we went for a walk. He was even given first pick of the cakes at tea-time! It makes me sick just to think about it.'

'Ruth!' Helen's face was white with shock and anger. 'How *dare* you talk about your father like that.'

'Because it's the truth – and before you start to criticise the way I am with Hugh, think about how you acted with Dad and then decide which of us is right. I'm pretty sure

Hugh loves me as much as I love him, but that doesn't make him perfect and it doesn't mean that I have to put him on a pedestal. Neither do I have to be a martyr and go along with everything he says when it's not what I want.'

'Yet you are going to Ireland with him!' Helen pronounced triumphantly.

'Of course I am! Like I said, he's human. If I let him go over there on his own for two years he may find someone else.'

'Ruth! Hugh hasn't got a roving eye already?' Helen exclaimed in dismay.

'Not as far as I know, but, as I said, he's only human. If I stay in England, when I could be over there with him, then I would only have myself to blame if he strayed.'

Desperately Helen tried to find the words she needed to counsel Ruth, to warn her that unless she treated Hugh more tolerantly she'd lose him anyway.

'You do tend to shout at him, Ruth,' she blurted out.

''Course I do. He's a soldier. Orders are all he understands. If I speak in a reasonable tone and ask him to do something he'll simply mumble "Yes" and go on reading or watching telly, or whatever. If I shout an order at him then he automatically springs to attention.'

'And you argue such a lot,' Helen persisted.

'He's got to learn what my opinions are, hasn't he?'

'But, Ruth . . .'

'Look Mum, we've only been married a couple of years, not a life-time like you and Dad. You knew what he felt about most things and you either shared his views or gave in quietly. I'm not like that, nor is Hugh. He doesn't want me to accept his opinions if I don't agree with them . . . and I don't intend to do so, anyway. OK we settle things rather noisily, but we do communicate. We're still individuals. I don't intend to end up as Hugh's shadow, without any opinions of my own, or being too scared to voice them.'

'I wasn't scared of your father . . .'

'Oh, come off it, Mum. You wouldn't ruffle his feathers no matter *what* the issue might be and you brought us kids up to be the same. As long as Dad didn't mind, we could do anything and go anywhere. The moment he raised so much as an eyebrow, it was taboo. We were shit-scared of him. The only good times were when he was away. Then we all breathed freely and even you became more human. When Dad was around you didn't even have Nesta Evans and Sheila Wilson in for coffee because you thought Dad mightn't like it.'

'The Wilsons and the Evans often came in for a meal . . .'

'Yes, as long as Jock and Taffy were there to keep Dad company. Then he'd play the big man of the house. You'd do all the work, all the cooking and baking, and he'd just pour the wine, or the beer, and lord it over everyone. And did he ever give you a hand with the clearing up afterwards?'

'Nesta and Sheila used to help.'

'Sometimes. More often than not the dishes were left until after they went home and then you were the one that did them. Well, it's not like that in my house. If we have friends in for a meal then Hugh plays his part. If he's at home he helps with the preparations as well as with the clearing up.'

'You seem to have it all worked out,' Helen murmured as they reached Aunt Julia's gate. 'I hope you've got it right. Time will tell. But all I can say is that my marriage was as near perfect as it was possible to be. Your father was a wonderful husband and I never had a moment's worry about him when he was away, whether it was a field exercise or a trip overseas. I hope you will be as lucky.'

'I hope so too, but, as I said, Hugh is only human.' Ruth grinned. 'And since he's not on a pedestal, he won't be able to fall off, will he?'

Chapter 20

Ruth found living in Northern Ireland very different from Chelsea. Hugh was stationed just outside Londonderry and they had been allocated a house in Robin Road, a cul-de-sac on the opposite side of the road to the barracks. A multi-stranded barbed-wire fence at the bottom of their garden and pill-box lookouts at the end of the road, segregated the Army property from that of the local inhabitants.

The road blocks were manned right around the clock and the soldiers on duty had the power to stop and search everyone using the road, as well as ask them for proof of identity. As it was, they quickly knew the people living there by sight and such formalities were generally overlooked.

Londonderry itself was in a state of siege. The bridge spanning the River Foyle formed a natural barrier. It divided Waterside, where the barracks were, from the main part of the city which was out of bounds to Army personnel.

The bridge leading into the city was heavily guarded both by the Army and the Royal Ulster Constabulary, who were responsible for carrying out searches. These were in addition to the searches made at various check-points in the city itself, as well as at the entrance to all shops and stores.

At first Ruth resented it when her shopping-bag and handbag had to be emptied out, so that the contents could be checked. After narrowly escaping a bombing incident inside a store, and reading almost daily of similar happenings, some of which killed and maimed women and children, she came to accept the need for such stringency.

Everybody was cautioned never to go out alone, not even in the streets on their own side of the river. It was even considered risky to go alone to the little local supermarket near the barracks.

When she first arrived in Derry, Ruth had thought it hilarious to see off-duty soldiers out walking in pairs, often pushing babies in prams. When Hugh had explained the reason was that if one of them was fired at, the other would be there as a witness and to fetch help, her amusement turned to incredulity.

The Army community was tight-knit and friendly. In less than a week, Ruth found she knew everyone living in Robin Road. Because of the restrictions about going out, or into the city, they made their own entertainment. They had organised a very active social club and they also visited each other's homes a great deal so that the children could play together.

Ruth never felt nervous about going out to the social club when Hugh was on duty, since she knew that at the end of the evening they all left together. When they reached their own homes they waited in the hallway, until the last of them had gone indoors and put on all the lights.

Transport was always provided when there were dances and social events at the barracks, although it was only a hundred yards or so away. On these occasions, since the men outnumbered the women by about five to one, Ruth usually found herself danced off her feet.

So much activity and entertainment helped to keep her mind off the dangers that surrounded them. Even so, she was always tense when Hugh was on duty. Coffee mornings were spiced with gruelling stories of border incidents, of men who had been injured, of IRA terrorist flare-ups, of petrol bombs, killings and mutilations. Yet, when once a week she travelled to Coleraine on the special shopping bus organised for the wives, the townspeople there all seemed so neutral that she found the reports of violence hard to believe or understand.

As Christmas approached, Ruth began to feel homesick.

The days were so short that there were only a few hours of daylight when it was safe to go out. No one dare chance going into Derry itself, as feelings between the British Army and the IRA were running high and wives were considered a fair target once they crossed over the bridge into the city. Even in Waterside, houses were daubed with anti-British slogans, and bombing campaigns were becoming more and more frequent, so that Ruth even felt nervous about shopping locally.

The weather was bitterly cold and a biting wind and driving rain kept her indoors most of the time, heightening her feeling of homesickness.

'Shall we ask my family to come over for Christmas?' she asked Hugh at breakfast one morning.

'We could, but I doubt if they would come. Who is going to milk the cows and feed them and see to all the other livestock?'

'Jim Baines.'

'On his own! Be too much for him. He *is* getting on in years, you know.'

'Well, let's just ask Mum and Lucy,' she pleaded.

'Your mother would never leave Mark by himself, not at Christmas-time.'

'And there's no chance of you getting any leave, so that we can go back to England and spend Christmas with them?'

'Not a hope. You go if you want to, though,' Hugh told her. 'I'll be on duty some of the time over Christmas, anyway. The IRA have already started to step up their campaign and it's bound to get worse over the holiday.'

Ruth shook her head, blinking back the sharp tears of disappointment. 'No, I wouldn't want us to spend Christmas apart.'

'We could have a party,' Hugh suggested, reaching across the table to take her hand and squeeze it reassuringly.

'We've received so many invitations to other people's parties we'd never manage to fit one in. No, forget it.'

'I must go. I'm going to be late on parade,' Hugh said, pushing back his chair. He ruffled her hair as he kissed her goodbye. 'You can always phone your mother on Christmas morning. If you're feeling lonely, how about inviting Gary Collins to come and stay over Christmas?'

Ruth's grey eyes widened with astonishment. At the mention of Gary's name, a mental picture of Hugh's tall, powerfully-built friend with the coppery-red hair and square, handsome face, flooded her mind and brought a tinge of colour to her cheeks.

Whenever she was in Gary's company she always felt breathlessly aware that he was paying her rather more attention than he should. There always seemed to be an unspoken message in his intensely blue eyes as they met hers, and, even though she told herself she was being fanciful, her pulse quickened whenever he was around.

For a brief moment, she wondered whether Hugh had noticed their attraction to each other and was trying to provoke her in order to find out how she felt about Gary.

She quickly dismissed the idea as nonsense, just her guilty conscience because of the rapport she sensed between herself and Gary.

There was something so dynamic about the man that even to be in the same room with him left her feeling bemused. To have him actually staying in their house would be out of the question. He might even think it was her idea and take it as an open invitation to extend his friendship.

'No, I don't think that's a very good idea,' she said firmly.

'Why not? He's a nice enough guy. I thought you got on very well with him,' Hugh said in genuine surprise.

Ruth didn't know what to say. How could she tell him that on more than one occasion Gary had come very near to making a pass at her and that far from resenting it, she'd found it quite flattering?

'Come on, where's your spirit of goodwill?' Hugh persisted. 'He mentioned it the other day. He wants to bring his girlfriend as well.'

'Oh!' Ruth felt so completely taken aback that her mind

went blank. The nerve of the man! To have chatted her up as he had done and then go behind her back and ask Hugh if he and his girlfriend could come and stay. Frantically she tried to think of a reason why they couldn't come. 'They couldn't both stay here . . . we've only got one spare bedroom,' she protested feebly.

'So? Gary won't mind about that!' Hugh grinned. 'Think about it. I must dash.'

A couple of days later, Hugh reminded her about their Christmas arrangements. 'Gary's girlfriend is flying in from London on Friday night.'

'You mean you've already said "Yes"?' Ruth stormed, her grey eyes darkening angrily.

'Not me, my darling,' Hugh told her laughing. 'Gary made all the arrangements and then thought to tell me. He said it would be OK by you so I thought you'd already hatched it all up between you.'

'Oh *really*!' For a moment Ruth felt so furious she could hardly speak.

Having Gary in her home would be bad enough, but having him sleeping there with his girlfriend was much worse.

As her anger at his cavalier treatment subsided, she reasoned that the outcome could work in her favour. He could hardly flirt with her if his girlfriend was there, so it should put an end to the feelings he engendered in her.

Sheila was about the same age as Ruth. She was so petite that her honey-blonde head barely came up to Gary's chest. Her huge, violet eyes dominated her heart-shaped face and gave her a fragile doll-like quality. She bubbled with Cockney good humour and Ruth found herself enjoying her company immensely. Having someone else in the house all the time took her mind off the rioting, the shootings and petrol bombs that raged in every part of Londonderry.

When Hugh and Gary were on duty the two girls had plenty of opportunity to get to know each other. Sheila talked non-stop and, since her favourite subject was Gary, Ruth was fascinated by what she learnt about his background.

'We've known each other ever since we were kids,' Sheila confided. 'His mum died just a couple of days after he was born. His granny brought him up, poor little devil.'

'Why, was she very strict with him?'

'Strict! That's a laugh. Half the time she didn't know where he was. She kept a pub, see. Real knees-up type of joint. Winter and summer, Gary used to be sent up to bed around seven o'clock so that he'd be safely out of the way before the pub got busy. Once his gran had been up to check he was asleep, Gary used to nip down the fire escape, and go back out to play. He'd have a right old time!'

'Where was his father?'

'Don't reckon he ever had one. Leastways, not that anyone knew. It was wartime, see. My mum went to school with Dora, that was Gary's mum. She said she couldn't believe it when she found out that Dora was in trouble.

'Even though she been brought up in a pub, and worked behind the bar and all that from the time she was fourteen, she wasn't a bit flighty. She was nice and friendly; everyone liked her and talked to her, but she didn't put it around or anything like that. My mum says she seemed to go the other way, as if all the drinking, and so on, had turned her off men, if you know what I mean. She did have a steady boyfriend, but he was killed.

'My mum says she reckoned Gary's dad was a bit special. She remembers Dora going on about this soldier and how good-looking and nicely-spoken he'd been. Seems he turned up at the pub one night, when Dora was working there on her own, feeling a bit sorry for himself and trying to drown his sorrows. He'd been trying to get home to see his wife who had just had a miscarriage, but he'd missed the last train. On top of that he'd just heard his kid brother had been killed. When it came to closing time he'd had a few too many, so Dora took him up to the flat to

155

try and sober him up. It seems he stayed the night and you can guess the rest. Next morning, of course, he's off back to his unit.'

'And that's the last Dora ever heard of him?'

'Right! Next thing is, Dora discovers she's pregnant. As soon as her mother finds out she goes mad and rants and raves and tells her she'd best have an abortion.'

'She wouldn't agree to that?'

'No! Everyone told her to get rid of it, but Dora wouldn't. She'd really fallen for this soldier. My mum says that Dora hoped right to the end that he would turn up again. Sad really, but ever so romantic.'

'And you say she died when Gary was born?'

'Well, within a couple of days. My mum reckoned it was from a broken heart.'

'And his grandma was left to bring him up. So now Gary has no family at all?' Ruth said sadly.

'His grandmother is still alive. Right old card, I can tell you. Still runs the pub. I think she hopes that one day Gary will go back and take over. I don't think he ever will, mind you. He loves the Army. Says it's in his blood because his father was a Guardsman.'

'Has he ever tried to find his father?' Ruth asked.

'Shouldn't think so. Nothing to go on, really. Dora didn't even know his name. The only thing she knew was that his younger brother, the one who'd just been killed, was called Gary. That's why, when she knew she was dying, she wanted the baby to be called that.'

'I don't think Hugh knows any of this,' Ruth said reflectively.

'Gary never talks about it, that's why. My mum only told me when she thought I was getting serious about him.'

'And are you serious about him?'

'Of course I am! Do you think I'd have come over here to spend Christmas with him if I wasn't?' Sheila's violet eyes grew dreamy. 'I'd marry him tomorrow if he asked me.'

'I wish you would,' Ruth said with feeling. 'Be great having you living here all the time.'

156

'You think Gary's extra special don't you?' Sheila remarked, looking directly at her.

'Well, yes. I suppose I do.' Ruth felt herself colouring under Sheila's scrutiny and wondered if her feelings for him showed, or whether Sheila was just probing. 'He is a bit of a flirt, though.'

'Rubbish!' Sheila giggled. 'That's just his way. Has he been chatting you up?'

'Well, not exactly. As you say, it's probably just his manner. He's sometimes a bit . . .' Ruth hesitated, not knowing quite how to explain the situation between herself and Gary.

'It's his animal magnetism, his sex appeal,' Sheila bubbled. 'It just gets to you. He's got a heart of gold, just like his mum. Think he must take after his dad in looks; he certainly isn't anything like his grandmother.'

'Perhaps he takes after her husband then . . . his grandfather.'

'No. There's a picture of him in the Saloon Bar and he was a small, dark chap with features as sharp as a ferret's. He's been dead for years. My mum remembers him from when she and Dora were kids and she says he was a bad-tempered devil. Not like my Gary.'

With Sheila for company, Ruth enjoyed Christmas much more than she had expected to. Although it was bitterly cold, and heavy snow made walking almost impossible, there was so much going on that both of them felt quite exhausted by New Year's Eve.

'I wouldn't mind a quiet night in,' Sheila said, yawning, as they went upstairs to get ready for the Troop Ball that was being held at the barracks.

'I had no idea there would be such a lot happening.' She groaned as she kicked off her shoes and stretched out on the bed. 'Are Army people always as crazy as this? All these parties and drinking sessions . . .'

'They work hard and they play hard.' Ruth laughed. 'You haven't seen anything yet. You should have been here for Hugh's birthday party. He bought a barrel of beer and invited the whole platoon. Mind you, only five of them turned up and one of those was Gary.'

'What a waste! What happened to all the beer?'

'They drank it, of course.'

'All of it!' She stared disbelievingly at Ruth.

'Every last drop. Then Hugh, Gary and the other lads all crashed out on the floor and they were still sleeping it off at lunch-time next day.'

'Do you think Hugh knew there would only be five of them coming?'

'Probably. He had to say the entire platoon were coming or I wouldn't have agreed to him getting in a full barrel of beer. It's a bit like when there's a stag night. Then they're all ordered to attend so that wives can't stop their husbands from going. And, of course, they always drink too much and end up legless. It's all part of their image. If they didn't put on an air of bravado, half of them would desert or just go to pieces, the stress over here is so great.'

'Yet the wives manage to stand it.'

'Not really. They go back to England for a break and the next thing their husbands know is that they aren't coming back again. I think while you are actually out here you just go on from day to day. When you get right away though, and you look back and remember all the shootings and atrocities that go on day in and day out, you wonder why the hell you put your life on the line all the time. Your nerve goes and you know you can't face it again.

'I wouldn't trust myself to go home to England on my own. I'm sure I wouldn't have the guts to come back again knowing what I do now. It gets the men the same way. They can't just stay in England, of course, because that would be desertion and they'd soon be picked up.'

'So what do they do?'

'Shoot themselves. Nothing very serious,' she added quickly, seeing Sheila's violet eyes darken with horror. 'A bullet through the hand or the foot, something like that.'

158

'Doesn't anyone suspect?'

'Of course they do. Usually the accident is faked so well that it's difficult for anything to be proved though. Recently one soldier who shot himself through the foot was put on a charge for damaging government property. They made him pay for damaging his boots!'

'You're joking!'

'This place really makes the toughest of them nervous wrecks because they have to be on the alert twenty-four hours a day, seven days a week. Even when they're off duty they're targets for the IRA.'

The New Year's Eve Ball proved to be quite eventful. Just before midnight, Hugh and Gary arrived unexpectedly.

'How on earth did you manage this?' Ruth asked in amazement.

'You have Gary to thank.' Hugh grinned. 'He managed to bribe a couple of the lads to stand in for us. They were only interested in the food so once the dancing started they were willing to take over our guard duties.'

'Does that mean you've finished for the night?'

'No! It just gives us a chance to see in the New Year with you.'

It was a momentous couple of hours. As the old year faded and a trumpeter heralded 1970, Sheila and Gary announced their engagement.

'I feel as excited as if it was someone in my own family,' Ruth exclaimed as, with tears in her eyes, she hugged and kissed Sheila.

'You will both come to our wedding . . . promise?'

'Of course they will,' Gary assured her. 'Hugh is going to be my best man.'

'It rather depends on when you decide to get married,' Ruth said hesitantly. 'The sooner the better . . .'

Sheila's eyes widened in delight. 'You're not! When?' she breathed ecstatically.

'What's going on?' Hugh asked, frowning as he looked from Ruth to Sheila and back again.

'You two hatching up something?' Gary asked, his intensely blue eyes puzzled.

Ruth turned to Hugh, her cheeks pink, biting her lip as she tried to find the right words.

As Ruth gazed at Hugh he looked perplexed, then, as realisation dawned, he took her tenderly in his arms. 'When, my darling?' he breathed, kissing her so ardently that she felt a dizzy uprush of emotion.

'In June, I think,' she whispered, her face radiant.

Chapter 21

Ruth was waiting on the doorstep for her mother and Lucy to arrive. It was a mild day in early May, but scudding rain clouds marred the pale blue sky, bringing frequent showers.

She felt exhausted. Hugh had laughed at the way she had cleaned the house from top to bottom in readiness for their guests.

'It's your mother who's coming, not a Sergeant-Major's inspection,' he told her when he had arrived home the previous evening to find her resting on the bed, still clutching a duster.

Ruth found it hard to explain to Hugh that, because it was her mother's first visit since they had been in Ireland, she felt it was important that their home looked its best.

It was almost six months since she had last seen any of her family and she felt both excited and apprehensive. She gazed down at her swollen figure and wondered how Lucy would react when she saw her. She tried to remember her own feelings when her mother had been expecting Lucy. Her memories of those days were hazy, overtaken as they were by her father's death, the time spent at Aunt Julia's, then the move to Bulpitts, and, later, after Donald Brady had died, to Hill Farm.

Her only clear recollection of that time was of waiting with Mark in Aunt Julia's sitting-room for her mother to come back from hospital. Lucy had been such a tiny scrap, wrapped up in a shawl inside a carrycot. And now she was already at school and would soon be an aunt. It seemed ludicrous.

Ruth looked at her watch and went inside to switch on the kettle. The waiting was making her feel edgy. Perhaps they should have stuck to the rules and let her mother and Lucy travel on the Army bus that went into Belfast airport to pick up soldiers returning from leave. It had been Gary's idea to collect them in his car, knowing the bus took so long. It used a devious route back to Londonderry in order to avoid the A1 out of Belfast, because that was a known IRA target.

'We'll be back here in just over half an hour of the plane landing,' he had assured her. 'I'll drive down the A1 so fast that not even a first-class sniper would stand a chance of getting us!'

A car pulling up outside announced their arrival. There were voices, people on the path and, suddenly, the hallway was crowded. Then Ruth was kissing her mother and Lucy and fighting back her tears of joy at being reunited with them both.

'Is that the baby in there?' Lucy asked in amazement, patting Ruth's distended stomach. 'He must be ever so huge!'

It wasn't until the meal was over, and Gary had left to go back on duty, that her mother seemed to relax fully. Ruth put it down to the journey, so she was surprised when, after they had tucked Lucy up in bed, and settled down in the sitting-room to have a coffee, her mother said sharply, 'He's not coming back again tonight, is he?'

'Who? Gary?'

Her mother nodded, tight-lipped, her grey eyes unfathomable.

'I shouldn't think so. Why?' Ruth asked in surprise.

Helen sighed softly and shook her head. 'I don't know . . . I just feel uneasy in his company.'

161

'What do you mean?' A flush stained Ruth's cheeks as she spoke.

'He's rather . . . strange. The way he dresses, for one thing. That flat cap and that violent red and black check jacket. In your father's day a Guardsman would never have dreamed of going out looking like that.'

Ruth choked back her giggles at the look of disdain on her mother's face. 'You haven't seen Hugh's "bookies' jacket" yet. Black, white and yellow check! It's outrageous – especially when he wears it with those grey and white striped trousers that he had on when he came to meet you!'

'Why *do* they dress like that?'

Ruth shrugged. 'They're all big kids at heart, aren't they? It's almost a competition to see who can look the most flamboyant. They work hard and dice with death when they're on duty so it's a form of escapism. Their way of letting off steam, I suppose.'

'Your father never behaved like that!'

'No, but then he wasn't constantly in danger. For most of his Army career he was a Training Sergeant at depot, a cushy routine number. He wouldn't dress like they do over here because he always felt he had to set the young crows an example, both on and off duty. Hugh and Gary and their mates don't have those sort of responsibilities, but they have other pressures. They work four hours on, four hours off, for ten days at a stretch. They're so exhausted that they fall asleep as they come through the door, before they can even eat a meal, or take their boots off. And they have to be back at the barracks again within four hours, remember.'

'Yes, I realise it must be hard on them but . . .'

'Hard!' Ruth challenged, her grey eyes steely. 'You don't know the half, Mum. Even when they've finished their ten days on rota they often go straight on stand-by. That means they can't go anywhere because they're on permanent call and can be called out at any time of the day or night if there is an incident. It happened last Sunday. I'd spent all morning cooking a roast and had just started dishing it up when Hugh was called out. Charlie, next door, and Stan, across the road, were called out at the same time, so I invited their wives in to help eat our dinner!'

'Yes, it must be very difficult.' Helen sighed.

'It is! As I said, drinking and dressing-up is their way of having fun and proving to themselves they're still alive, if you like. They do everything to excess. They drink too much, smoke too much and behave like overgrown kids. It's their way of forgetting the danger they're in every time they go on duty. They all do it. There's no "keeping up with the Jones's" over here, like there is in civvy street, because they all get the same money, live in the same kind of houses and have identical furniture. Even their Army uniform is standard issue. The hard part is remembering that you *are* an individual. I sometimes think the men manage it better than the women.'

'I'm sure what you say is right, but it still doesn't make me like Gary Collins any better,' Helen said firmly.

'Well, you will probably see quite a lot of him while you're here because he's Hugh's best friend. His girlfriend, Sheila, stayed with us over Christmas and we had a great time.'

'I thought he must be the Cockney chap you wrote and told me about. His father was in the Guards and disappeared before he was born?'

'That's right.'

Helen's face grew even more stony. She stood up. 'I've got a dreadful headache, Ruth. I think I'll have an early night.'

Bemused by her mother's reaction, Ruth talked it over with Hugh. He could offer no explanation and thought Ruth was being fanciful.

'You're imagining it.' He smiled. 'Your mother is probably just tired after her journey.'

Next morning Helen seemed to be her normal self, so Ruth pushed the matter from her mind and concentrated on making her mother's and Lucy's stay as enjoyable as possible. There was a lull in IRA activities, so Ruth

163

suggested they should go into Londonderry. She warned her mother that they would be searched and persuaded her to empty everything out of her handbag except her purse and some form of identity.

As they crossed the bridge over the River Foyle, Helen was shocked at the sight of so many heavily-armed soldiers on duty.

'Just look at them; they're only young boys!' she exclaimed.

'Most of them are nineteen,' Ruth said nonchalantly. She had seen them so many times before, that now she scarcely noticed them.

Having been thoroughly searched before they crossed the bridge, Helen was taken aback when they were again checked, this time by the RUC, when they reached the other side. Even Lucy's tiny handbag was turned out. For a moment she was in tears when the few coins she had in it rolled onto the pavement. They were quickly retrieved and returned to her by people queuing to pass through the turnstile and she was soon smiling again.

Helen was appalled by the devastation in the centre of Derry, the boarded-up windows, the gaping holes and the buildings cordoned off because of unexploded bombs or dangerous masonry.

'Let's go back,' she urged. 'There's really no pleasure in shopping here. I don't like having to turn out my bag every time we go inside a shop or pass through one of these check-points. They seem to have them all over the place.'

Ruth readily agreed. She wasn't feeling too well. The tension she felt, knowing she was responsible for the safety of her mother and Lucy, together with the heat and dust, had brought on a headache that was getting worse all the time.

Taking Lucy's hand, she led them down a side street which she knew would bring them out at the check-point nearest the bridge. There was a queue and, as they stood waiting to pass through, she heard the sound of running feet and the sharp report of hand-guns firing. Her anxiety made her heart pound. The queue began to move forward and, to her dismay, she saw that it meant going through a turnstile. Knowing she would have difficulty she tried to back off, urging Lucy and her mother forward in her place.

'Wait for me on the other side,' she told them. 'I'd get stuck in that so I'll walk round it.'

The moment she began to edge away a policeman's hand clamped down on her shoulder. There were angry murmurs from the crowd and Ruth felt herself being roughly pushed and shoved, while in the background the sound of shooting and general commotion became louder.

Urgently she explained her predicament. The policeman looked suspicious but called a woman colleague over and she was taken to one side, where she was searched and then escorted to the far side of the check-point to where Helen and Lucy were waiting.

Trembling, Ruth leant on her mother's arm as they hurried over the bridge. The incident had upset her so much her legs felt like jelly.

'You need a brandy or something,' Helen said, concerned. 'Is it safe to go into one of the pubs now we're back in Waterside?'

Ruth shook her head. 'Let's just get through the check-point on the other side of the bridge and I'll be OK,' she said.

As they reached it, she felt waves of nausea sweeping over her. 'I feel sick,' she gasped, leaning against the barricade for support. 'You'd better let me through before I throw up.'

The middle-aged policeman eyed her distrustfully but let her pass without searching her. She stumbled as far as the nearest building then leaned up against the wall, closing her eyes because she felt so faint.

'Would you be wanting a drink of water?' a man standing in the doorway asked. He was unshaven and in shirt-sleeves and she hesitated before answering.

He disappeared inside the building and returned with a tin mug. 'Are you English then?' he asked as she took the cup from him.

She nodded.

'From the Army barracks?'

'Visiting,' she said cautiously.

He stared at the three of them with narrowed eyes, then rubbed a gnarled hand over his bristling chin as he took the mug back and turned away.

'Come on,' Helen grabbed Ruth's arm. 'Let's get out of here; let's get home.'

Behind them, across the water in Derry city, they could still hear spasmodic gunfire.

From then on, they stayed on their own side of the river. There was plenty to do: all Ruth's neighbours were delighted to meet visitors from England, so there was no lack of callers or invitations and even Lucy enjoyed herself, playing with all the children.

The only discordant note was when Gary came to the house during Helen's visit. It was so marked that even Gary noticed it.

'I don't think your mother approves of me,' he remarked ruefully to Ruth.

'Nonsense!' Ruth tried to laugh it off, but she knew the tell-tale colour in her cheeks gave her away.

'Oh, I've seen the way her mouth tightens whenever I'm around and the hostile look in her eyes.' He shook his head in bewilderment. 'As far as I know, I've never said or done anything to upset her, so what's it all about?'

'You've just got a complex,' Ruth teased.

'No. When she stepped off the plane, and Hugh introduced us, she looked at me as if she was seeing a ghost. Then her face tightened and she kept staring at me as if I'd got three eyes or something!'

'You're imagining it!' Ruth told him, but deep inside her she knew it was true. Her mother didn't like Gary. She bristled whenever he came near her; even her voice became sharper.

The situation came to a head the night of the party. They had invited most of the people in Robin Road as well as Gary, and one or two of Hugh's other unmarried friends.

Towards the end of the evening, someone asked Helen if she and Lucy would be on the Army bus next day, or whether Gary was taking them to the airport in his car.

'We're going on the bus,' Helen said quickly.

Ruth and Hugh exchanged looks but before either of them could speak Gary said, 'No need, I'll take you.'

Helen gave him a long, level look, then said coldly, 'Hugh's on duty and Ruth isn't up to the journey.'

'Well, I'll take you on my own.' Gary smiled.

'No, thank you!'

Her frosty reply was like a slap in the face.

There was a stunned silence, then everyone began talking at once, but the happy atmosphere was gone. Everyone was curious as to why she had refused so adamantly and Gary looked as bemused as the rest of them.

Ruth could barely keep back her tears. She had noticed all evening that her mother had seemed to be watching Gary intently, her face growing more and more taut, her lips tightening into a thin, hard line, and she felt completely bewildered by her mother's attitude.

Gary was the last to leave. Rather hesitantly he held out his hand to Helen. When she completely ignored him he stuffed his hand back into his pocket and Ruth could see him clenching and unclenching it as he struggled to control his feelings.

'I'm sorry you won't let me give you a lift in the morning, Mrs Woodley. I hope you have a pleasant journey. I expect we'll meet again.'

To Ruth's amazement and embarrassment her mother didn't answer, or manage even a glimmer of a smile.

'What on *earth* got into you, tonight, Mum?' she asked furiously, after he had gone. 'You didn't have to make it quite so obvious that you don't like Gary.'

Helen stared at Ruth for a long time, then she said wearily, 'I can't explain . . . not now, anyway. And if I did you wouldn't believe me.' Without another word she turned on her heel and went upstairs to bed.

Their leave-taking next morning was rather subdued. Ruth kissed and hugged Lucy and, because it would be her birthday a few days later, gave her a present of a baby doll.

'Now I've got a new baby just like you'll have!' Lucy exclaimed delightedly. 'Are you going to have a little girl, Ruth? Then I can give my doll the same name as your baby.'

'We'll have to wait and see.' Ruth smiled gently at her golden-haired little sister. 'I hope she'll be as pretty as you are,' she said, pulling Lucy close and kissing her again.

'Are you going to call her Lucy?'

'No. I think one Lucy in the family is enough!' Ruth laughed. 'No, we've decided that if it's a girl then we shall call her Sally. If it's a boy . . .' she paused and looked straight at her mother, '. . . if it's a boy then we're going to call him Gary.'

'Not after *that* Gary,' her mother exclaimed in shocked tones.

'No,' Ruth told her coolly, 'after Dad's brother . . . the one who was killed in the war.'

Helen looked at her speechlessly.

'Dad once told Mark and me all about him – how much he loved him and how close they'd been as boys. I always felt he would have liked Mark to have been named after him,' Ruth explained defiantly.

Helen didn't answer; her face had gone an ashen grey. She bent down and picked up her suitcase. 'Come on Lucy,' she said, refusing to meet Ruth's eyes. 'It's time we were going home.'

Chapter 22

Helen found the journey back to England extremely tedious. It took twice as long to reach Belfast airport by bus as it would have done in Gary's car and, when she and Lucy arrived there, they found there was no plane for almost two hours.

After they had had something to eat and drink, Helen found a quiet corner and made Lucy as comfortable as possible, rolling her anorak up as a cushion under her head, so that she could sleep. Then Helen tried to read, but her thoughts kept going back to Ruth and her friends, and to Gary Collins in particular.

She knew she had behaved badly, but she had felt powerless to change her attitude towards Gary. She had never felt so overwhelmingly hostile towards another person in her life. From the moment when she had first seen him with Hugh she had felt threatened.

There had been something about his face, with its strong square jawline, vivid blue eyes under straight, dark brows, his wide mouth and finely-chiselled lips, that had stirred deep memories. Her breath caught in her throat as in a flash she realised that it was his uncanny likeness to Adam!

The only thing that was different was the colour of his hair. She had never known anyone with hair that bright, rich coppery shade before . . . except in a photograph. A faded, much-handled photograph that Adam had always carried in his wallet. It had been a picture of his younger brother who had been killed before she had ever had a chance to meet him . . . and his name had been Gary.

The revelation stunned her. Her emotions in chaos, she tried to recall every detail Adam had ever told her about his brother. She was almost certain that Gary had never married, never even had a serious girlfriend. He had only been twenty when he had been killed. Still, it had been wartime and he could have fathered a child. If he had then surely Adam would have known about it, since they were so close.

She went over in her mind what she knew about Gary Collins. He was about six months younger than Hugh, which meant he must have been born around September 1944. Adam's brother had been killed just a few days before Christmas 1943. It was possible!

She held her breath as she counted up the months, then remembered he had been in France for quite some time before he'd been killed.

169

Her relief at knowing that Adam's brother couldn't possibly be Gary Collins' father was short-lived, as she began having crazy thoughts. She tried to put them from her mind, as a cold sweat sent trickles of perspiration down her body. She wondered whether it was her imagination playing tricks, or if she was going mad. Being on her own so much, with only Mark and Lucy for company, was making her fanciful. Yet, as she went over the facts again and again, the same answer faced her.

She recalled the events in her own life around that time. Her miscarriage just a few days before Christmas, that had prevented her meeting Adam in London. And it was while he'd been there that he had heard his young brother Gary had been killed. And that was around the time Gary Collins was conceived! Try as she might to put the idea aside, she felt an overpowering conviction that it wasn't just coincidence that they bore such a striking resemblance to each other.

While she had been lying in hospital after her miscarriage, not even aware that his brother had been killed, had Adam found comfort in someone else's arms to try to ease the pain that must have been burning inside him?

The thought sent chill shivers through her, but the more she thought about it the more possible it seemed to be. The dates fitted so perfectly. Adam had been in London at that time . . . and on his own. When he had come to see her in hospital he had stayed only a very short time, and she had been too sedated to talk rationally. It was the last time they had seen each other before he had gone overseas.

After the war was over, Adam had never talked about Gary. It was one of the reasons she had been so surprised to hear he had told Ruth and Mark about him. And Ruth's remark that she thought he would have liked Mark to be named for his dead brother, had been like a knife turning. She had never even thought of it. Had Adam suggested it, she would gladly have consented.

Again, disturbing thoughts filled her mind. Had he not mentioned it to her because there was already a child named Gary, a love-child that she knew nothing about?

The thought tormented her so much that she was unable to sit still. Gently releasing Lucy's hand she stood up and began pacing restlessly up and down, feverishly going over every aspect of the facts as she knew them.

When she sat down again she was clear in her own mind that the pieces fitted as smoothly as any jigsaw. She saw it all now. The night Adam had stayed over in London he had found solace in Dora's arms. It all fitted: the dates, the place, Gary's intensely blue eyes, the shape of his mouth, the way he laughed, even his mannerisms. She couldn't possibly be mistaken. Every detail was there. Meeting him was like seeing Adam reincarnated. She was surprised she hadn't realised it before and that Ruth hadn't been aware of it.

She had felt uneasy about the closeness of Ruth's friendship with Gary. She'd even suspected they might be having a mild flirtation. Now she understood the empathy between them. The bond that existed was closer than any friendship.

The announcement that their plane was ready to depart distracted Helen's thoughts. For the next few hours the journey home – the noise and confusion at Heathrow airport, the rush for the train at Waterloo Station, and coping with their luggage – took all her attention.

When she went to bed that night, however, Helen found that, even though she felt exhausted, sleep eluded her. She lay there in the darkness, going over what she knew and trying to work out what she ought to do.

After tossing and turning for hours, she finally went downstairs to make herself a drink. Sitting at the kitchen-table, she planned how she would go about getting proof to substantiate her conviction that Gary was Adam's son. Until then she would keep the knowledge to herself, she decided. Sooner or later, though, she would face Ruth and Mark, as well as Gary, with the truth. It was only right that they should be told. It might sully Adam's memory, but Gary Collins was entitled to know the identity of his father. And he would learn that the Guardsman he had held in such high esteem all his life had feet of clay after all, she thought savagely.

171

Bitterly, she realised that she was out for revenge. She felt deeply hurt, not so much because Adam had cheated on her, but that he had been able to put it so completely out of his mind. Never once when recounting all the things that had happened to him while he was waiting to be sent to Europe, or during his service in the Army of Occupation, had Adam ever hinted that there had been another woman in his life.

Perhaps Dora Collins was only one of many, she told herself resentfully. While she had been patiently waiting for him to come home again he'd probably been consoling himself with girls in France, Belgium and even in Germany, she thought with annoyance.

If he'd strayed once and as far as he knew got away with it so successfully, why not twice, a dozen times, hundreds of times even? She even began to wonder whether he had been unfaithful to her after the war was over, when he was away on exercises or overseas.

Angrily, she pushed her empty cup away. Her life had suddenly turned sour. She had always held Adam in such high esteem, placed him on a pedestal, in fact, and now it had come crashing down. And to think she had refused Donald's offer of marriage in order to stay true to Adam's memory, because she believed that it was what he would have done if she had been the one to die first!

Hate and bitterness overwhelmed her. She wanted to scream, to shout the truth. Tears blinded her. How could she have been so gullible all these years? She recalled Ruth's plain speaking just before she had gone out to Ireland. Perhaps Ruth had more sense than she did, after all. At the time she had treated her remarks with scorn but now she didn't feel nearly so sure of herself.

The shrilling of the telephone brought her to her senses. It was only six o'clock. Who on earth could be phoning so early? she wondered as she went to answer it.

'Hello Grandma!'

'Who . . . who is that? Are you sure you have the right number?'

'I hope I have . . . at this time in the morning. It's Hugh.

172

I'm ringing to let you know you're a grandmother. Ruth went into labour last night. The baby was born at four o'clock this morning.'

'Is everything all right? How is Ruth?'

'Absolutely fine. No complications of any kind.'

'And the baby?'

'Quite perfect. A little girl. She weighed in at seven pounds. Looks just like Ruth. Dark hair, same shaped face. She's gorgeous.'

'That's wonderful, Hugh. I'm so relieved. I do wish it had happened before we left. Do . . . do you want me to come back?'

'No need. Ruth's returning to England for a spell, just as soon as she comes out of hospital. It's not really safe for her and the baby out here. We had a lot of bombing last night. Our social club was hit, several of our friends have been badly injured. It's upset Ruth . . .'

'How awful! Of course she must come back to England at once. Are you sure you wouldn't like me to come and fetch her? She's not fit to travel on her own.'

'Give it a few days and she'll be OK. Don't worry, she'll have someone to travel across with when she's ready. A lot of wives are packing it in over here now that things have started to really hot up. I'll phone you again when I know when she will be coming.'

Hugh's call suddenly changed everything. With a sense of relief, Helen pushed to one side her own problem. There were far more important things to do now than brood about the past. She must get everything ready for when Ruth arrived. The days ahead would be busy ones with a young baby in the house.

Since Gary had never known who his father was there was nothing to be gained by telling him, or anyone else, about it at the moment. She would give it more thought . . . when she had less on her mind. It might be better for everyone if it remained her secret.

Chapter 23

Helen idolised Sally from the first moment she set eyes on her. As she cradled the tiny bundle in her arms and gazed down at the mass of brown hair that curled over the baby's tiny ears and forehead, she was filled with a deep tenderness.

Sally was a happy, contented baby, sleeping right through the night and quickly settling into a routine, so that it seemed to Helen she had always been there.

It was a wonderful summer and Sally grew plump and golden as she lay outside in her pram, kicking her tiny arms and legs. Helen kept a watchful eye on her from the kitchen window, and Lucy was in constant attendance as soon as she came home from school. Even Mark made frequent detours so that he could stop by the pram.

Sally thrived on such attention. She smiled readily and her eyes, which were now a soft brown with golden flecks in them, followed every movement around her.

Ruth, too, seemed to be enjoying her new role. Her only disappointment was the fact that Hugh hadn't managed to get any leave, so he hadn't seen the baby since she'd left Ireland. Just after Ruth had come back, fresh disturbances had broken out and in Derry over three hundred people had been injured, so she knew Hugh would be needed there for quite a long time.

'Sally will be walking and talking before he sees her,' she grumbled, as she put down a letter she had just received from Hugh.

'Well, you know what the Army's like!' Helen reminded her.

'I can still grumble, can't I?' Ruth grinned. 'I can re-member the way you used to carry on when you thought

Dad was coming home and instead he was sent off on a course or an exercise!'

'Yes, it can be infuriating. You make all the preparations, spend hours cooking, and then they don't turn up,' Helen said grimly.

'I don't,' Ruth laughed. 'Hugh has to take pot luck. If there's no food in the house then we go to the pub, or I send him out to get a take-away.'

Helen was about to voice her disapproval, then held back, remembering all the frustration she had known when she had prepared for Adam's homecoming, only to be disappointed. At the time she had blamed the vagaries of the Army. Now she wasn't so sure that it had always been duty that had detained Adam. Perhaps Ruth had the right attitude after all.

Briskly she turned her mind to other things. Knowing what she did now, such thoughts only embittered her. Given her life over again, she wouldn't have been so gullible. Her lips tightened, hard lines forming on either side of her mouth, visibly ageing her.

Turning stones was dangerous, she decided, and she wished she had never delved into Gary Collins' background. Everything pointed to him being Adam's son. If only she could have talked to someone about it, she thought, just to ease the gnawing doubts in her own mind. Resolutely, though, she had made up her mind not to involve the rest of the family and, difficult though it was, she had kept to her decision. She intended to let them keep the image they had of their father as being a good and honourable man.

Three weeks later, with baby Sally sound asleep, and Lucy also tucked up in bed, Helen was making her way across the meadow, to pen up the hens and geese for the night, when she heard a car draw up outside the house. Since Mark and Ruth were both there she didn't turn back, but it puzzled her just who the caller could be at that time of the evening.

175

The car was still there when she got back and its long black outline seemed vaguely familiar. As she went indoors she could hear voices and laughter coming from the sitting-room and paused to tidy her hair before joining them.

'Is that you, Mum? Come and see who's here,' Ruth called excitedly.

'Hugh!' Delighted for Ruth's sake that he had managed to get home at last, Helen hugged him enthusiastically.

Then, as she became aware of someone else, she stiffened. It was like a bad dream. The man who had filled her thoughts ever since her return from Ireland was there, greeting her like an old friend, putting his arm around her and kissing her on the cheek.

'I'm afraid I had to bring Gary. It was the only way I could get a lift,' Hugh joked.

'Gary's always welcome,' Ruth said warmly, smiling up at him. 'We're thinking of adopting him. I shall teach Sally to call him "Uncle" just as soon as she can talk.'

'I don't think children should be encouraged to call strangers "Uncle". It only confuses them,' Helen said tightly and was immediately aware of Ruth's puzzled stare. 'I'll go and prepare a meal for you both,' she said to hide her confusion.

'Don't bother,' Hugh said quickly. 'We'll drive down to the pub later on and get something to eat there.'

'Mum won't let you do that.' Ruth laughed. 'She thinks I'm a dreadful wife because I don't have a meal waiting to pop on the table at any hour of the night or day, just in case you should turn up. She always used to for Dad.'

'You nag me now if I'm five minutes late!' Hugh laughed. 'I can't bear the thought of what you'd say if I didn't turn up at all.'

'I certainly wouldn't be as patient as Mum was with Dad. I'd probably throw it at you. She used to pander to his every whim; his word was law.'

Helen went into the kitchen and closed the door firmly, shutting out the laughter that followed Ruth's remarks.

Automatically she began to prepare some food, but her mind was in a turmoil at the thought of Gary being there in her home. Meeting him in Ireland had been bad enough, but to have him under her own roof was a bitter pill to swallow, now that she was so sure he was Adam's son. It was probably only for a couple of days, she reminded herself. Surely she could keep a still tongue in her head for just that length of time.

Their short leave passed better than Helen dared hope. Gary kept out of her way, as if sensing her antagonism towards him, even though she did her utmost to conceal it. He spent most of his time out on the farm with Mark.

Yet even that irritated Helen. She brooded over the way they had taken to each other so readily.

Watching them walk around the farmyard together she was struck by the similarities between them; their height and the breadth of their shoulders was almost identical. Although he was only nineteen, working on the farm had developed Mark's muscles and he carried himself like a military man.

Helen wasn't surprised, only numbly resigned, when Mark remarked conversationally, after Gary and Hugh had gone roaring off in Gary's car when their leave was over, that someone had thought Gary was his brother.

'Funny thing to say, wasn't it?' he persisted. 'It was old Bill Thatcher that said it. Gary and I were standing at the bar in the Lion and old Bill was sitting in his usual seat by the fireplace. He stared across at us, and then pointed at Gary with that old pipe of his and said, "This ain't your Ruth's husband." I told him it wasn't and he sat there for a minute or so, drawing on his pipe, and then he said, "Be your brother, is it? Never knew before that you had an older brother."'

'Silly old man!' Helen exploded.

'When I told him I hadn't got a brother, he just sat there nodding and shaking his head as if he was having an argument with himself and then he said, "Well, you have now."'

'And then I suppose you bought him a pint?' Ruth said scornfully.

'Gary did. He seemed tickled pink at the idea of being my brother.'

Helen walked away. She didn't want Mark to see the misery in her eyes but his words, 'Gary seemed tickled pink at the idea of being my brother', echoed over and over in her head. Yes, she thought, he would do. Deep down he knows the truth and wants to be recognised as one of the family.

Gary's image filled her mind. He was so like Adam in everything except the colour of his hair, that of course old Bill Thatcher, who claimed the gift of 'second sight' would see the resemblance when the two of them were standing side by side. They even had Adam's vivid blue eyes and straight dark brows. Of course they looked like brothers! It was there for anyone to see and it worried her in case he went round voicing his suspicions. She could only hope that if he did, his babblings would fall on deaf ears, or be regarded as a sign that he was getting old and muddled.

She was determined not to be undermined by gossip. Adam was dead and his past could remain that way, too. She had no intention of drawing anyone else into her private hell. Except Gary! She would dearly love to make him suffer!

Her own bitterness frightened her. Gary could hardly help his parentage. She should be feeling sorry for him because he had been denied a father, not constantly seeking revenge.

But had he? The question burned in her mind. Had Adam visited him when he was a child? Helen remembered Adam's frequent long absences, the times when she didn't see him for weeks, or even months. Work had always been given as the reason, and accepted without question. But had he sometimes spent weekends in London, visiting his son, watching him grow into a sturdy boy and then into manhood? Had his regular visits impressed the boy so much that he had determinedly followed his father into the Army?

There was only one way to find out . . . to ask Gary. She shrank from doing so, afraid that once she started talking to him about his childhood, she might disclose what she thought to be the truth about his father. It was torture enough having him in her own home and seeing him on intimate terms with her own three children. To openly admit he really was a blood relation was out of the question.

Helen could see that Hugh's leave had unsettled Ruth, so it was no surprise when, at the end of the summer, since things had quietened down in Northern Ireland, she decided to rejoin him. Sally was over three months old and Hugh had only seen her once in all that time.

Helen missed Ruth and Sally even more than she had thought she would, and she hoped Hugh's tour of duty in Ireland would soon come to an end. Having them at Hill Farm had kept her so busy that she hadn't had time to dwell on what she now thought of as Adam's betrayal. Apart from that, she had actually enjoyed having a baby around the place, and it had been fun for Lucy.

She felt cheated a few months later when Gary Collins was posted back to Chelsea Barracks while Hugh remained in Northern Ireland. Although things were still fairly quiet in Derry, she still felt anxious about them being there.

Now that he was back in England, the farm became a second home to Gary. Whenever he was free he drove there, ostensibly to see Mark, but all the time he was in the house Helen felt he was watching her. Sometimes she caught a strange look in his vividly blue eyes, almost as if he knew her secret. It worried her, too, that Mark had begun to model himself on Gary, smoking as well as drinking.

Before Gary had appeared on the scene Mark had rarely gone to the village pub. Now he went there most Saturday evenings. Encouraged by Gary, he had started picking up girls and this also worried Helen, even though she realised that, since he was twenty, it was only natural. She wouldn't have minded so much if he had found a steady girlfriend. It was the type of girls, and the casualness of it all, that bothered her. She felt his cavalier treatment of women was a flaw in his nature, and feared it had been inherited from Adam.

Gary was an unsettling influence in other ways. When Ruth had married Hugh, Mark had given up all thought of joining the Army. Without any pressure from her he had decided to make farming his life. Now, regaled by Gary's anecdotes, and talk of Army life in general, his interest had been rekindled and she could sense his unrest.

Her resentment against Gary and the way he was affecting her family increased until she could barely manage to be civil to him. Every visit he made inflamed her. She looked forward to the weekends when he was on duty, the weeks when he was away on exercises or courses.

She was surprised when Ruth wrote to tell her that Gary had at last married Sheila. He had never mentioned it to her or Mark, as far as she knew. According to Ruth's letter, no one had known about it until Gary was charged with not asking his CO's permission to get married. When Gary was marched in to his CO's office, a soldier on either side of him, and the charge had been read out, he had been reprimanded and warned, 'Don't do it again.'

The two men standing stiffly to attention on either side of him, Ruth wrote, had laughed at the CO's comment and, as a result, found themselves on a charge, while Gary had been let off with nothing more than a caution.

As Helen read the news, she hoped that marriage would keep Gary away from Mark. In that she was mistaken. Gary still turned up regularly at the farm and always on his own. Sheila, he explained, was helping at the pub, and since Gary's grandmother was now in her seventies, that meant Sheila was more or less running the place.

Gary's influence on Mark became more and more noticeable. He began to change from a likeable, willing young man to a hard drinking womaniser. He grew increasingly restless and moody. Helen suspected he regretted his commitment to the farm and, given the slightest provocation, would get rid of it when it legally became his on his twenty-first birthday. She dreaded that happening, since it made her own future so insecure.

Often, when Lucy was in bed, and Mark out, Helen would sit down with pen and paper trying to work out whether, if Mark did sell the farm, she could afford to buy a small cottage for herself and Lucy.

She wished there was someone with whom she could talk it over, but pride wouldn't let her go outside the family for advice. She didn't want to talk to Mark about it, in case he felt she was trying to pressurise him. That only left Ruth.

When she phoned to ask her to come for a holiday, her own immediate problem went right out of her mind at Ruth's news.

'Must be telepathy,' Ruth chuckled. 'I was just about to ring you.'

'Oh?'

'I'm expecting another baby, Mum. Hugh and I are over the moon.'

Chapter 24

Ruth's second baby, Anna, was completely different from Sally. Her hair was fair and straight, her face round and chubby and her eyes a vivid forget-me-not blue. She reminded Helen of Lucy as a child, although she was quite different in temperament.

Right from the moment she was born Anna commanded attention. And, because of her appealing eyes and winsome manner, she always got it. Angelic-looking she might be, but she could be capricious as well as lovable. Helen thought she was spoilt, much preferring Sally, who was far less demanding.

Ruth and Hugh wouldn't hear a word spoken against

Anna. She could twist Hugh around her little finger and, as she grew from a chubby toddler into a dainty little girl, she frequently did.

When Anna was three, Hugh was posted to Hong Kong and, since it was for a two-year period, they decided that Ruth and the children would go as well.

Helen heard the news with mixed feelings. She knew Lucy would miss Sally very much, since they were so close, yet, in a way, she was relieved that their friendship was being temporarily halted. Sally was very grown-up for a seven-year-old, but she felt it would be better for Lucy to mix more with girls her own age. Spending so much time with Sally was making her childish and also very bossy since, being older, she always took the lead.

Helen welcomed the news that Gary Collins would also be going to Hong Kong for two years. In the seven years since she had first met Gary, her belief that he was Adam's illegitimate son had grown stronger. Although she had guarded her secret for all that time it was a heavy burden. She still thought he was a bad influence on Mark and wished he would stop coming to the farm.

She hoped that if Gary was out of the country for a couple of years Mark might settle down. He was twenty-six and she felt it was time he was married. It irked her to see the way he tried to identify with Gary, soaking up his tales of Army life, remembering incidents from the time they had lived in quarters.

Although Mark ran the farm efficiently it was with no real enthusiasm and Helen often wished that he had gone into the Army when he had first been keen. Now, it was too late. Even if he was fit enough for that kind of life he was too old. At present, his entire life seemed to consist of the farm and weekend drinking binges, often with Gary. With Gary out of the way, he might find a steady girlfriend, and settle down.

Far from helping Mark to settle, Gary's absence only seemed to make him more discontented. He and Lucy

182

quarrelled incessantly. Mark grumbled because Lucy wouldn't help with chores, but she was adamant. She hated Hill Farm and not only wanted nothing to do with it, but couldn't wait to get away.

'As soon as our Ruth gets back, I'm moving in with her,' she stormed after one of her frequent rows with Mark.

'Don't talk stupid.' Mark sneered. 'She won't have room for you.'

'I'll share a room with Sally.'

'A young kid like that! She'll be *great* company.'

'She'll be almost ten when they come home from Hong Kong in October.'

Mark refused to take her seriously but, like her, he was counting the days until Hugh and Gary arrived back in England. On his own, drinking and pulling the girls didn't have the same appeal.

Due to last-minute delays it was mid-December before Hugh's company eventually returned to England. The moment Ruth phoned, Helen asked whether they were all coming to Hill Farm for Christmas and the New Year.

'I was counting on you asking us!' Ruth laughed. 'We've nowhere else to go.'

Helen breathed a sigh of relief. It was going to be a real family Christmas after all. She suddenly realised how much she had missed Ruth and the children, and how dismal even the farm had become in their absence. Having children around the place would be a tonic for them all.

'Give us a few days to settle into our quarters, so that we don't come back into complete chaos, and we'll be with you. The whole company has leave, but Hugh will be one of the last to get away. He has a lot of extra responsibility now he's a sergeant,' she added a little smugly. 'It really has changed him. He's become terribly conscientious.'

'He's a sergeant! You never mentioned it in your letters.'

'He was only made up just before we left Hong Kong.'

Helen looked forward with increasing pleasure to having the entire family at home. She thought wistfully of just how much Adam would have enjoyed it.

She went into the kitchen and busied herself. It didn't do to sit and think about Adam; it always brought on the great yearning that she had never quite managed to erase, even though he had been dead now for fifteen years. Theirs had been such a perfect marriage . . . while he had been alive.

It was only since he'd been killed that the obnoxious doubts had soured her mind. And even those couldn't obliterate the love she'd had for him, or cancel out the longing she still felt to have his arms around her, and know his strength.

Perhaps she should have married again, made a new life for herself, she thought pensively. Staying alone, devoting herself to Lucy and Mark had, in some ways, been short-sighted. Lucy would soon be working and earning enough to be self-sufficient. Mark didn't need her, that was for sure. They only tolerated each other these days; there was no bond of understanding between them.

Helen sighed as she reached for a mixing-bowl and began measuring flour into it. She knew Mark would like nothing better than to sell the farm. His enthusiasm was gone; it was just a job that had to be done each day and, although he applied himself methodically, the work was done automatically, without any real enjoyment or satis-faction.

If only she had let him go in the Army. She hoped he would be less morose once the others arrived, and the house was alive again with voices, laughter, and children playing. She wondered what sort of change she would see in Sally and Anna.

The first year Ruth had been out in Hong Kong she had written almost every week and often sent photographs. After that her letters had become less frequent and there were no more photos. Still, Helen thought, it didn't matter

184

now and it would make seeing them again all the more interesting.

It was going to be a memorable Christmas. Mark had brought a seven-foot fir tree indoors and Helen and Lucy had decked it with tinsel and piled presents for everyone underneath. Helen also had two special gifts for the children – a kitten each. There was a fluffy grey one for Sally and a ginger and white one for Anna. She didn't know if Ruth would let them take them back to quarters, but it didn't matter. There was plenty of room for them on the farm and they would be there next time the girls came to visit.

The night before Ruth and her family were due to arrive, Helen set the alarm clock for seven, half an hour earlier than usual. She wanted to have all the chores done and lunch ready when they arrived. Ruth had said she wasn't sure what time they would get away but that they would phone from London so she could meet the train.

The morning dragged. Twice Mark came in for coffee, and to check if there had been a phone call.

'Perhaps there wasn't a box they could use at the station . . . you know how they get vandalised,' Lucy said moodily.

'What are you doing about lunch, Mum?' Mark asked, coming into the kitchen again around midday.

'Well, the table's laid in the dining-room, ready for when they arrive, but if you don't want to wait, you can have yours in the kitchen.'

She was just reaching into the oven for the casserole, to dish some out for Mark, when they heard the car.

'Who on earth. . . ?'

'Mum, it's them, it's them!' Lucy called excitedly from the landing and came racing down the stairs to greet them.

Confusion reigned. Helen bent down to hug the two small girls. Sally, with her serious brown eyes and mane of thick, dark hair that curled in tiny tendrils over her forehead, Anna with her huge forget-me-not blue eyes and blonde hair that flowed like a silken curtain over her

185

shoulders. She held them at arms' length to admire Sally's pink dress with its pleated skirt and Anna's matching one in blue.

Then, as Lucy scooped them both up and took them into the sitting-room where the log fire crackled and glowed, Helen hugged and kissed Ruth, her eyes misty with tears of happiness.

It wasn't until Helen turned to greet Hugh that she saw Gary standing beside him.

'Surprise, surprise?' He laughed, and his intense blue eyes were mocking as they met hers.

'Yes,' Helen said stiffly. 'Ruth didn't mention you were coming.'

'Always been one of the family, you know,' he quipped.

Helen stiffened, biting her bottom lip to check the sharp retort she'd been about to make. Turning away she said over her shoulder, 'The meal is all ready. I'll have it on the table by the time you've taken off your coats.'

Back in the privacy of the kitchen, Helen leant against the oven, trying to quell the fury that seethed inside her. With his firm square jaw and intensely blue eyes it was almost like welcoming Adam back into the house.

The breadth of the man, the strength of him as he towered above her, brought alive feelings that she had long considered dormant. Seeing him evoked mental torment, the self-inflicted torture that had gnawed at her happiness ever since she had first realised Gary's parentage.

Resolutely, she pushed these thoughts out of her mind and concentrated on dishing up the meal. Then she called out to Lucy to help carry the plates and dishes and asked Mark to see they were all seated round the dining-table.

'Where are you sitting . . . you've put me in your place, haven't you?' Gary asked, his eyes challenging as Helen finally came to the table.

'I . . . I'll squeeze in between the two girls. They'll make room for me.'

'Nonsense! This is your place. I remember you always like to sit here so that you can pop back out to the kitchen

186

without disturbing anyone . . . see what a memory I have?' Gary said lightly. 'I'll push in between Mark and Lucy.'

Helen's heart jolted uneasily as she saw how Lucy's cheeks turned pink as she made room for Gary to sit next to her.

The meal passed without incident. There was so much to be said, so many questions to be asked and answered, that it was mid-afternoon before they moved from the table.

Mark suddenly pushed back his chair and stood up. 'I must get back to the yard and see to the milking,' he told them.

'I'll come and give you a hand if you like,' Gary volunteered.

'Wait for me,' Lucy said, rising from her chair before Helen could recover from her surprise.

As Ruth helped her clear away, Helen kept looking out of the window to where Gary and Lucy were carrying feed across the meadow to the chickens. It was a task that Lucy had always steadfastly refused to do. In fact, as far as work on the farm was concerned, she had long ago made it quite clear that she wasn't interested.

Helen knew she should feel grateful since it was one job less for her to do, but she would have far rather gone out and tended to the hens herself than see Lucy and Gary together. She was more than relieved when they came back indoors and Gary said he must be getting back to London, as Sheila would be expecting him.

Once Gary had left, Helen was perfectly happy and contented. She had her family around her, the spirit of Christmas pervaded the house, there was plenty of food and fun and everyone was happy.

Sally and Anna had only vague memories of the farm but took to it enthusiastically, eager to be out of doors with the animals from the moment they were awake in the morning until it was dark. Hugh helped Mark around the farm, leaving Helen the opportunity to have Ruth to herself. And Helen was pleasantly surprised by the empathy between them. Ruth had matured during her two years in Hong

187

Kong. She seemed not only more gentle, but far more tolerant and understanding.

The happy, relaxed atmosphere also brought Helen and Hugh closer. In the past she had avoided his company because of his air of superiority. She always felt that he was secretly gloating because Ruth had married him in spite of her strong opposition.

Now, Helen saw him in a new light. What she had taken for arrogance she now realised was quiet reserve and that, beneath his handsome exterior, he was in fact quite shy. There was also, from time to time, a deep, brooding sadness in his dark eyes and this worried her so much she mentioned it to Ruth, concerned that there might be a problem.

'It was Northern Ireland.' Ruth said, sighing. 'He saw some terrible sights there. Savage killings, people maimed and blown apart; he still has nightmares about it even now. The trouble is, he won't talk about it.'

'How do you know that is what's troubling him then?'

'From Gary.' Ruth laughed. 'You know what he's like. He doesn't brood like Hugh. He's talked it out of his system. And, anyway, he wasn't over in Ireland as long as Hugh was. Perhaps if they had been together out there the whole time Hugh wouldn't be feeling it all so badly now. I think after Gary left he became stressed. The conditions out there and worrying about me and the baby . . .' she shrugged helplessly. 'It's all in the past, so it's no good going on about it now. Perhaps I shouldn't have come back home with Sally. If I'd been there, and he'd had someone to come home to when he was off duty, it might have made things easier for him.'

'You did the right thing. It was no place to be with a new baby,' Helen defended.

'Yes, I suppose you're right. I do wish Hugh would talk about it; I'm sure it would help. Perhaps in time he will.' Impulsively she hugged Helen. 'Come on, forget it. Don't let it spoil our holiday.'

Despite his moods, Helen found Hugh more approachable. They had never been really close but they had always had a healthy respect for each other. His ways were not hers but she had never interfered. She was pleasantly surprised to find he had turned out to be a wonderful father, combining patience with discipline. And he was always ready to show a lively interest in whatever the girls were doing.

Anna's mischievous ways still seemed to captivate him, but Helen noticed that, now Sally was older, she and Hugh seemed to have a special rapport. Not only did she take after him in looks with her dark hair and eyes, but she had his quiet, serious manner. Listening to them talking, or Hugh explaining something, warmed Helen's heart.

It was a wonderful Christmas for them all. On Christmas day a light snow fell, gilding the trees and hedges. More snow fell overnight and, by morning, there was at least three inches on the ground. The girls were entranced. When the milking was done and the cattle attended to, Mark dragged out a sleigh from the depths of the barn and he and Hugh spent an energetic morning giving the girls rides on it. Ruth and Lucy joined in later as they built an enormous snowman and finally took sides for a full-scale snowball fight.

Watching them all playing together, Helen smiled happily. It was the first time for years that she had her complete family around her. She was enjoying the experience so much that, when Ruth told her Gary had volunteered to come and pick them up at the end of their stay, she suggested that perhaps he and Sheila might like to come for New Year's Eve.

'Are you sure that's what you want?' Hugh asked in surprise.

Helen flushed, remembering the many times Hugh had witnessed her antagonism to his friend, but she refused to be drawn.

'I think it will be a wonderful end to our holiday,' Ruth told Helen, giving her a quick hug. 'You'll like Sheila; she's great. We had a wonderful time together out in Hong Kong. The children adore her and she's very good with them. It's a pity she can't persuade Gary to start a family.'

'Perhaps he doesn't like children.'

'He's very fond of our two.'

'Not quite the same thing, is it? You don't have any responsibility when they're someone else's.'

'It's not that. It's something much deeper . . . something he won't talk about – even to Sheila. You don't want to let that brash way of his fool you, you know. Underneath he's quite susceptible.'

Remembering how much her opinion of Hugh had changed during the past week, Helen wisely said nothing. She began to wish she hadn't invited Gary and Sheila for New Year's Eve, but knew she could hardly change her mind now.

Chapter 25

Sally and Anna were allowed to stay up on New Year's Eve to see 1979 in. Hugh let in the New Year, and, after they had all joined in the traditional first-footing festivities, Ruth suggested that the two girls should go to bed. They were so worn out that they agreed fairly readily. Sally insisted that Lucy should take her up to bed, but Anna wanted Gary to do it.

'We'll both do it,' Lucy said, grabbing their hands. 'Come on Gary.'

He obeyed with alacrity. Helen held her breath, waiting for Sheila, Ruth or Hugh to object, but Mark was refilling their glasses and none of them seemed to be taking any notice.

Helen bit her lip, and refused to have any more wine. She waited with growing irritation for Gary or Lucy to return to the room.

After five minutes, she commented on their absence.

'Probably telling them a story,' Ruth said, smothering a yawn. 'He often does.'

190

Another five minutes passed and, feeling uneasy, Helen went upstairs to find out where they were. It was very quiet. She walked into the bedroom that Anna and Sally were sharing and found they were both fast asleep, Sally with one hand underneath her cheek, Anna on her back, her golden hair spread out like a halo.

They stirred slightly as she gently kissed them both, but were much too tired to return her caress. As she came out of their room, wondering where Gary and Lucy could be, she heard a giggle coming from Lucy's room. Apprehensively she pushed open the door. Gary was sitting on the side of the bed, leaning over Lucy, who lay there giggling. Supporting himself on one elbow, he was running a finger teasingly around her chin and neck. For a moment Helen froze, then suddenly exploded with anger.

'Get out!' she hissed.

Gary stumbled to his feet, backing away towards the door.

Lucy also swung from the bed, her blue eyes blazing. 'Mother, what *do* you think you're doing walking into my bedroom like this?'

'What are *you* doing might be more to the point?' Helen snapped.

'Not what you seem to think!' Lucy exclaimed, her cheeks pink, her blue eyes flashing angrily.

'Lucy's right. We were only planning an outing for the two girls,' Gary said quickly.

'Really!' The scorn and disbelief in Helen's voice brought a dark flush to his face.

'What on earth's going on? What's all the shouting about? You'll wake the girls in a minute.' Ruth asked as she came running up the stairs.

'It's Mum and Gary . . . she's always picking on him,' Lucy said tearfully.

Ruth's grey eyes were puzzled as she looked questioningly at her mother.

'Mum walked into my bedroom and because Gary was there she blew her top.' Lucy sniffed. 'We were only making plans to take the girls to the pantomime, but Mum won't believe us,' Lucy gabbled on.

Helen turned away, too choked to speak. She realised she'd been hasty, but the sight of Gary and Lucy lying there had brought such mixed feelings that she had been unable to control her outburst.

The tension in the room was electric. Helen knew Ruth was waiting for some sort of explanation and that Gary, and possibly even Lucy, deserved some kind of apology from her. Yet she couldn't bring herself to speak.

'Lucy, I've just made the coffee,' Ruth said. 'Why don't you and Gary go on down and have yours with the others? I'll bring Mum's up here.'

'I'm sure it's just a misunderstanding, Lucy,' Helen heard Ruth say as the three of them went down the stairs. 'Mum's worn out with so many of us here over Christmas. You go and have your coffee with the others and forget the whole thing. I'll have a chat with Mum.'

Helen felt sick as she waited for Ruth to bring up her coffee. The torment inside was more than she could bear alone. If only Adam were there to advise her. Mark wouldn't understand. He never did see things her way. She could imagine the cold stare he would give her, the slight curl to his top lip as he listened, then the imperceptible shrug of his shoulders before he walked away. She couldn't stand that kind of rejection. If only Adam was here, she thought sadly. Yet it was Adam who was the root cause of her problem, she reminded herself bitterly.

She went into her own bedroom and sat down at the dressing-table. The face that stared back at her disturbed her. Her hair was not just streaked with grey but almost white. There were a myriad lines around her grey eyes; her mouth was tightly pursed and she looked old.

'I shouldn't look like this at fifty-four,' she murmured aloud. 'What's happening to me?'

She combed her hair, then outlined her mouth with fresh lipstick, and applied some blue eye-shadow to liven up the dullness of her grey eyes.

'You look better now,' Ruth said cheerfully, putting a cup of coffee down on the dressing-table. 'You quite frightened me when I walked into Lucy's room. You looked so upset. Now, what's all the fuss about? I'm sure Gary wasn't seducing young Lucy. Not that I'd altogether blame him if he was; she's been playing him along ever since he arrived.' She sat down on the edge of the bed and sipped her coffee. 'Lucy's right though, you never have liked Gary. What's wrong with him?'

Helen slowly turned to face Ruth. She tried to speak, but couldn't, then, suddenly, she was in floods of tears. All the pent-up misery of the years since she had first suspected that Gary was Adam's child, was finally released. Her shoulders slumped and her entire body shook with sobs.

'Mum!' Ruth put her arms round her mother. Gently she led her over to the bed. 'Lie down, I'll get Hugh,' she said helplessly.

'No, no.' Desperately Helen restrained her. 'Shut the bedroom door . . . lock it. I don't want anyone coming in here and seeing me like this.'

Ruth did as Helen asked, then came and stood uncertainly near the bed.

'Drink your coffee, and pass me mine,' Helen said in a choked voice. 'I'll be all right in a minute.'

'You've been overdoing things Mum. We'd better go home. It's too much for you . . .'

'No, no. It's not that at all, Ruth. You just don't understand. Give me a minute and I'll try and explain.'

The coffee steadied Helen's nerves and brought the colour back into her cheeks.

'Well?' Ruth asked curiously, as Helen put her cup down on the bedside-table.

Helen looked at her in silence, trying to find the right words. She felt she owed Ruth an explanation, and she hoped she would understand her dilemma, and why she had acted as she did.

'It's to do with Gary,' Helen said and paused.

'I rather gathered that,' Ruth said wryly. 'Go on.'

'You probably don't remember the first time I met him . . .'

'Yes I do. It was when you came over to see me in Ireland.'

'You'd told me all about him before then; that he'd come from London, that his mother had died when he was born and he'd never known who his father was . . .'

'Well, what about it?'

Helen didn't reply. She got up and pulled an old leather handbag from her wardrobe. Inside the bag was a framed photograph which she gave to Ruth.

'This is a picture of Dad isn't it? I've never seen it before.'

'It was taken just after we first met. He had it done especially for me,' Helen said, holding out her hand to take the photo back. 'Does it remind you of anyone?'

'Mark, I suppose,' Ruth said with a light shrug. 'Except that Dad's eyes were a different sort of blue to Mark's and, as far as I remember, Dad's hair was more bushy.'

'No one else?'

'Let's have another look.' Ruth held out her hand for the photograph. She sat staring at it for a minute or two, then looked up, frowning, her grey eyes questioning. Without speaking she shook her head and passed the photograph back.

'Come on,' Helen challenged.

'I know what you want me to say,' Ruth said in a shaky voice, 'but it's nonsense. His eyes are like Dad's and there *is* a resemblance, but that's probably because they're both in Guards' uniform . . . his hair's the wrong colour, anyway.'

'Look at this.' Helen handed her an old, faded photo. She saw Ruth's eyes widen as she took it. Then Ruth stood up and took it across to the light, staring at it and shaking her head as if refusing to believe the evidence of her own eyes.

'Have you told Gary?' Ruth whispered. 'Oh Mum!' Her face was contorted as she looked up at Helen. 'You don't know what a relief this is.'

'Relief?' Helen looked bewildered.

'I've always had such strong feelings for Gary, ever since we first met. It used to worry me, especially if he called round and Hugh was away. Sometimes I even thought I'd like him to make a pass at me. Now I know why I felt the way I did. It was perfectly natural, the sort of feeling you would have for a cousin.'

'For a cousin!' Helen stared at her perplexed.

'Well, if he's Dad's brother's son then that would make him our cousin, wouldn't it?'

Helen didn't answer. She wanted to scream the truth at Ruth, but commonsense prevailed. It was enough if she understood why Gary must never get involved with Lucy.

'You must tell Gary. It will mean so much to him to know who his father was,' Ruth said eagerly.

Helen held out her hand for the snapshot. 'Let's leave things as they are.'

Ruth looked down at the faded piece of pasteboard. Slowly she turned it over, reading the writing on the other side. She suddenly froze, her brows furrowed in a frown. When she looked up, Helen was startled by the abject misery in their grey depths.

'It wasn't Dad's brother who was Gary's father, was it?' she whispered, aghast. 'It couldn't have been . . . he was killed in France . . .' she stopped as she read the answer in her mother's eyes.

'Oh, Mum . . . Mum . . .' She put her arms around Helen and held her close.

'Are you sure?'

Helen nodded. 'I've been over it all so many times. It all fits . . .' she stopped, choked by tears. Then, taking a deep breath she told Ruth all she knew.

Ruth was silent for a few minutes after Helen had finished. Then she said in a flat voice, 'You can't *really* be certain though, can you? I agree it all seems to fit, but it is so out of character for Dad. He was always such a stickler for the truth and doing one's duty and all the rest of it.'

'The proof is here, isn't it?' Helen said, taking the photograph out of Ruth's hand.

'They say everyone has a double,' Ruth defended weakly.

'In looks, perhaps,' Helen agreed. 'But Gary has all Adam's mannerisms as well. When I see Gary walk in the house it's almost like seeing your father come home. He gets more like him all the time.'

'And you are determined not to tell him the truth?'

'There's nothing to be gained by doing so.'

'Not for you, perhaps. It would set Gary's mind at rest though . . . and Sheila's.'

'No. If you tell either of them I'll never forgive you, Ruth. Promise me you'll say nothing.'

'Just tell me why, Mum. Perhaps then I'll understand,' Ruth pleaded.

Helen shook her head wearily. 'I don't know. It's just that I feel a sense of evil every time I look at Gary. I think it's the thought that I have been deceived. I know it's not his fault, but I feel the only weapon I have is to withhold the knowledge from him.'

'I think you should see a psychiatrist . . . you need help,' Ruth told her.

'The only help I need you can give me.'

'What do you mean?'

'Just keep Gary away from here. Don't bring him with you next time you come down.'

'But, Mum . . .'

'As long as I don't see him I can forget. The bitterness goes, the hurt inside me fades. The moment I am in the same room with him my mind is full of recriminations against your father.'

'Well, I'll do my best,' Ruth said cautiously. 'Both Gary and Sheila will think it strange, though. And so will Hugh . . . unless I give them some sort of explanation.'

'No! Hugh is *not* to be told, nor anyone else. All I'm asking is that you try and keep Gary away.'

'You won't be able to stop Mark seeing him.'

'No, I know that,' Helen said resignedly. 'After this holiday though I don't think Mark will be too keen on

196

bringing him here. He likes having Gary to himself, so that they can go drinking. He's resented Sheila being here as well as the way Lucy has monopolised Gary.'

'We'd better go back downstairs. The others will wonder what we're doing,' Ruth told her, standing up and collecting the coffee cups.

'You go on. I'll be down in a minute. You won't forget your promise, Ruth, will you? I don't want anyone told . . . not even Hugh.'

Chapter 26

Her mother's disclosures about Gary troubled Ruth and she longed to be able to confide in Hugh. In the thirteen years they had been married she had never kept any secrets from him. Nor he from her, as far as she knew.

This was where she differed from her mother, Ruth thought. Although they were so alike in looks, they were totally opposite in temperament. Her mother would go to almost any length to ensure there was no bickering between herself and Mark, especially when their father had been around. She couldn't ever remember a family argument. Her mother liked an harmonious life and had always ensured that their home was a haven of peace and happiness.

Ruth remembered how she had found it hard to stand up for herself. When she visited other families, it had frightened her if a grown-up shouted at them because they were doing something wrong. And she had been shocked when her friends argued with their parents.

Looking back, she was sure her confrontation with her mother, when she had wanted to marry Hugh, had succeeded partly because she'd never acted in that way before. It was a weapon she learned to value and one which she used whenever necessary.

197

She knew her mother thought she was now much too frank and outspoken, but it worked for her and Hugh. They never bore grudges, or sulked, or held private vendettas. If Hugh annoyed her she let him know; if she upset him, he was equally candid. If there was provocation, they shouted at each other and cleared the air.

She knew her mother deplored their behaviour and thought it in very bad taste, especially in front of the children.

When she tried to explain to her that things were different from when she was first married, her mother would only shake her head and her mouth would tighten in disapproval.

Ruth knew she was right. Life had changed, even in the Guards. If her father had spoken to his officers in the way Hugh did then he would probably have been on a charge for insubordination, she thought wryly.

For several weeks after her mother's revelations, Ruth found herself watching Gary closely whenever they met. Sometimes she wondered if she was imagining there were facial and physical resemblances to her father, simply because she wanted them to be there. She also became acutely conscious of his mannerisms, especially when they identified with those of Mark or her father.

As she tried to analyse her own feelings towards Gary, it made her moody and introspective.

'Are you broody or something?' Hugh joked when he arrived home late one evening, after Sally and Anna were in bed, to find her sitting in the dark.

'No, just thinking. Do you want some supper?'

'In a moment.' He sat down on the settee and drew Ruth into the curve of his arm. 'What's wrong? You seem to have been in some kind of a daze ever since we arrived back from Hong Kong. Missing the sun?'

'No, not really.'

'Not fed up with me, are you?' His lips sought hers in a deep warm kiss.

'Oh Hugh, you are an idiot!' She sighed as she relaxed against his hard body. 'Why on earth should I be?'

'I don't know. There's something strange about you. I was

198

beginning to wonder if you'd gone overboard for our friend Gary.'

'What!'

Ruth shot upright, turning to stare at him in dismay.

'Well, every time he's in the house you devour him with your eyes and he seems to have all your attention.'

'Rubbish! Absolute rubbish!' she exclaimed heatedly.

'That's all right then.' He drew her back into his arms, his fleeting kisses covering her eyes, her forehead, her face, finally coming to rest on her lips.

Their love-life had always been good, and now Ruth found release from the tension that had built up inside her as she responded to Hugh's love-making.

There had never been any other man for her and, as far as she knew, there had never been anyone else in Hugh's life, certainly not since they'd been married.

Or had there? As she lay there, her limbs entwined with his, a shadow of doubt crept into Ruth's mind.

Why should Hugh be any different from other men? Who would have believed that her father, so upright and honest, and always such a stickler for the truth, would have had an affair? Yet Gary was living proof of his infidelity.

This disturbing thought haunted her and she became less responsive to Hugh during the weeks that followed. He sensed the change in her and it mystified him. An estrangement developed between them. Ruth was often aware that Hugh was watching her, a puzzled expression in his dark eyes. She longed to fling her arms around him and blurt out all her mother had told her. Her promise to keep silent about Gary weighed heavily, making her snappy and irritable with Sally and Anna.

She even found herself wondering what Hugh was up to when he was working. She became devious, questioning other wives about where their husbands were, just to see if it all tied in when Hugh told her he was on a course or exercise. Afterwards, she despised herself for checking on him. Yet the next time he was absent she found herself resorting to the same subterfuges.

199

'If you were any older I'd say you were going through the change,' Hugh told her sourly after one of their bitter exchanges. 'You're becoming as shrewish as your mother.'

'My mother – shrewish!' Ruth stared at him in amazement. 'You don't know what you're saying!'

'I do, you ask Gary. Since her outburst at New Year, it's put him off going to the farm. He meets Mark in town or at a pub somewhere. I don't know what Gary has done to deserve it, but nowadays you don't seem to have any time for him either. I suppose it's all to do with your mother finding him in Lucy's bedroom. Gary swears they were only planning an outing for our girls and I believe him.'

'Of course Mum was upset,' Ruth defended. 'Lucy's a very attractive teenager.'

'She's just a kid. And a spoilt one at that. She's at the stage where she thinks she has only to flutter her eyelashes and open wide those blue eyes of hers and men will fall at her feet. Well, she may find it works with the boys at the youth club but not with an old soldier like Gary! Anyway, he's a happily-married man!'

'And happily-married men don't have affairs?'

'Not when they know their wives are checking up on them,' he told her with a mocking grin.

'How did you know?' Ruth flushed angrily.

'You didn't think you could keep something like that secret, not amongst Army wives, did you?' Hugh sneered. 'A really juicy bit of gossip that made in the Mess.'

Worried by what her mother's secret was doing to her own marriage, Ruth decided to go and talk to her and try to persuade her to agree that she could tell Hugh about Gary. Hugh was away on an exercise so she made Lucy's eighteenth birthday an excuse to take the two girls on a visit.

It was early April, and the blue sky was patterned with fluffy white clouds. The birds were singing and the sun was warm on their faces as they waited at the station to be collected. Ruth prayed her mother would understand.

What better time than now, with spring burgeoning all around them, to clear the air between herself and Hugh. If the weather held she would be able to take Sally and Anna walking. It suddenly seemed important to her that they should know and love the countryside around Sturbury just as she had done as a girl.

They were all up early on the morning of Lucy's birthday. Sally and Anna were dancing with excitement at the sight of all the cards and presents piled on Lucy's chair.

When Lucy finally arrived at the breakfast-table, she was wearing a black skirt with a deep side slit and a low-necked white blouse. Her shoulder-length blonde hair fanned over her shoulders like a glittering golden shawl.

'You look more as if you were dressed for a party than going to work in a hairdresser's,' Ruth joked as she kissed her younger sister and handed her a prettily-wrapped box.

'That reminds me,' Lucy exclaimed, looking at her mother, 'I may be rather late home tonight. The girls at work are taking me for a birthday drink.'

'Oh, Lucy, no!' Sally and Anna exclaimed in unison. 'What about your birthday tea?'

Lucy smiled apologetically. 'Sorry, but I made this arrangement long before I knew you were coming. There's still the party on Saturday. Tell you what, I'll bring you both a bag of crisps,' she said lightly.

Ignoring their cries of 'big deal', she pushed back her chair and went to fetch her coat.

Ruth could see that Sally and Anna were almost in tears so she hastily concocted an outing to take their minds off their disappointment.

'Come on,' she said as she began stacking the breakfast dishes. 'We'll wash up and then I'll take you out.'

'Where are we going?' Sally asked, her face lighting up with anticipation.

'That's a secret,' Ruth told her mysteriously.

'Give us one clue,' Anna begged, but Ruth refused to be drawn.

'How can we get ready when we don't know where

we're going?' Anna grumbled. 'We don't know whether to keep on our jeans or change into a dress.'

'What you've got on will be fine. But bring a warm sweater,' Ruth told them.

She had absolutely nothing in mind, so the moment they were out of the room she sought her mother's advice.

'Why don't you borrow the car and take them to Stourton Tower and then to Stourton Gardens afterwards? They've opened up a restaurant in what used to be the stables, so you could have a snack lunch there and I'll have a proper meal waiting when you get home. Make a day of it.'

'Why don't you come with us?'

Helen hesitated and Ruth could see she was tempted by the idea. Then she shook her head slowly. 'No. Mark has the vet coming this morning. I ought to be here to make them coffee. I'll have an easy day . . . the rest will do me good.'

'Finding us a bit too much for you?' Ruth asked sympathetically.

'No, of course not. But I still have some baking to do for Lucy's party on Saturday. Go on, enjoy yourselves. This is supposed to be a holiday for those two girls of yours, you know.'

For the three of them it was a memorable day. Sally and Anna found everything excitingly new. For Ruth, it was sheer nostalgia, a trip back in time.

'I bet Grandma has been worrying in case we've broken down or something,' Ruth commented as they pulled up outside the farm. 'It's almost seven o'clock!'

'It's been great. Much better than sitting around waiting for Lucy to get back from work. I bet she's the one waiting for us,' Anna exclaimed triumphantly.

Helen looked relieved to see them but more than a little surprised that Lucy wasn't with them.

'I thought you must have decided to go and collect her when she didn't ring in for a lift,' she remarked.

'I never even thought about it,' Ruth said a little guiltily. 'The bus from Winton leaves at half-past six, doesn't it?'

202

'She's missed that and there's not another one tonight,' Helen said, concerned.

'Shall I go and pick her up?' Ruth volunteered. 'There are only three pubs in Winton so it shouldn't be too difficult to find her.'

'Sit down and have your meal first,' Helen replied. 'It's all ready. Mark and I have been waiting for you.'

'Oh, sorry! You should have had yours.'

'Mark's not long finished outside. He said he'd go and get changed but he should be down any minute. If Lucy hasn't phoned by the time we've finished then probably Mark will go and look for her.'

They had finished eating and were having coffee when they heard the commotion outside. Mark sprang to his feet and went to investigate. Within seconds he was back, followed by Gary who was supporting a rather dishevelled-looking Lucy.

'Hi, everybody!' She waved a hand in greeting, then collapsed against Gary, giggling.

'How ever many drinks have you had?' Mark asked, frowning.

Lucy giggled louder, waved her hand dismissively and said in a slurred voice, 'I'm OK . . . and I have the crisps.' She tried to focus her eyes on Sally and Anna, 'Gary,' she said, clutching at him wildly, 'give 'em their crisps. Go on. I promised I'd bring them some and Lucy never breaks a promise, does she, girls?'

'They can have them in the morning. They're just on their way up to bed,' Helen said in an icy voice.

'No we weren't . . .' Anna began but her grandmother silenced her with a look.

'Go on,' Ruth urged, giving them both a gentle push. 'I'll be up in a minute to kiss you goodnight.'

Anna hesitated, ready to argue, but Sally had seen the warning signals in her mother's eyes and hurried her younger sister away.

Helen stayed silent until Sally and Anna had left the room, then she turned on Gary, her face white and tense, her mouth a thin, hard line.

203

'I'm sure you have an explanation for bringing Lucy home in this state,' she said, cuttingly, 'but I don't want to hear it. Get out and stay away from here, I never want to see you again.'

'Look, Mrs Woodley . . .'

'Get out!' Helen hissed.

Gary paused for a moment, then with a slight lift of his shoulders turned on his heel. As the door slammed behind him, Mark went after him, calling his name, shouting to him to stop. There was a sound of a car engine being revved, of tyres spinning on the pathway and then silence. Ruth went to the window in time to see the tail of the car as it turned into the main road.

'Mark's gone with him,' she said quietly.

'I never want to see Gary ever again,' Helen said in a low, hard voice. 'He's caused nothing but trouble.' She turned to Lucy who was looking at her in bewilderment. 'And I won't have you seeing him behind my back . . . you understand?'

'Why not?'

The shock of Gary's dismissal seemed to have sobered Lucy. 'All he did was to give me a lift home!'

'You mean he wasn't at the pub drinking with you?' Ruth asked in surprise.

'Of course he wasn't! It was an all-girls "do". I felt a bit queer when I came out. I knew I'd had too much to drink so I thought I would walk home.'

'Walk!' Helen exclaimed disbelievingly. 'It's almost four miles.'

'Well, I did tell you I'd had too much to drink,' Lucy said, pulling a face. 'At that moment I thought I could walk it. I'd just reached the edge of town when Gary's car pulled up. I thought you'd sent him to meet me.' She pouted.

'Well, we'll say no more about it,' Helen said, mollified by Lucy's explanation. 'Just remember, though. I don't want Gary here again.'

'But he's promised to take me to the Troop Ball,' Lucy sulked. 'Does that mean I have to meet him in London?'

'What Troop Ball?' Ruth asked sharply. 'Hugh hasn't mentioned there's to be one.'

'In a fortnight's time. The Spring Ball. Gary says it lasts all night and there will be breakfast at four o'clock the next morning.' Her blue eyes were wide and excited, 'Can you imagine it! It sounds absolutely fantastic. I've never been to a real ball. I'll need a new dress, Mum. I haven't got a long one,' she said in a wheedling tone, 'unless, of course, Ruth has one I can borrow.' She looked appealingly at her elder sister.

'Lucy, didn't you hear what I said? I don't want Gary here ever again and I don't want you . . .'

'Then I'll go and stay with Ruth for the weekend and go from there,' Lucy said quickly before her mother could finish.

'Why don't you both come and stay with us?' Ruth said quickly.

'Are you going to this ball, then?' Helen asked.

'Probably.'

'What do you mean "probably"? Either you are or you aren't,' Helen said irritably.

'We usually go to those sort of functions. Hugh has to pay whether he attends or not, so we might just as well go along and enjoy ourselves.'

'But hasn't Hugh said if you're going?' Helen persisted.

'No, he hasn't, but that's not surprising since he's away, now is it?' Ruth snapped. 'I don't even know if he will be back from the exercise in time for it.'

She was as surprised as her mother that Hugh hadn't mentioned the ball, but she had no intention of going into it then. She wanted to face Hugh first and find out why he hadn't told her about it or checked with her if she wanted to go.

There were niggling doubts at the back of her mind. Having been away in Hong Kong for over two years, she hadn't any very close friends amongst her neighbours, so if Lucy hadn't mentioned the Troop Ball she might never have known about it until it was over. Was Hugh taking a chance on that . . . planning to take someone else?

The moment the thought came into her mind she felt angry. Hugh had never cheated on her in the whole of the time they'd been married so why should he start now?

'Does Sheila know that Gary has invited you, Lucy?' she asked, in what she hoped was a casual voice.

'I don't know,' Lucy's blue eyes widened innocently. 'He never even mentioned if Sheila was going.'

Tight-lipped, Ruth began stacking the dirty dishes as she tried to quell the suspicions racing inside her head. As she began to pile them on a tray to take them through to the kitchen, she found her mother watching her through narrowed eyes and knew from her expression that she, too, was thinking along exactly the same lines.

Chapter 27

Helen woke in a cold sweat, the horrifying dream still vivid in her mind. She struggled to sit up in bed and groped for the light-switch on the bedside lamp. She stared around the unfamiliar room wondering where she was and trying to collect her thoughts. Feeling exhausted, she lay back against the pillows, trying to control the rapid thumping of her heart by breathing slowly and deeply. Gradually her limbs stopped trembling, but she felt completely drained.

The mattress on the narrow bed was harder than she was used to, so probably that was what had caused her bad dream. Ruth had separated the bunk beds for her and Lucy to sleep more comfortably. Sally and Anna were using sleeping-bags in the tiny front boxroom. Helen pushed back the duvet and swung her legs over the side of the bed, groping for her slippers and dressing-gown.

As quietly as possible she made her way downstairs to the kitchen. She realised she would never get back to sleep so she decided to make herself a hot drink. Everyone should be home very soon, she thought, glancing at the clock. Breakfast at a Troop Ball was usually served around four in the morning and it was now almost half-past five.

The front door opened and Ruth and Hugh walked into the kitchen just as the kettle boiled.

'Oh dear, couldn't you sleep?' Ruth sympathised. She kicked off her high-heeled sandals and wriggled her toes with a sigh of relief.

'I had a bad dream. It must be coming back here. It's the first time I've slept at Pirbright since . . . since your father was killed.'

'Oh, Mum!' Ruth's grey eyes glistened with tears as she went across to her mother and hugged her. 'I never thought of that . . .'

'Why on earth should you? It happened eighteen years ago,' Helen said quickly. 'Forget I said it, I'm all right. Let's have that coffee.'

Ruth spooned instant coffee into three mugs and filled them with water. She reached for the biscuit-barrel and held it out to her mother.

'No thanks. I'll wait till breakfast-time. I don't suppose you two will want a second breakfast?'

'Well, I certainly won't!' Hugh laughed. 'Two eggs, bacon, fried bread, kidney and two sausages. I think that should keep me going until lunch-time!'

'I take it you both enjoyed yourselves?'

'Very much. One of the best balls I've been to,' Ruth said enthusiastically. She bent down and rubbed her ankles. 'My feet are killing me though. I think we must have danced every dance.'

'Where's Lucy? Hasn't she come back with you?' Helen looked enquiringly at Hugh and Ruth.

'Sit down Mum. We've got something to tell you,' Ruth said. 'I'll make another drink.' She turned away and began to fill the kettle, while Hugh pulled out one of the kitchen chairs and sat down.

'I don't want any more coffee. Just tell me what's happened. Has there been an accident . . . is she hurt?'

Helen asked anxiously, the memory of the violent dream that had woken her still vivid in her mind.

'No, no. Nothing like that,' Hugh said quickly. 'Just a spot of explaining to do, and Lucy thought it might be better coming from us.'

'Well, go on. I'm listening,' Helen said impatiently. She sensed from their attitude that whatever it was they had to say to her, was something she wasn't going to like.

Ruth and Hugh exchanged glances, each waiting for the other to speak. 'Lucy wants to get married,' Ruth blurted out. 'She asked us to tell you.'

Helen's face went deathly white. Even the thin, tight line of her lips was bloodless as she looked from one to the other, fear in her grey eyes. 'Oh no! She's not . . . she's . . .'

'No, she's not pregnant.' Ruth laughed gently, patting her mother's hand.

'That wasn't what I was trying to say,' Helen said slowly. 'She's not . . . not involved with Gary is she?'

Ruth blanched, but she shook her head. 'No, Mum, of course she isn't.'

'Gary?' Hugh looked puzzled, but Ruth silently signalled to him not to say anything more.

'Who does she want to marry then?' Helen asked, as the colour slowly came back into her cheeks.

'It's worse than her wanting to marry Gary,' Hugh said angrily. 'She wants to marry Russell Campbell . . . he's one of our officers!'

Helen stared at them blankly.

'You do understand what that means?' Hugh said sharply, his dark brown eyes blazing.

'Of course Mum understands, Hugh. Don't forget my Dad was in the Guards, and discipline and protocol were much more strict then than they are now,' Ruth exclaimed sharply.

'I've tried to explain to Lucy what it means, not just to her, but to the rest of us as well, if she marries him,' Hugh went on, ignoring Ruth's outburst. 'She seems to think it won't make any difference. She's wrong, of course! For a

208

start, she won't be able to socialise with Ruth. I won't be able to have anything to do with her either – nor for that matter will Gary. You can't keep something like that a secret when you're living and working with the same people all the time. It won't be easy for Lieutenant Campbell, but he's an arrogant bastard anyway, so he can probably handle it.'

'How did she come to meet him? Did you introduce them, Hugh?' Helen asked in a bewildered voice.

'Me! Good heavens no. I hardly ever speak to the man.'

'Then who did?'

Ruth shook her head. 'I've seen him around camp but I didn't even know his name until tonight.' She looked at Hugh. 'How did Lucy come to meet him?'

'Through Gary I suppose. He was dancing with Lucy early on in the evening and I saw Campbell go across and speak to them. Then a bit later on I noticed that Lucy was dancing with Campbell.'

'I might have known Gary would be involved,' Helen said bitterly.

'He didn't have much option if Campbell came over and spoke to them . . . and asked to be introduced to Lucy,' Ruth protested lamely.

'Are you telling me that Lucy met this Russell Campbell for the very first time just a few hours ago and now she wants to marry him!' Helen exclaimed incredulously. 'She must be out of her mind! And, for that matter, so must you to come and ask me such a question. You might know what my answer would be.'

Hugh and Ruth exchanged uneasy glances. 'Lucy is quite serious, Mum,' Ruth told her. 'And so is Lieutenant Campbell.'

'It's absolute nonsense,' Helen snapped. 'Lucy probably thinks she'll cause a sensation by aping what you did at her age. Well, I refuse to agree . . . not this time!' she added angrily, half to herself.

'It worked well enough for us,' Ruth said quietly. 'And for you,' she added, as her mother glared at her.

209

'I only thought it did,' Helen reminded her acidly.

'Look, we can't just sit here arguing about it,' Hugh said uncomfortably. 'Lucy's outside.'

'For goodness' sake . . . bring her in. I'll soon make her see sense,' Helen vowed.

'Russell Campbell is with her.'

Helen looked at Hugh stonily, refusing to let him see how distressed she felt. 'Well, I've got to meet him sometime. I suppose now is as good a time as any other.'

'Mum . . . you will be careful what you say to him? He *is* one of Hugh's officers remember,' Ruth pleaded.

'Ruth, I'm not a *complete* fool,' Helen said tartly.

'I know that Mum, I only meant . . .'

'I know!' Helen stood up and put an arm around Ruth's shoulder. 'I was an Army wife for too long not to know what the consequences of all this can be.'

'Shall I call them?' Hugh asked, moving towards the door. He wanted desperately to get the matter settled. As far as he could see, he was on the losing side whatever happened. Like Helen, he thought Lucy was being impetuous. Ruth might have been only eighteen when they married but she had been far more grown-up than Lucy was. He was fond of his little sister-in-law but he still thought of her as a child, and a very spoilt one at that. Helen was a good mother but, in his opinion, she was far too lenient with Lucy, and Mark had no authority whatsoever over her.

'Just a minute. It might be better if Mum got dressed first,' Ruth suggested as Hugh made for the door.

Helen looked down at the warm red dressing-gown she'd wrapped round her and then back at Ruth.

'Go on, Mum. First impressions count,' Ruth urged.

As she stood in front of the mirror, combing her greying hair, Helen tried to compose her thoughts. In her heart she knew the odds were against her if Lucy had set her mind on marrying Russell Campbell. Ruth had married Hugh, she reminded herself, in spite of all her threats and Lucy was far more spoilt and self-assured than Ruth had ever been.

210

What's wrong with my girls? she wondered. Why did they have to throw their lives away like this? Marriage was all very well, but why didn't they enjoy their independence first, not tie themselves down to a husband and a family?

Ruth was just thirty-one, yet sometimes she seemed quite middle-aged. She was a good wife and mother, but what had she got to look forward to? She had no career, and very few friends or interests outside her immediate family. Helen felt it was all wrong.

It reminded her of her own life, and she thought how different that could have been if she hadn't rushed into marriage so young. Her parents had probably been right and she should have gone to university. The way things had worked out, she would have completed her time there before Adam came home. But things had been rather different for her . . . she had been pregnant. Ruth didn't have that kind of pressure, nor, it seemed, did Lucy.

Looking into the mirror she was aware of how the passing years had left their mark. She was grey-haired, her face was lined, and she was putting on weight. She picked up a lipstick to try and give her face a little more colour before she went downstairs.

Russell Campbell was bold, handsome and arrogant. He was well over six foot tall, slim, with broad shoulders, and he seemed to fill the room with his presence. Helen felt his green eyes sweeping over her critically, as he took her outstretched hand in his strong grasp. Helen was glad she had taken Ruth's advice; she would have felt even more at a disadvantage in her dressing-gown.

'Nice of you to see me without warning, Mrs Woodley.' He greeted her in a deep, cultured voice. He smiled, showing his strong white teeth. 'Ruth's told you that Lucy and I are going to be married . . . as soon as possible.'

Helen returned his stare, conscious that his astute green eyes were watching her closely.

She felt irritated by the way Lucy was clinging to his arm, gazing up into his strong-boned face so adoringly. Was it sexual attraction, or was Lucy flattered by his attention because he was an officer? she wondered. Lucy couldn't be in love with him, not on such a brief aquaintance, she thought stubbornly. Why marriage anyway? It seemed crazy for a man of his type to want to rush headlong into something so serious and binding.

'Lucy is eighteen, legally old enough to decide such issues for herself, so she doesn't need my permission, does she?' Helen said coolly.

Russell Campbell's sandy eyebrows raised enquiringly and his mouth twitched in a slight smile. 'Does that mean you would withhold it if we did, Mrs Woodley?'

'I would prefer Lucy to think it over and be sure that she knew exactly what she was doing.'

'Mum, of *course* I know what I'm doing!' Lucy's blue eyes glistened, her lips pouted. 'Stop treating me like a child.'

Russell Campbell patted Lucy's hand reassuringly, but his gaze remained fixed challengingly on Helen.

'Right, Mrs Woodley. Then I take it that we can go ahead with our plans?' he said crisply.

'White wedding . . . Guards' Chapel . . . Guard of Honour . . .' Lucy breathed excitedly, her face radiant, her blue eyes suddenly sparkling.

'All the trimmings,' he assured her. 'And for our honeymoon . . . Venice . . . Paris . . . wherever you wish.'

Helen's legs suddenly felt weak and she groped for a chair and sat down. It was like the re-run of a film she'd seen before. How could this be happening? It was madness! They didn't know the first thing about each other.

She looked helplessly at Ruth and Hugh but, like her, they seemed to have been swept along by Russell Campbell's decisive manner and supreme confidence. He'll go far, Helen thought grudgingly. But was he the right man for Lucy? Once the glamour of the situation paled, would Lucy yield to his dominance? Helen didn't think so; it wasn't in Lucy's nature to do so. If only she could persuade her to wait.

212

As she looked at their eager faces, she could hear her own voice, begging her parents to let her marry Adam. And she remembered Ruth, on the day she'd returned from Brecon, making threats about what she would do if she wasn't allowed to marry Hugh. I must be getting old; I'm not even going to put up a fight this time, she thought resignedly.

As she looked again at the tall, haughty young officer, so resplendent in his Mess dress, she knew it would be useless. He looked so devastatingly handsome that Lucy was bound to think herself in love with him. She could only pray that it would turn out all right and that the inevitable rift between Ruth and Lucy wouldn't cause too much heartbreak. Even if they managed to meet in private with the barriers down, the gulf between officer and men had to be observed when they were on duty.

Helen felt the only good that would come from it was the barrier it would create between Gary and Lucy. For a long time now she had worried about the closeness between them and wondered whether the time had come to break her silence. Now she felt relieved that it wasn't going to be necessary.

The burden of Adam's unfaithfulness was heavy for her to bear, but it was her cross. She didn't want to blight Lucy's life with such knowledge. She wished she had never told Ruth. She had never dreamed it would make her regard Hugh with suspicion. She must talk to Ruth and try and convince her that she had nothing to worry about where Hugh was concerned; of that she was certain.

Ruth and Hugh's ways were not hers, but she was confident that their relationship was sound. Ruth mustn't let doubts ruin it. She had always boasted that if anything troubled either of them, they always brought it out in the open and talked it over. Perhaps it would be best if Ruth *did* tell Hugh about Gary; perhaps she had been wrong in making her promise not to speak to him about it.

Sometimes, when she lay awake at night, pondering over Adam's behaviour, Helen wished he could return and

213

tell her exactly what had happened. They had been so very much in love with each other and their marriage had seemed to be so secure, that deep in her heart she still found it hard to believe that he had let her down. Perhaps it had just been an isolated incident.

She knew that if only she could convince herself of that, then, knowing the strain he had been under at that time, she would have been able to understand and forgive him.

Chapter 28

Lucy's wedding had a fairy-tale quality; the sort of wedding most girls only dream about. Helen wasn't sure whether it was the magnificent setting of the Guards' Chapel, or the knowledge that Wellington Barracks was only just across the road from Buckingham Palace, that gave added splendour to the occasion.

The sheer grandeur, though awe-inspiring, had a calming effect. As they waited for Lucy to arrive, Helen remembered that the last time she'd been there had been for Ruth's wedding to Hugh. That had been memorable, but this time it was all on a much grander scale; everything was so much more opulent. Even the flowers were in greater profusion, and there were three times as many people.

It was Russell's friends and family that filled almost one half of the huge chapel, she reflected a little ruefully, while their own occupied a mere three pews and most of those were Lucy's friends.

As she studied the women's expensive furs and stylish clothes, their smart hats and glittering jewellery, she truly felt a country cousin by comparison.

She was irked to see that Gary had been invited. She still held him responsible for Lucy rushing into marriage. If Gary hadn't introduced her to Russell Campbell, then she would probably have gone on to finish her training as a hairdresser.

Like Hugh, Gary was not in uniform because they differed in rank to Russell. Grudgingly, Helen had to admit that Gary looked extremely handsome in his well-tailored grey suit, and his likeness to Adam brought a lump to her throat.

Her curiosity was aroused by the stout, elderly woman, with a very colourful floral hat, seated next to Gary. From the way she kept asking him questions in a sibilant whisper, Helen assumed it must be one of his relations.

She asked Ruth, only to be met with a negative shake of the head. 'Perhaps it's Sheila's mother,' Ruth whispered.

Helen put the matter out of her mind as the music changed, heralding the arrival of the bride. The soft murmur of voices died away, as the waiting congregation turned to watch Lucy make her entrance.

She looked breathtakingly lovely, her white silk gown billowing ethereally about her, as she walked down the aisle on Mark's arm. The lace veil that covered her golden hair was held in place with a circlet of white rosebuds, which matched the posy she was carrying.

Russell Campbell and his best man, both resplendent in their full dress uniform of red and blue, lavishly trimmed with gold braid, were waiting at the foot of the altar steps.

Sally and Anna walked sedately behind Lucy. Sally in a long dress of pale, dusky pink which set off her dark hair; Anna in Wedgwood-blue which made her shoulder-length fair hair appear almost silver. On their heads they wore tiny circlets of white rosebuds and carried matching posies.

The entire ceremony went as smoothly as any television spectacular. The only discordant sound was the faint whirring of cine-cameras being operated from high up in the gallery.

As they emerged from signing the register, Lucy, with her veil now thrown back, looked radiant. She clung to Russell's arm, gazing up at him adoringly, her pink lips slightly parted, her forget-me-not blue eyes sparkling with happiness.

Outside, in the paved courtyard, was the official photographer and hoards of amateurs, eager to capture the colourful scene for themselves.

215

Passers-by in the road outside stopped to gaze through the railings, delighted at the colourful spectacle, as Russell and Lucy posed, again and again, for the clicking cameras.

Helen had never seen Lucy so vivacious. She prayed that the marriage would work out, but she felt apprehensive about the different life style Lucy would be adopting. She had only met Russell's parents briefly, but she suspected they thought their only son was marrying beneath him.

Colonel Campbell was an ex-Guardsman, every inch a military man, with his bristling moustache and ramrod back. Only recently retired, he now lived in the country where, in season, he hunted twice a week and, for the rest of the year, amused himself playing golf or attending race-meetings.

His wife, with her fashionable blue rinse and elegant designer clothes, came from a titled family. She was involved with numerous charitable committees and had seemed astounded when Helen had confessed that she had little time for such activities, because she was too busy helping Mark with the day-to-day running of the farm.

The reception was as lavish as the ceremony. Champagne flowed freely, punctuating the speeches and toasts. Helen drank sparingly, resenting the fact that Russell's family were paying, when she should have been.

Colonel Campbell had been insistent. 'Can't take it with us, so we may as well spend some of it now! Russell's our only child, dammit – only right that we give him a good send off. He'll get the lot once we die, so think of it as an advance!' He had boomed with laughter at his own macabre joke.

Standing there, sipping her glass of champagne, and looking around the noisy, crowded room, heavy with the smell of expensive perfume and cigar smoke, Helen sensed there were two camps. The small group that comprised Lucy's relations and friends, were from a different world to Russell's family and friends, who were all so self-assured, so egotistical. They all seemed to be rich and successful; people who either knew where they were going in life or who had already arrived.

With Lucy gone she would now be very much on her own,

she thought. She recalled with a feeling of apprehension Lucy's teasing comment to Mark as they were about to leave the farm for London. 'Next time you walk down the aisle it had better be as a bridegroom,' she had joked.

He had grinned and shaken his dark head emphatically. 'No chance of that. As soon as we get rid of you I'm through with the farm. I can't stand Sturbury any longer.'

'What are you going to do?' she'd asked in surprise. 'Join the Army?'

'I wish I could.' His blue eyes had clouded. 'I've left it too late though; I'm too old now. No, I'll probably emigrate to South Africa, or Australia, or just become a hobo!'

They'd both laughed, but Helen had heard the desperation in his voice and knew that he meant it. She blamed Gary for Mark's discontent. His constant talk about Army life had made Mark envious and restless.

She felt saddened and bitter that her entire family had this obsession with the Army, although, she supposed, it was only natural since, with the exception of Lucy, they'd been brought up in married quarters. Even Sally and Anna were planning to be Army wives.

She'd overheard them talking together when they had been standing outside the Guards' Chapel, posing for the photographers. Sally had said wistfully, 'Only another seven years and I'll be able to get married.'

Anna had looked at her in surprise. 'Who will you marry?' she'd asked in a puzzled voice.

'A soldier of course,' Sally replied scornfully. 'It's a family tradition, isn't it?'

Young as they were, they had realised that, Helen thought resignedly, and the prospect dismayed her. People began to drift away after Lucy and Russell left for their honeymoon in Paris. Helen went across the room to where Ruth was sitting talking to someone. As she reached them she was surprised to see it was the elderly woman in the flowered hat she'd noticed earlier in the chapel.

'Mum, this is Mrs Collins . . . Gary's grandmother.'

Hesitantly, Helen took the small, gnarled hand. She felt

she'd suffered enough humiliation for one day. Her pride had already been bruised by Russell's family. Now, face to face with the woman who might well know the truth about Adam's unfaithfulness, it could be dented further.

'Been a wonderful day, 'asn't it?' the old woman said, in a strong Cockney voice. 'Can't think when I've been to a more lovely wedding. All we wants now is a good old knees-up to finish it off!' She gave a ribald cackle, that had heads turning in their direction.

'Better not let my Gary hear me say things like that or he'll be ashamed of me!' She looked proudly across to the other side of the room, where Gary was talking to Hugh and Mark. 'He don't half fit in well with your lot! Always talking about you all!' The bird-bright eyes in the plump, round face studied Helen closely.

For a wild moment Helen wanted to ask her about Gary's father. This woman must have the key to the truth, something she yearned to know so desperately.

'We used to see quite a lot of Gary before he went out to Hong Kong,' Helen murmured uncomfortably. 'Since then . . .' her voice trailed away, as Gary walked across to join them, his blue eyes fixed on her challengingly.

'Reckon you've bin like a family to 'im,' the old woman went on garrulously, smiling up at Gary as he towered over her, his arm affectionately around her shoulders.

'Well . . . I don't know about that . . .'

'Poor little devil, never 'ad a real family of 'is own,' Mrs Collins sniffed. 'Not with 'is ma dying like she did when 'e were born and me having to bring him up more or less on me own. Mischievous little bugger 'e could be an all, I can tell you. Never had a man around, no dad to keep him in order; that was part of the trouble.' She sniffed loudly, then rummaged in her large, black handbag for a tissue to dry her eyes.

'Still,' she added, smiling up at him, her voice filled with pride, ''e's not turned out too bad, 'as 'e . . . not for a one-night stand.'